Also by MARY HIGGINS CLARK

ASPIRE TO THE HEAVENS
WHERE ARE THE CHILDREN?

Mary Higgins Clark

A STRANGER

IS WATCHING

SIMON AND SCHUSTER · NEW YORK

Designed by Dianne Pinkowitz
Manufactured in the United States of America
  2 3 4 5 6 7 8 9 10

Library of Congress Cataloging in Publication Data

Clark, Mary Higgins.
  A stranger is watching.

  I. Title.
PZ4.C5942St [PS3553.L287]   813'.5'4   77-20505
ISBN 0-671-23071-9

In joyful memory of Warren
and for
Marilyn, Warren, David, Carol, and Patricia

You are your parents' glass and I in you
Call back the lovely April of our prime.

1

He sat perfectly still in front of the television set in room 932 of the Biltmore Hotel. The alarm had gone off at six but he was awake long before that. The wind, cold and forbidding, rattled the windowpanes and that had been enough to pull him out of the uneasy sleep.

The *Today* show came on but he didn't adjust the barely audible sound. He didn't care about the news or the special reports. He just wanted to see the interview.

Shifting in the stiff-backed chair, he crossed and uncrossed his legs. He'd already showered and shaved and put on the green polyester suit he'd worn when he'd checked in the night before. The realization that the day had come at last made his hand tremble and he'd nicked his lip when he shaved. It bled a little and the salty taste of blood in his mouth made him gag.

9

He hated blood.

Last night at the desk in the lobby, he'd seen the clerk's eyes sliding over his clothes. He'd carried his coat under his arm because he knew it looked shabby. But the suit was new; he'd saved up for it. Still the clerk looked at him like he was dirt and asked if he had a reservation.

He'd never checked into a real hotel before but knew how to do it. "Yes, I have a reservation." He said it very coldly and for a minute the clerk looked uncertain but when he didn't have a credit card and offered to pay cash in advance, the sneer was back. "I will check out Wednesday morning," he told the clerk.

The room cost one hundred forty dollars for the three nights. That meant he only had thirty dollars left. But that would be plenty for these few days and by Wednesday he'd have eighty-two thousand dollars.

Her face floated across his mind. He blinked to force it away. Because just as always the eyes came after it; the eyes like great lamps that followed him, that were always watching him, that never closed.

He wished he had another cup of coffee. He'd sent for room service, reading the instructions how to call for it very carefully. He'd had a large pot of coffee and there'd been a little left but he'd already washed the cup and saucer and orange juice glass and rinsed out the coffeepot before putting the tray on the floor in the hall.

A commercial was just ending. Suddenly interested he leaned forward to get nearer to the set. The interview should be next. It was. He twisted the volume knob to the right.

The familiar face of Tom Brokaw, the *Today* anchorman, filled the screen. Unsmiling, his voice subdued, he began to speak. "The restoration of capital punishment has become the most emotional and divisive issue in this country since the Vietnamese War. In just fifty-two hours, at eleven-thirty A.M. on March 24th, the sixth execution this year will take place when nineteen-year-old Ronald Thompson dies in the electric chair. My guests . . ."

The camera dollied back to include the two people seated on either side of Tom Brokaw. The man to his right was in his early thirties. His sandy hair was streaked with gray and somewhat disheveled. His hands were together, fingers spread apart and pointing upward. His chin rested on the fingertips, giving him a prayerful stance that was accentuated by dark eyebrows arcing over winter-blue eyes.

The young woman on the other side of the interviewer sat stiffly erect. Her hair, the color of warm honey, was pulled back in a soft chignon. Her hands were knotted into fists in her lap. She moistened her lips and pushed back a strand of hair from her forehead.

Tom Brokaw said, "On their previous appearance here, six months ago, our guests made a very strong case supporting their views on capital punishment. Sharon Martin, syndicated columnist, is also the author of the best-selling book, *The Crime of Capital Punishment*. Steven Peterson, the editor of *Events* magazine, is one of the most articulate voices in the media to urge restoration of capital punishment in this country."

His tone became brisk. He turned to Steve. "Let's start with you, Mr. Peterson. After having witnessed the emotional public reaction to the executions that have already taken place, do you still believe that your position is justified?"

Steve leaned forward. When he answered, his voice was calm. "Absolutely," he said quietly.

The interviewer turned to his other guest. "Sharon Martin, what do you think?"

Sharon shifted slightly in her chair to face her interrogator. She was achingly tired. In the last month she'd worked twenty hours a day, contacting prominent people—senators, congressmen, judges, humanitarians, speaking at colleges, at women's clubs, urging everyone to write and wire the Connecticut governor and protest Ronald Thompson's execution. The response had been enormous, overwhelming. She had been so sure that Governor Greene would reconsider. She found herself groping for words.

"I think," she said, "I *believe* that we, our country, has taken a giant step backwards into the Dark Ages." She held up the newspapers at her side. "Just look at this morning's headlines. Analyze them! They're bloodthirsty." Quickly, she leafed through them. "This one . . . listen . . . *Connecticut Tests Electric Chair*, and this . . . *19-Year Old Dies Wednesday*, and this, *Doomed Killer Protests Innocence.* They're all like that, sensational, savage!" She bit her lip as her voice broke.

Steve glanced at her swiftly. They'd just been told that the Governor was calling a press conference to announce her absolute refusal to grant Thompson another stay of execution. The news had devastated Sharon. It would be a miracle if she didn't get sick after this. They never should have agreed to come on this show today. The Governor's decision made Sharon's appearance pointless, and God knows Steve didn't want to be here. But he had to say something.

"I think every decent human being deplores sensationalism and the need for the death penalty," he said. "But remember it has been applied only after exhaustive consideration of extenuating circumstances. There is no *mandatory* death sentence."

"Do you believe that the circumstances in Ronald Thompson's case, the fact that he committed the murder only days after his seventeenth birthday, making him barely eligible for adult punishment, should have been considered?" Brokaw asked quickly.

Steve said, "As you know, I will not comment specifically on the Thompson case. It would be entirely inappropriate."

"I understand your concern, Mr. Peterson," the interviewer said, "but you had taken your position on this issue several years before . . ." He paused, then continued quietly, "before Ronald Thompson murdered your wife."

Ronald Thompson murdered your wife. The starkness of the words still surprised Steve. After two and a half years, he could still feel the sense of shock and outrage that Nina had died that way, her life snuffed out by the intruder who came into their home, by the hands that had relentlessly twisted her scarf around her throat.

Trying to blot the image from his mind, he looked directly ahead. "At one time, I had hoped that the ban on executions in our country might become a permanent one. But as you point out, long before the tragedy in my own family, I had come to the conclusion that if we were to preserve the most fundamental right of human beings . . . freedom to come and go without fear, freedom to feel sanctuary in our homes, we had to stop the perpetrators of violence. Unfortunately the only way to stop potential murderers seems to be to threaten them with the same harsh judgment they mete out to their victims. And since the first execution was carried out two years ago, the number of murders has dropped dramatically in major cities across the country."

Sharon leaned forward. "You make it sound so reasonable," she cried. "Don't you realize that forty-five percent of murders are committed by people under twenty-five years of age, many of whom have tragic family backgrounds and a history of instability?"

The solitary viewer in Biltmore's room 932 took his eyes

from Steve Peterson and studied the girl thoughtfully. This was the writer Steve was getting serious about. She wasn't at all like his wife. She was obviously taller and had the slender body of someone who might be athletic. His wife had been small and doll-like with rounded breasts and jet black hair that curled around her forehead and ears when she turned her head.

Sharon Martin's eyes reminded him of the color of the ocean that day he'd driven down to the beach last summer. He'd heard that Jones Beach was a good place to meet girls but it hadn't worked out. The one he'd started to fool with in the water had called "Bob!" and a minute later this guy had been beside him, asking what his problem was. So he'd moved his blanket and just stared out at the ocean, watching the changing colors. Green. That was it. Green mixed with blue and churning. He liked eyes that color.

What was Steve saying? Oh yes, he'd said something about feeling sorry for the victims, not their murderers, "for people incapable of defending themselves."

"My sympathies are with them too," Sharon cried. "But it's not either/or. Don't you see that life imprisonment would be punishment enough for the Ronald Thompsons of this world?" She forgot Tom Brokaw, forgot the television cameras as once again she tried to convince Steve. "How can you . . . who are so compassionate . . . who value life so much . . . want to play God?" she asked. "How can anyone presume to play God?"

It was an argument that began and ended the same way as it had that first time six months ago when they'd met on this program. Finally Tom Brokaw said, "Our time is running out. Can we sum up by saying that notwithstanding the public demonstrations, prison riots and student rallys that are regularly occurring all over the country, you still believe, Mr. Peterson, that the sharp drop in random murder justifies execution?"

"I believe in the moral right . . . the duty . . . of society to protect itself, and of the government to protect the sacred liberty of its citizens," Steve said.

"Sharon Martin?" Brokaw turned quickly to her.

"I believe that the death penalty is senseless and brutalizing. I believe that we can make the home and streets safe by removing violent offenders and punishing them with swift, sure sentences, by voting for the bond issues that will build the necessary correctional institutions and will pay the people who staff them. I believe that it is our reverence for life, *all* life, that is the final test of us as individuals and as a society."

Tom Brokaw said hurriedly, "Sharon Martin, Steven Peterson, thank you for being with us on *Today*. I'll be back after this message . . ."

The television set in room 932 of the Biltmore was snapped off. For a long time the muscular, thick-chested man in the green-plaid suit sat staring straight ahead at the darkened screen. Once again he reviewed his plan, the plan that began with putting the pictures and the suitcase in the secret room in Grand Central Station and would end with bringing Steve Peterson's son Neil there tonight. But now he had to decide. Sharon Martin was going to be at Steve's house this evening. She would be minding Neil until Steve got home.

He'd planned simply to eliminate her there.

But should he? She was so beautiful.

He thought of those eyes, the color of the ocean, churning, caring.

It seemed to him that when she looked directly into the camera she had been looking at *him*.

It seemed as though she wanted him to come for her.

Maybe she loved him.

If she didn't it would be easy to get rid of her.

He'd just leave her in the room in Grand Central with the child on Wednesday morning.

Then at 11:30 when the bomb went off, she, too, would be blown to bits.

2

THEY LEFT THE STUDIO TOGETHER, walking a few inches
apart. Sharon's tweed cape felt heavy on her shoulders. Her
hands and feet were icy. She pulled on her gloves and
noticed that the antique moonstone ring Steve had given
her for Christmas had smudged her finger again. Some
people had such a high acid content they couldn't wear
real gold without that happening.

Steve reached past her and held the door open. They
stepped into the windblown morning. It was very cold and
just beginning to snow; thick, clinging flakes that chilled
their faces.

"I'll get you a cab," he said.

"No . . . I'd rather walk."

"That's crazy. You look dead tired."

"It will help clear my head. Oh Steve, how can you be so positive . . . so sure . . . so relentless?"

"Don't let's start again, dear."

"We have to start again!"

"Not now." Steve looked down at her, impatience mingling with concern. Sharon's eyes looked strained, fine, red lines threaded through them; the on-camera makeup she was wearing had not covered the paleness that became accentuated as snow melted on her cheeks and forehead.

"Can you go home and get some rest?" he asked. "You need it."

"I have to turn in my column."

"Well, try to get a few hours' sleep. You'll get up to my place by about quarter of six?"

"Steve, I'm not sure . . ."

"I am. We haven't seen each other for three weeks. The Lufts are counting on going out for their anniversary and I want to be in my home tonight with you and Neil."

Ignoring the people scurrying into the Rockefeller Center buildings, Steve put his hands on Sharon's face and lifted it. Her expression was troubled and sad. He said gravely, "I love you, Sharon. You know that. I've missed you terribly these past weeks. We've got to talk about us."

"Steve, we don't think alike. We . . ."

Bending down he kissed her. Her lips were unyielding. He felt her body tense. Stepping back he raised his hand to signal a passing cab. When it pulled over to the curb, he held the door for her and gave the driver the address of the *News Dispatch* building. Before he shut the door, he asked, "Can I count on you for tonight?"

She nodded silently. Steve watched the cab turn down Fifth Avenue, then quickly walked west. He had stayed overnight at the Gotham Hotel because he had to be at the studio at 6:30, and was anxious to call Neil before he left for school. Everytime he was away from home, he worried. Neil still had nightmares, still woke up with suffocating attacks of asthma. Mrs. Lufts always called the doctor quickly but even so . . .

The winter had been so damp and cold. Maybe in the spring when Neil could get out more, he'd build up a little. He looked so pale all the time.

Spring! My God, it *was* spring. Sometime during the night the vernal equinox had taken place and winter had officially ended. You'd never guess it from the weather prediction.

Steve reached the corner and turned north, reflecting that he and Sharon had been seeing each other exactly six months now. When he picked her up at her apartment that first evening, she'd suggested walking through Central Park to the Tavern on the Green. He warned her that it had become much cooler in the last few hours and reminded her it was the first day of fall.

"Wonderful," she said. "I was just getting bored with summer." For the first few blocks they'd been almost silent. He studied the way she walked, easily in stride with him, her slender frame accentuated by the belted tawny gold suit that exactly matched the color of her hair. He remembered that the sharp breeze was pulling the first dead leaves from the trees and the setting sun accentuated the deep blue of the autumn sky.

"On a night like this, I always think of that song from *Camelot*," she told him. "You know the one, *If Ever I Would Leave You*." She sang softly, "How I'd leave in autumn, I never would know. I've seen how you sparkle when fall nips the air. I know you in autumn and I must be there . . ." She had a lovely contralto voice.

If ever I would leave you . . .

Was that the minute he fell in love with her?

That evening had been so good. They'd lingered over dinner talking while the people at other tables left, and new people came.

What had they talked about? Everything. Her father was an engineer for an oil company. She and her two sisters were born abroad. Both sisters were married now.

"How have you escaped?" It was a question that he had to ask. They both knew what he was really asking, "Is there anyone important in your life?"

But there wasn't. She'd traveled almost constantly for her last newspaper before she started writing the column. It was interesting and lots of fun and she didn't know where the seven years since college had vanished.

They walked back to the apartment and by the second block they were holding hands. She invited him up for a nightcap. There was the slightest emphasis on *nightcap*.

While he made drinks, she touched a match to the kindling in the fireplace and they sat side by side watching the flames.

Steven could still remember vividly the feeling of that night, the way the fire brought out the gold in her hair, threw shadows on her classic profile, highlighted her sudden beautiful smile. He'd ached to put his arms around her then but simply kissed her lightly when he left. "Saturday, if you're not busy. . ." He waited.

"I'm not busy."

"I'll call you in the morning."

And on the drive home, he'd known that the restless, ceaseless heart hunger of the last two years might be ending. If ever I would leave you . . . Don't leave me Sharon.

It was quarter of eight when he turned into the building at 1347 Avenue of the Americas. *Events* magazine staffers were not noted for their early arrivals. The corridors were deserted. Nodding to the security guard at the elevator, Steve went up to his thirty-sixth-floor office and dialed his home.

Mrs. Lufts answered. "Oh, Neil's fine. He's just eating his breakfast, or picking at it, I should say. Neil, it's your dad."

Neil got on. "Hi, Dad, when are you coming home?"

"By eight-thirty sure. I have a five o'clock meeting. The Lufts still want to go to the movies, don't they?"

"I guess so."

"Sharon will be up before six so they can leave."

"I know. You told me." Neil's voice was noncommittal.

"Well have a good day, son. And dress warmly. It's getting pretty cold down here. Is it snowing up there yet?"

"No, it's just sort of cloudy."

"All right. See you tonight."

"Bye, Dad."

Steve frowned. It was hard to remember that at one time Neil had been such a vibrant, happy-go-lucky kid. Nina's death had changed that. He wished that Neil and Sharon would get closer. Sharon was trying, really trying, to break through Neil's reserve, but he just wouldn't give an inch, at least not so far.

Time. Everything took time. Sighing, Steve turned to the table behind his desk and reached for the editorial he had been working on the night before.

3

THE OCCUPANT OF ROOM 932 left the Biltmore at 9:30 A.M. He exited by the Forty-fourth Street door and headed east toward Second Avenue. The sharp, snow-filled wind was hurrying pedestrians along, making them shrink within themselves, tuck their necks into upturned collars.

It was good weather for him, the kind of weather when people didn't bother to notice what other people were doing.

His first stop was a thrift shop on Second Avenue below Thirty-fourth Street. Ignoring the buses that passed every few minutes, he walked the fourteen blocks. Walking was good exercise and it was important to keep in shape.

The thrift shop was empty except for the elderly sales-clerk who sat listlessly reading the morning paper. "Anything particular you want?" she asked.

"No. I'll just look around." He spotted the rack with the

women's coats and went over to it. Pushing through the shabby garments, he selected a dark gray tent-shaped wool coat that looked long enough. Sharon Martin was fairly tall, he reflected. There was a tray of folded kerchiefs near the rack. He reached for the largest one, a faded bluish rectangle.

The woman stuffed his purchases in a shopping bag.

The Army-Navy store was next. That was easy. In the camping-gear section he bought a large canvas duffel bag. He selected it carefully, making sure it was long enough to hold the boy, thick enough that you couldn't tell from the shape what he'd be carrying, wide enough to let sufficient air in when the drawstring was loose.

In a First Avenue Woolworth's, he bought six rolls of wide bandage and two large spools of thick twine. He brought his purchases back to the Biltmore. The bed in his room was made and there were clean towels in the bathroom.

His eyes darted around for signs that the maid had gone through the closet. But his other pair of shoes was right there, exactly as he had left them, one a hairsbreadth behind the other, neither quite touching the old black double-locked suitcase that was standing in the corner.

Slipping the deadlock on the room door, he placed the bags with his purchases on the bed. With infinite care, he lifted the suitcase from the closet and laid it on the foot of the bed. Reaching into a compartment in his wallet, he extracted a key and opened the suitcase.

He made a thorough check of the contents, the pictures, the powder, the clock, the wires, the fuses, the hunting knife and the gun. Satisfied, he closed the bag again.

Carrying the suitcase and the shopping bag, he left the room. This time he went into the lower lobby of the Biltmore to the underground arcade which led to the upper level of Grand Central Station. The early morning commuter rush was over but the terminal was still filled with people scurrying to and from trains, people using the station as a shortcut to Forty-second Street or Park Avenue, people on their way to arcade shops, to the off-track betting center, the quick-service restaurants, the newsstands.

Moving quickly, he went down the stairs to the lower level and drifted over toward platform 112 from which Mount Vernon trains arrived and departed. There was no train due for eighteen minutes and the area was deserted. Glancing around swiftly, he made sure no guard was looking in his direction and disappeared down the stairs to the platform.

The platform extended in a U shape around the end of the tracks. From the other side a sloping ramp led into the depths of the terminal. Hurrying around the tracks, he made his way to that ramp. Now his movements became quicker, furtive. The sounds became different in this other world of the terminal. Overhead the station was bustling with the comings and goings of thousands of travelers. Here a pneumatic pump was throbbing, ventilating fans were rumbling, water was trickling across the damp floor. The silent, starved forms of beggar cats slithered in and out of the nearby tunnel under Park Avenue. A continuing dull railroad sound came from the loop where all the trains, beginning their outgoing journey, turned and chugged in gathering momentum away from the terminal.

He continued his gradual descent until he was at the foot of a steep iron staircase. He hurried up the metal steps, carefully placing one foot silently on the rung above. An occasional guard wandered through this area. The light was poor but even so . . .

At the head of the small landing there was a heavy metal door. Carefully depositing the suitcase and the shopping bag on the landing, he fished for and found the key in his wallet. Quickly, nervously, he inserted it in the lock. Reluctantly, the lock yielded its authority and the door swung open.

Inside it was pitch black. He fumbled for the light switch, found it, and keeping one hand firmly on it, reached down and lifted the suitcase and shopping bag into the room. He let the door close noiselessly.

The dark now was absolute. He could see the outlines of the room. The musty smell was overwhelming. Letting out a protracted sigh, the intruder consciously tried to relax. Deliberately he listened for the station sounds but they were far off, discernible only when a distinct effort was made to hear them.

It was all right.

He flicked the switch and the room became gloomy-bright. The dusty fluorescent lamps glared on the peeling ceiling and walls, casting deep shadows in the corners. The room was L-shaped, a cement room with cement walls from which thick layers of gray, moisture-repellent paint were hanging in jagged flaps. An ancient, outsize pair of laundry tubs were to the left of the door. Dripping water from the faucets had streaked their insides with canals of rust through thick layers of caked dirt. In the middle of the room, uneven, tightly nailed boards entombed a chimney-like object, a dumbwaiter. A narrow door off the far right of the L-shaped room was ajar, revealing a grimy toilet.

He knew the toilet worked. He'd come into this room last week for the first time in over twenty years and checked the lights and plumbing. Something had made him come here, had reminded him of this room when he was making his plan.

A rickety canvas army cot leaned lopsided against the

far wall, an overturned orange crate next to it. The cot and crate worried him. Someone else, sometime, had stumbled onto this room and stayed in it. But the dust on the cot and the stale dampness could only mean the room had been unopened for months at least, maybe years.

He hadn't been here since he was sixteen, more than half a lifetime ago. That was when this room was used by the Oyster Bar. Located directly below the Oyster Bar kitchen, the old boarded-up dumbwaiter used to bring mounds of greasy dishes to be washed in the deep sinks and dried and sent back upstairs.

Years ago the Oyster Bar kitchen had been renovated and dishwashing machines installed. And this room sealed off. Just as well. No one would work in this smelly hole.

But it could still serve a purpose.

When he'd pondered where he could keep Peterson's son until the ransom was paid, he'd remembered this room. He'd investigated it and then realized how well it fit into his plan. When he'd been working here, with his hands all swollen from irritating detergents and scalding water and heavy wet towels, all through the terminal well-dressed people had been rushing home to their expensive houses and cars, or sitting in the restaurant eating the shrimp and clams and oysters and bass and snapper he'd had to scrape off their plates, never caring about him at all.

He'd make everyone in Grand Central, in New York, *in the world* notice him. After Wednesday they'd never forget him.

It had been simple to get into this room. A wax impression in the door of the rusty old lock. Then he'd made a key. Now he could come and go as he pleased.

Tonight Sharon Martin and the boy would be here with him. Grand Central Station. The world's busiest railroad terminal. The best place in the world to hide people.

He laughed aloud. Now that he was here, he could begin to laugh. He felt clear and brilliant and stimulated. The peeling walls and sagging cot and leaking water and splintered boards excited him.

Here he was the master, the planner. He'd arrange to get his money. He'd close the eyes forever. He couldn't stand dreaming about the eyes anymore. He couldn't stand it. And now they had become a real danger.

Wednesday. Eleven-thirty Wednesday morning was exactly forty-eight hours away. He'd be on a plane leaving for Arizona where no one knew him. It wasn't safe for him in Carley. There were too many questions being asked.

But out there, with the money . . . and the eyes gone . . . and if Sharon Martin was in love with him, he'd bring her with him.

He carried the suitcase past the army cot and carefully laid it flat on the floor. Opening it, he removed the tiny cassette recorder and camera and put them in the lefthand pocket of his shapeless brown overcoat. The hunting knife and gun went into the righthand pocket. No bulges showed through the deep, thick pockets.

He picked up the shopping bag and methodically spread its contents on the cot. The coat and scarf and twine and tape and bandage rolls, he stuffed into the duffel bag. Finally he reached for the packet of neatly rolled posters. He opened them, smoothing them down, bending them to reduce the curling. His eyes lingered on them. A smile, reminiscent, thoughtful, extended his narrow lips.

The first three pictures he hung on the wall, over the cot, securing them carefully with surgical tape. The fourth he studied, and slowly rolled up again.

Not yet, he decided.

Time was passing. Carefully he turned out the light

before opening the door a few inches. He listened intently, but there were no footsteps in the area.

Slipping outside, he noiselessly descended the metal steps and hurried past the throbbing generator, the rumbling fans, the yawning tunnel, up the ramp, around the Mt. Vernon tracks, up the steps to the lower level of Grand Central Station. There he became part of the flow of people, a barrel-chested man in his late thirties with a muscular frame, a stiff, straight carriage, a chapped, puffy, high-cheekboned face with narrow lips that he pressed together and heavy lids that only partially concealed the pale eyes that darted from side to side.

A ticket in his hand, he hurried to the gate on the upper level where the train was leaving for Carley, Connecticut.

4

Neil stood on the corner waiting for the school bus. He knew Mrs. Lufts was watching him from the window. He hated that. None of his friends' mothers watched them like Mrs. Lufts did. You'd think he was a kindergarten baby instead of a first-grader.

Whenever it was raining, he had to wait in the house until the bus came. He hated that too. It made him look like a big sissy. He tried to explain that to his father but Dad hadn't understood. He'd just said that Neil had to take some special care because of his asthma attacks.

Sandy Parker was in the fourth grade. He lived on the next street but got on the bus at this stop. He always wanted to sit next to Neil. Neil wished that he wouldn't. Sandy always talked about things Neil didn't want to talk about.

Just as the bus turned the corner, Sandy came puffing up, his books sliding around in his arms. Neil tried to head for an empty seat near the back but Sandy said, "Here, Neil, here are two seats together." The bus was noisy. All the kids talked at the tops of their voices. Sandy didn't talk loud but you couldn't miss a single word he said.

Sandy was bursting with excitement. They'd barely sat down when he said, "We saw your father on the *Today* show when we were having breakfast."

"My father?" Neil shook his head. "You're kidding."

"No, I'm not. That lady I met at your house was on it too, Sharon Martin. They were arguing."

"Why?" Neil didn't want to ask. He was never sure if he should believe Sandy.

"Because she doesn't believe in killing bad people and your father does. My dad said that your dad's right. He said that the guy who killed your mother should fry." Sandy repeated the word with emphasis, *"Fry!"*

Neil turned to the window. He leaned his forehead against the cool glass. Outside it looked so gray and it was just starting to snow. He wished it were tonight. He wished his dad had been home last night. He didn't like being just with the Lufts. They were both nice to him but they argued a lot and Mr. Lufts went out to the bar and Mrs. Lufts was mad even though she tried not to show it in front of him.

"Aren't you glad they're going to kill Ronald Thompson Wednesday?" Sandy persisted.

"No . . . I mean . . . I don't think about it," Neil said in a low voice.

That wasn't true. He did think about it a lot. He dreamt about it all the time too, always the same dream about that night. He was playing with his trains up in his room.

Mommy was in the kitchen putting away the shopping. It was just getting dark out. One of his trains went off the track and he switched off the power.

That was when he heard the funny sound, like a scream but not a loud scream. He'd run downstairs. The living room was almost dark but he'd seen her. Mommy. Her arms were trying to push someone back. She was making awful, choking sounds. The man was twisting something around her neck.

Neil had stood on the landing. He wanted to help her but he couldn't move. He wanted to shout for help but he couldn't make his voice work. He started to breathe like Mommy, funny, gurgly sounds, then his knees went all crumbly. The man turned when he heard him and let Mommy fall.

Neil was falling too. He could feel himself falling. Then the room got brighter. Mommy was lying on the floor. Her tongue was sticking out, her face was blue, her eyes were staring. The man was kneeling beside her now; his hands were all over her throat. He looked up at Neil and started to run but Neil could see his face clearly. It was all sweaty and scared.

Neil had had to tell all about that to the policemen and point out the man at the trial. Then Daddy said, try to forget it, Neil. Just think of all the happy times with Mommy. But he couldn't forget. He kept dreaming about it all the time and he'd wake up with asthma.

Now maybe Daddy was going to marry Sharon. Sandy had told him that everybody said his dad would probably get married again. Sandy said that nobody wants other women's kids, especially kids who are sick a lot.

Mr. and Mrs. Lufts kept talking about wanting to move to Florida. Neil wondered if Daddy would give him to

33

the Lufts if he married Sharon. He hoped not. Miserably, he stared out the window, so deep in thought that Sandy had to poke him when the bus pulled up in front of their school.

5

THE CAB SCREECHED TO A STOP at the *News Dispatch* building on East Forty-second Street. Sharon rummaged in her handbag, pulled out two dollars and paid the driver.

The snow flurry had stopped for the moment but the temperature was still dropping and the sidewalk felt slick underfoot.

She went directly to the newsroom that was already bustling with preparations for the afternoon edition. There was a note in her box to see the City Editor immediately.

Disturbed by the implied urgency, she hurried across the noisy room. He was alone in his small, cluttered office. "Come in and close the door." He waved her to a seat. "Got your column for today?"

"Yes."

"Any reference to telegraphing or phoning Governor Greene to commute Thompson's sentence?"

"Certainly. I've been thinking about it. I'll change the lead. The fact that the Governor said she won't stop the execution might be a break. It might jog a lot more people into action. We've still got forty-eight hours."

"Forget it."

Sharon stared. "What do you mean, 'forget it'? You've been right with me all through this."

"I said, forget it. After the Governor made her decision, she personally called the old man and blasted him. Said that we were deliberately creating sensationalism to sell papers. She said that she doesn't believe in capital punishment either but she has no right to interfere with the sentence of the court without new evidence. She said if we wanted to campaign to amend the Constitution, it was our right and she'd help us every step of the way, but to pressure her to interfere in one particular case had the effect of trying to apply justice capriciously. The old man ended up agreeing with her."

Sharon felt her stomach twist as though she'd been kicked. For an instant she was afraid she was going to get sick. Pressing her lips together, she tried to swallow over the sudden constriction in her throat. The editor looked at her closely. "You all right, Sharon? You look pretty pale."

She managed to force back the brackish taste. "I'm all right."

"I can get someone to cover that meeting tomorrow. You better take a few days off."

"No." The Massachusetts legislature was debating outlawing capital punishment in that state. She intended to be there.

"Have it your way. File your column and go home."

His voice became sympathetic. "I'm sorry, Sharon. A constitutional amendment could take years to get passed and I thought if we got Governor Greene to be the first one to commute a death sentence, the same approach could be used case by case across the country. But I can understand her position."

Sharon said, "I understand that legalized murder is not to be protested anymore except in the abstract." Without waiting for his reaction, she abruptly got up and left the room. Going to her desk, she reached into the zipper compartment of her oversized shoulderbag and pulled out the folded typewritten pages that contained the article she had worked on most of the night. She carefully tore the pages in half, then in quarters, finally in eighths. She watched as they fluttered into the battered wastebasket next to her desk.

Putting a fresh sheet of paper in the typewriter, she began to write. "Society is again about to exercise its recently regained prerogative, the right to kill. Almost four hundred years ago, the French philosopher Montaigne wrote, 'The horror of one man killing another makes me fear the horror of killing him.'

"If you agree that capital punishment should be outlawed by the constitution. . . ."

She wrote steadily for two hours, slashing whole paragraphs, inserting phrases, rewriting. When she had completed the column, she retyped it quickly, turned it in, left the building and hailed a cab. "Ninety-fifth Street just off Central Park West, please," she said.

The cab turned north at the Avenue of the Americas, entered the park at Central Park South. Sharon watched somberly as new snow flurries settled over the grass. If this kept up, by tomorrow, children would be sleighriding here.

Just last month Steve had brought his ice skates down and

they'd gone skating at Wollman Rink. Neil was supposed to have come with him. Sharon had planned that after skating, they'd go to the zoo and then have dinner at the Tavern on the Green. But at the last minute, Neil claimed he didn't feel well and stayed home. He didn't like her, that was obvious.

"Okay, Miss."

"What? Oh, I'm sorry." They were turning onto Ninety-fifth Street. "The third house on the left." She lived in the ground-level-with-garden apartment of a renovated brownstone.

The cab pulled in front of it. The driver, a slight, graying man, looked over his shoulder at her quizzically. "It can't be all that bad, lady," he said. "You sure look down."

She attempted a smile. "It's that kind of day, I guess." Glancing at the meter, she fished in her pocket for money, making the tip generous.

The driver reached back and opened the door for her. "Boy, this weather is going to have a lot of people in the dumps by rush hour. Supposed to really start snowing. If you're smart, you'll stay inside from now on."

"I'm driving up to Connecticut later."

"Better you than me, lady. Thanks."

Angie, her two-mornings-a-week cleaning woman, had obviously just left. There was a faint smell of lemon polish; the fireplace had been swept; the plants trimmed and watered. As always the apartment offered a restful welcome to Sharon. The old oriental rug that had been her grandmother's had mellowed into soft shades of blue and red. She'd reupholstered in blue the couch and chair she bought secondhand, a labor of love that had taken the better part of four weekends but turned out well. The pictures and prints on the walls and over the fireplace she'd selected one by one, in small antique shops, at auctions, on trips abroad.

Steve loved this room. He always noticed even the smallest change in it. "You have a way with a home," he told her.

Mechanically, she walked into the bedroom and began to undress. She'd shower and change and make tea and try to sleep for awhile. She couldn't even think coherently now.

It was nearly noon when she got into bed and she set the alarm for three-thirty. For a long time sleep didn't come. Ronald Thompson. She'd been so *sure* the Governor would commute his sentence. There was no question that he was guilty, and lying about it had certainly hurt him. But except for that one other serious episode when he was fifteen, his record was good. And he was so *young*.

Steve. It was people like Steve who were molding public opinion. It was Steve's reputation for integrity, for fair play that made people listen to him.

Did she love Steve?

Yes.

How much?

Very, very much.

Did she want to marry him? They were going to have to talk about that tonight. She knew that was why Steve wanted her to stay at his place. And he wanted so much for Neil to begin to accept her. But it wouldn't work; you can't force a relationship. Neil was so standoffish with her, so rejecting. Was it that he didn't like her or would he react the same way to any woman who took his father's attention from him? She wasn't sure.

Did she want to live in Carley? She loved New York so much, loved it seven days a week. But Steve would never agree to move Neil to the city.

She was just beginning to make it as a writer. Her book was in its sixth printing. It had been published as a paperback; no hardcover house had been interested, but the reviews and sales had been unexpectedly good.

Was this the time to get involved in marriage—marriage to a man whose child resented her?

Steve. Unconsciously she touched her face, remembering the feeling of those big, gentle hands warming it as he said goodbye to her this morning. They were so desperately attracted to each other . . .

But how could she accept the uncompromising, stubborn side of him when he made up his mind on an issue?

Finally she dozed off. Almost immediately she began to dream. She was writing a column. She had to finish it. It was important to finish it. But no matter how frantically she pressed the typewriter keys no impressions were being made on the paper. Then Steve was in the room. He was pulling a young man by the arm. She was still trying to make the words come out on the paper. Steve made the boy sit down. "I am so sorry," he kept saying to him, "but it is necessary. You must understand this is necessary." Then while Sharon tried to scream, Steve fastened the boy's arms and legs in shackles and reached for a switch.

Sharon was awakened by the sound of a hoarse voice, her own, shrieking, "No . . . No . . . No . . ."

6

AT FIVE MINUTES OF SIX the few people in the streets of
Carley, Connecticut, were hurrying from cars to stores,
heedless of anything except the bitter, snowy night.

The man standing in the shadows near the edge of the
Cabin Restaurant parking lot was completely unobserved.
His eyes constantly roved the area as pelting snow blew
in his face. He'd been there nearly twenty minutes and
his feet were freezing.

Impatiently, he shifted and his toe touched the duffel bag
at his feet. He felt for the weapons in the pocket of his
coat. They were at his fingertips and he nodded, satisfied.

The Lufts should be along any minute. He'd phoned
the restaurant and confirmed the six o'clock reservation.
They were planning to have dinner and then go to see the
Selznick's *Gone With the Wind*. It was playing in the

41

Carley Square Theater diagonally across the street. The 4:00 P.M. performance was on now. They were going to the 7:30 showing.

He stiffened. A car was coming down the block, was turning into the parking lot. He shrank behind the spruce trees edging the area. It was their stationwagon. He watched as they parked near the restaurant entrance. The driver got out and went around to help his wife who was clumsily stepping onto the slick tarpin. Their bodies bent against the wind, their gait awkward, his hand under her elbow, the Lufts moved with cautious haste toward the door of the restaurant.

He waited till they were safely inside before bending down and picking up the duffel bag. Moving swiftly, he circled the parking lot, keeping well behind the shrubbery. He cut across the street and hurried behind the moviehouse.

There were about fifty cars parked in the lot. He headed toward an eight-year-old dark-brown Chevrolet sedan parked unobtrusively in the far right corner.

In an instant he had the door unlocked. He slipped into the seat, put the key in the ignition and turned it. The engine purred with quiet pep. With a slight smile and a last overall glance at the deserted surroundings, he started the car. He did not turn the lights on as he drove past the theater into the quiet street. Four minutes later the shabby brown sedan pulled into the circular driveway of the Peterson home on Driftwood Lane and parked behind a small red Vega.

7

THE DRIVE FROM MANHATTAN TO CARLEY usually took less than an hour but the ominous weather forecast had sent commuters scurrying to their cars early. The traffic buildup combined with icy spots on the parkways made Sharon's trip to Steve's house last nearly an hour and twenty minutes. But she was almost unaware of the maddening delays. All the way up, she rehearsed what she would say to Steve, "It won't work for us. . . . We don't think alike. . . . Neil will never accept me . . . it will be easier if we don't see each other any more . . ."

Steve's house, a white clapboard colonial with black shutters, vaguely depressed Sharon. The porchlight was too bright. The foundation shrubs were too high. Sharon knew that Steve and Nina had lived in this house only a few

43

weeks before her death and that he hadn't done any of the renovating they'd planned when they bought it.

She parked just past the porch steps and unconsciously braced herself for Mrs. Lufts' rapid-fire greeting and Neil's coolness. But this would be the last time. That thought deepened her depression.

Mrs. Lufts had obviously been watching for her. The front door was yanked open as she got out of the car. "Miss Martin, my, it's nice to see you." Mrs. Lufts' stocky frame filled the doorway. Her small-featured face was squirrel-like with bright, inquisitive eyes. She was wearing a heavy red-plaid coat and galoshes.

"How are you, Mrs. Lufts?" Sharon stepped past her into the house. Mrs. Lufts had a habit of always standing close to the person she was with so that contact with her invariably had a smothering effect. Now she moved back barely enough to let Sharon squeeze past.

"It's awfully nice of you to come," Mrs. Lufts said. "Here, let me take your cape. I love capes. Make you look sweet and feminine, don't you think?"

Sharon set her pocketbook and overnight bag down in the foyer. She pulled off her gloves. "I guess so. I've never really thought about it . . ." She glanced into the living room. "Oh . . ."

Neil was sitting, cross-legged, on the carpet, magazines scattered around him, a pair of blunt scissors in his hand. His sandy hair, exactly the shade of Steve's, fell over his forehead, leaving his bent neck thin and vulnerable. His bony shoulders stuck out under a brown-and-white flannel shirt. His face looked thin and pale except for the red streaks around the enormous dark brown eyes that were welling with tears.

"Neil, say hello to Sharon," Mrs. Lufts commanded.

44

He looked up, listlessly. "Hello, Sharon." His voice was low and quivering.

He looked so little and scrawny and woebegone. Sharon ached to put her arms around him but knew that if she did, he'd only pull away from her.

Mrs. Lufts made a clicking sound with her tongue. "I'll be blessed if I know what the trouble is. Just started crying a few minutes ago. Won't tell me why. You never can figure what goes on in that little head. Well, maybe you or his dad can get it out of him." Her voice rose an octave, "Billlllll . . ."

Sharon jumped, her eardrums ringing. Hastily she went into the living room and stood in front of Neil. "What are you supposed to cut out?" she asked.

"Just some dumb pictures with animals." Neil did not look at her again. She knew he was embarrassed to be seen crying.

"Why don't I get myself a sherry and then give you a hand. Want a coke or something?"

"No." Neil hesitated, then reluctantly added, "Thank you."

"Just help yourself," Mrs. Lufts said. "Make yourself at home. You know where everything is. I got everything on the list Mr. Peterson left, steak and salad makings and asparagus and ice cream. It's all in the refrigerator. I'm sorry to be rushing but we do want to have dinner before the movie. Bill . . ."

"I'm coming, Dora." There was annoyance in the voice. Bill Lufts came up the stairway from the basement. "Just wanted to check on the windows," he said, "make sure they're locked. Hello, Miss Martin."

"How are you, Mr. Lufts?" He was a short, thick-necked man in his mid-sixties with watery blue eyes. Tiny broken capillaries formed telltale patches on his cheeks and nostrils, reminding Sharon that Steve was worried about Bill Lufts' heavy drinking.

"Bill, get a move on will you?" His wife's voice was edged with impatience. "You know how I hate to gulp my food, and we're running late now. The only time you take me out is our anniversary, seems to me, and I do think you could hurry . . ."

"All right. All right." Bill sighed heavily and nodded to Sharon. "See you later, Miss Martin."

"Have a good time." Sharon followed him into the foyer. "And, oh yes, happy anniversary."

"Wear a hat, Bill. You'll catch your death . . . What? Oh, thank you, thank you, Miss Martin. Soon as I sit down and get a rest and something to eat, I'll start feeling like an anniversary. Right now with all this rushing . . ."

"Dora, you're the one who wants to see this movie . . ."

"All right. I've got everything. Have a nice time, to-gether, you two. Neil, show your report card to Sharon. He's a real bright boy, no trouble either, are you, Neil? I gave him a snack to hold him over till dinner but he hardly touched it. Don't eat enough to keep a bird alive. All right, Bill, all right!"

They were finally off. Sharon shivered as a chilly blast of air rushed into the foyer before she could close the door after them. She went back into the kitchen, opened the refrigerator and reached for the bottle of Bristol cream sherry. She hesitated, then took out a carton of milk. Neil might have said he didn't want anything but she was going to make him some hot cocoa.

While she waited for the milk to heat, she sipped the sherry and glanced around. Mrs. Lufts did her best but she wasn't a good housekeeper and the kitchen had a vaguely untidy look. There were crumbs spilling around the toaster on the counter. The top of the stove needed a good scrubbing. Really the whole house needed a facelifting.

Steve's property backed onto Long Island Sound. "I'd cut all those trees that block the view," Sharon thought, "and enclose the back porch and make it part of the living room with floor-to-ceiling windows, and knock out most of the walls and put in a breakfast bar . . ." Sharply she checked herself. It was none of her business. It was just that the house and Neil and even Steve had such a neglected look.

But it was not for her to change. The thought of not seeing Steve again, not expecting his call, not feeling those strong, gentle arms around her, not watching that suddenly carefree look light up his face when she said something that amused him, filled her with bleak loneliness. This is how it feels to know you have to give up someone, she thought. How does Mrs. Thompson feel, knowing that her only child will die day after tomorrow?

She knew Mrs. Thompson's number. She'd interviewed her after deciding to get involved in Ron's case. A number of times during this last trip, she'd tried to phone Mrs. Thompson to share the news that so many important people had promised to contact Governor Greene and urge clemency. But she'd never caught her home. Probably because Mrs. Thompson had been working on a petition for clemency from the people in Fairfield County.

That poor woman. She'd been so hopeful when Sharon visited her, then seemed so upset when she realized that Sharon didn't think Ron was innocent.

But what mother could believe her son was capable of murder? Maybe Mrs. Thompson was home now. Maybe it would help just to talk with someone who had worked to save Ronald.

Sharon lowered the flame under the saucepan, went over

to the wall-phone and dialed the number. The phone was answered on the first ring. Mrs. Thompson's voice was surprisingly steady. "Hello."

"Mrs. Thompson, this is Sharon Martin. I had to call to tell you how sorry I am, to ask if there's anything I can do..."

"You've done enough, Miss Martin." The bitterness in the woman's voice stunned Sharon. "If my boy dies Wednesday, I want you to know that I hold you responsible. I begged you to keep out of this."

"Mrs. Thompson ... I don't know what you mean ..."

"I mean, that in all your columns you have over and over again written that there was no question of Ronald's guilt but that wasn't the issue. It *is* the issue, Miss Martin!" The woman's voice became high-pitched. "It *is* the issue. There were many people who know my boy, who know that he's incapable of hurting anyone, who were working to get him clemency. But you ... you've forced the Governor not to examine his case just on its own merits ... We're still trying, and I don't believe God will do this to me, but if my son dies, I don't think I'll be responsible for what I might do to you."

The connection was broken. Bewildered, Sharon stared at the receiver in her hand. Could Mrs. Thompson really believe...? Numbly she replaced the receiver on the hook.

The milk was almost boiling in the saucepan on the stove. Mechanically, she reached for the box of Quik in the cabinet and scooped a heaping teaspoon of it into a mug. She poured the milk in, stirred it, and put the pot in the sink to soak.

Stunned by the implication of Mrs. Thompson's attack, she started for the living room.

The bell rang.

Neil scrambled for the door before she could stop him. "Maybe it's my dad." He sounded relieved.

He doesn't want to be alone with me at all, Sharon thought. She heard him click the double lock and a sense of alarm jangled through her. "Neil, wait a minute," she called. "Ask who it is. Your dad would have his key."

Hastily she set down the cocoa mug and sherry glass on a table near the fireplace and ran into the hall.

Neil obeyed her. He had one hand on the knob but hesitated and called "Who is it?"

"Is Bill Lufts there?" a voice called. "I have the generator he ordered for Mr. Peterson's boat."

"Oh, that's all right," Neil told Sharon. "Mr. Lufts is waiting for that."

He turned the handle of the door and was starting to pull it open when it was pushed in with violent force, slamming Neil back against the wall. Stunned, Sharon watched as a man stepped into the foyer and with a lightning-quick movement closed the door behind him. Gasping, Neil fell to the floor. Instinctively, Sharon ran over to him. She helped him to his feet, and keeping one arm around him, turned to face the intruder.

Two distinctively separate impressions burned into her consciousness. One was the glittering stare in the stranger's eyes. The other was the thin, long-barreled pistol he was pointing at her head.

8

THE MEETING IN THE CONFERENCE ROOM of *Events* magazine lasted until 7:10 P.M. The main topic of conversation was the just-released Nielson report that had been highly favorable. Two out of three of the surveyed college graduates in the twenty-five to forty age bracket preferred *Events* to *Time* or *Newsweek*. Besides that, the paid circulation was up fifteen percent over the previous year and the new regional advertising was working well.

At the end of the meeting, Bradley Robertson, the publisher, stood up. "I think we can all take a great deal of pride in these statistics," he said. "We've been working hard for nearly three years but we've done it. It's not easy to launch a new magazine these days and I, for one, want to say, that in my mind, the creative direction of Steve Peterson has been the decisive factor in our success."

After the meeting, Steve went down in the elevator with the publisher. "Thanks, again, Brad," he said, "that was very generous of you."

The older man shrugged. "It was honest of me. We've made it, Steve. We'll all be able to start taking some decent money soon. It's about time, too. I know it hasn't been easy for you."

Steve smiled grimly, "No, it hasn't."

The elevator door opened in the main lobby.

"Goodnight, Brad. I'm going to run. I want to catch the seven-thirty . . ."

"Wait a minute. Steve, I saw you on the *Today* show this morning.

"Yes."

"I thought you were excellent, but so was Sharon. And, personally, I confess I go along with her thinking."

"A lot of people do."

"I like her, Steve. She's as bright as they come . . . damn good-looking too. And a real lady."

"I agree."

"Steve, I know how much you've been through the last couple of years. I don't want to butt in, but Sharon would be good for you . . . and for Neil. Don't let issues, no matter how compelling, come between you."

"I pray they don't," Steve answered quietly. "And at least now I'll be able to offer Sharon something more than a financially strapped guy with a ready-made family."

"She'd be darn lucky to get both you and Neil! Come on, my car's outside. I'll drop you off at Grand Central."

"Great. Sharon is up at my place and I don't want to miss the train."

Bradley's limousine was at the door. The driver quickly began to thread through the snarled midtown traffic. Steve leaned back and unconsciously sighed.

"You look tired, Steve. This Thompson execution has got to be getting to you."

Steve shrugged. "It is. Naturally it brings everything back. Every paper in Connecticut is rehashing the . . . Nina's death. I know that the kids have to be talking about it in school. I worry about how much Neil is hearing. I'm desperately sorry for Thompson's mother . . . and for him too."

"Why don't you take Neil and get away for a few days until this is over?"

Steve considered. "I might do that. It probably would be a good idea."

The limousine pulled up to the Vanderbilt Avenue entrance to Grand Central. Bradley Robertson shook his head. "You're too young to remember, Steve, but during the thirties, Grand Central was the hub of transportation in this country. There even used to be a radio series . . ." He closed his eyes. "'Grand Central Station, crossroads of a million private lives,' that was the blurb for it."

Steve laughed. "And then along came the jet age." He opened the door. "Thanks for the lift."

Pulling out his commuter book, he walked quickly down into the terminal. He had five minutes till train time and decided to phone home to tell Sharon he was definitely making the 7:30 train.

He shrugged. Don't kid yourself, he thought. You just want to talk to her, to make sure she didn't change her mind about coming. He stepped into a phonebooth. He didn't have much change and made the call collect.

The phone rang once . . . twice . . . three times.

The operator came in. "I am rrringing your number but there is no answer."

"There has to be someone there. Keep trying, operator, please."

"Certainly, sir."

The jabbing sound continued. After the fifth time, the operator came back on. "There is no answer, sir. Will you place your call later, please?"

"Operator, would you mind checking the number? Are you sure we're ringing 203-565-1313?"

"I'll dial it again, sir."

Steve stared at the receiver in his hand. Where could they be? If Sharon hadn't come up, would the Lufts have perhaps asked the Perrys if Neil could stay with them?

No. Sharon would have phoned him if she decided not to go to his house. Suppose Neil had had an asthma attack . . . suppose he'd had to be rushed to the hospital again?

An attack wouldn't be surprising if he'd heard any talk in school about the Thompson execution.

Neil had been having more frequent nightmares lately.

It was 7:29. The train was leaving in one minute. If he tried to phone the doctor or the hospital or the Perrys, he'd miss the train and have to wait forty-five minutes for the next one.

Perhaps there was trouble with the phone lines because of the storm. That didn't always show up at once.

Steve started to dial the Perrys, then changed his mind. He replaced the phone on the hook, then raced across the station in long, sprinting strides. Taking the stairs down to the platform two at a time, he barely reached the train as the doors were closing.

At that same instant, a man and woman passed in front of the phonebooth he had just abandoned. The woman was wearing a long, shabby gray coat. Her head was covered with a soiled, bluish kerchief. The man's arm was through hers. Under his other arm, he clutched a heavy khaki duffel bag.

9

SHARON STARED AT THE POWERFUL HANDS that held the gun,
at the eyes that slithered from side to side, into the living
room, up the staircase, over her body.

"What do you want?" she whispered. Within the crook
of her arm, she could feel the violent trembling of Neil's
body. She tightened her grip, pressed him to her.

"You're Sharon Martin." It was a statement. The voice
was a monotone, without inflection. Sharon felt a pulse
pounding in her throat, closing it. She tried to swallow.
"What do you want?" she asked again. The persistent soft
whistle in Neil's breathing . . . suppose he was frightened
into one of his asthma attacks? She would offer cooperation. "I have about ninety dollars in my purse . . ."

"Shut up!"

The evenly spoken words chilled her. The stranger

dropped the bag he was carrying. It was a large khaki duffel bag, the kind military personnel used. He reached into his pocket and pulled out a ball of thick twine and a roll of wide bandages. He dropped them next to her. "Blindfold the boy and tie him up," he ordered.

"No! I won't."

"You'd better!"

Sharon looked down at Neil. He was staring at the man. His eyes were cloudy; the pupils enormous. She remembered that after his mother's death he'd been in deep shock.

"Neil, I . . ." How could she help him, reassure him?

"Sit down." The intruder's voice was a sharp order to Neil. The child looked up beseechingly at Sharon, then obediently sat on the bottom step of the staircase.

Sharon knelt beside him. "Neil, don't be afraid. I'm with you." Her hands fumbled as she reached for one of the bandages and wound it around his eyes, tying it at the back of his head.

She looked up. The intruder was staring at Neil. The gun was pointed at him. She heard a click. She pulled Neil against her, shielding him. "No . . . no . . . don't."

The intruder looked at her; slowly he lowered the gun letting it dangle from his hand. He would have killed Neil, she thought. He was ready to kill him . . .

"Tie up the boy, Sharon." There was an intimacy about the command.

With hands that fumbled at the ropes, she obeyed. She tied Neil's wrists together, trying to leave the bindings loose enough to allow for circulation. After she fastened his wrists, she pressed her hands on his.

The stranger reached past her, cut the end of the twine with a knife. "Hurry up . . . tie his feet!"

She heard the edginess in the tone. Quickly she obeyed.

Neil's knees were trembling so. making his legs jerk apart. She wound the twine around his ankles and knotted it.

"Gag him!"

"He'll choke; he has asthma . . ." The protest died on her lips. The man's face was different somehow, whiter, strained. His high cheekbones were throbbing under stretched skin. He was near panic. Desperately, she bound Neil's mouth, leaving the gag as loose as she dared. If only Neil didn't struggle . . .

A hand shoved her away from the child. She toppled to the floor. The man was leaning over her. His knee dug into her back. He pulled her arms behind her. She felt the twine biting her wrists. She opened her mouth to protest, felt a wad of cloth stuffed into it. He yanked a strip of gauze over her mouth and cheeks, knotted it at the back of her head.

She couldn't breathe. Please . . . No . . . Hands slid over her thighs, lingered. Her legs were pulled together; twine cut through the soft leather boots.

She felt herself being lifted. Her head fell backward. What was he going to do to her?

The front door was opened. Cold, wet air stung her face. She weighed 120 pounds but the abductor was rushing down the slippery porch steps as though she were weightless. It was so dark. He must have turned off the outside lights. She felt her shoulders hit against something cold, metallic. A car. She tried to inhale deeply through her nostrils; to adjust her eyes to the darkness. She must clear her head; stop panicking, think.

The grating sound of a door being opened. Sharon felt herself falling. Her head glanced against an open ashtray. Her elbows and ankles took the force of the jolt as she hit the musty smelling floor. She was in the back of a car.

She heard crunching footsteps retreating. The man was going back into the house. Neil! What would he do to Neil? Frantically Sharon tried to wrench her hands free. Pain shot through her arms. The rough twine bit deeply into her wrists. She thought of the way the intruder had stared at Neil, had released the safety catch on the gun.

Minutes passed. Please, dear God, please . . . The sound of a door opening. Crunching footsteps coming toward the car. The front right door swung open. Her eyes were adjusted to the darkness. Through the shadows, she could see his outline. He was carrying something . . . the canvas bag. Oh, God, Neil was in that bag! She knew it.

He was leaning into the car, dropping the bag onto the seat, pushing it down on the floor. Sharon heard the dull thud. He'll hurt Neil. He'll hurt him. A door closed. Footsteps scurried around the car. The driver's door opened, clicked shut. The shadows moved. She heard harsh breathing. He was leaning down, looking at her.

Sharon felt something fall on her, something that scratched her cheek . . . a blanket or a coat. She moved her head trying to free her face from the choking, acrid smell of stale perspiration.

The engine started. The car began to move.

Concentrate on directions. Remember every detail. Later the police would want to know. The car was turning left onto the street. It was cold, so cold. Sharon shivered and the tremulous movement tightened the knots, causing the cords to dig tighter into her legs and arms and wrists. Her limbs shrieked a protest. Stop moving! Calm. Be calm. Don't panic.

Snow. If it was still snowing, there might be tracks for a while. But no. There was too much sleet mixed in with the snow. She could hear it on the windows. Where were they going?

The gag. It was choking her. Breathe slowly through the nostrils. Neil. How could he breathe inside that sack? He would suffocate.

The car picked up speed. Where was he taking them?

10

ROGER PERRY STARED UNSEEINGLY out the window of his living room on Driftwood Lane. It was a rotten night and it was good to be home. He became aware of how much faster the snow was falling even in the fifteen minutes since he'd been in.

Funny, all day a sense of apprehension had been making him edgy. Glenda hadn't looked well these past couple of weeks. That was it. He always teased her that she was one of those lucky women who grew better looking with every birthday. Her hair, now pure silver, strikingly accentuated her cornflower-blue eyes and lovely complexion. She'd been a size 14 when the boys were growing up but ten years ago had slimmed down to a size 8. Just want to look good in my declining years, she'd joked. But this morning when he'd brought coffee to her in bed, he noticed how deadly pale she was, how thin her face looked. He'd phoned the doctor from the office and they'd agreed that it was the execution Wednesday that was weighing on her mind. Her testimony had helped convict the Thompson boy.

Roger shook his head. It was a dreadful business. Dreadful for that unfortunate boy, for everyone connected with it. Steve . . . little Neil . . . the Thompson boy's mother . . . Glenda. Glenda couldn't take this kind of strain. She'd had a coronary right after she testified at the trial. Roger pushed back the fear that another attack might kill her. Glenda was only fifty-eight. Now that their boys were raised, he wanted these years with her. He couldn't do without her.

He was glad that she'd finally agreed to hiring a daily housekeeper. Mrs. Vogler was to start in the morning and work weekdays from nine till one. That way Glenda could rest more without worrying about the house.

He turned when he heard Glenda come into the room: She was carrying a small tray.

"I was just about to do that," he protested.

"Never mind, you look as though you can use this." She handed him a bourbon old-fashioned and stood companionably beside him at the window.

"I do need it. Thank you, dear." He noticed that she was sipping a coke. If Glenda didn't have a pre-dinner cocktail with him, it meant only one thing. "Chest pains today?" But it was not a question.

"Just a few . . ."

"How many nitros did you take?"

"Only a couple. Don't worry, I'm fine. Oh look! That's funny."

"What is?" Don't change the subject, Roger thought.

"Steve's house. The outside lights are off."

"That's why it just seemed so dark to me," Roger said.

He paused. "I'm positive Steve's lights were on when I came home."

"I wonder why anyone would turn them off." Glenda's voice was troubled. "Dora Lufts is so nervous. Maybe you should take a walk over . . ."

"Oh, I don't want to do that, dear. I'm sure there's a simple explanation."

She sighed. "I suppose. It's just that . . . well, what happened . . . has been on my mind so much these days."

"I know it has." He put a comforting arm around her shoulders, felt the tension in her body. "Now, let's sit down and relax . . ."

"Wait, Roger, look!" She leaned forward. "There's a car pulling out of Steve's driveway. The headlights aren't on. I wonder who . . ."

"Now you just stop wondering and sit down." Roger's tone was firm. "I'll get some cheese."

"The Brie is out on the table." Ignoring the gentle tug of his arm on her elbow, Glenda reached into the pocket of her long quilted skirt and pulled out her glasses. Slipping them on, she bent forward again and stared at the dark, quiet outline of the house diagonally across the road. But the car she'd noticed coming from the Peterson driveway had already passed her window and was disappearing down the block into the swirling snow.

11

"AFTER ALL, TOMORROW IS ANOTHER DAY." Crouched on
the staircase, a lilt of hope in her voice, Scarlett O'Hara
murmured the final words and the music rose to a crescendo
as the picture on the screen dissolved into a long view of
Tara.

Marian Vogler sighed as the music faded out and the
lights in the theater went up. They don't make pictures
like that any more, she thought. She absolutely didn't want
to see the sequel to *Gone With the Wind*. It would just
have to be a letdown

She got to her feet reluctantly. Time to come to earth.
Her pleasant, freckle-spattered face slipped back into
worried lines as she walked up the carpeted, sloping floor
to the back of the theater.

Every one of the kids needed new clothes. Oh well, at

least Jim had agreed that she could take that housekeeping job.

He'd arranged to get a ride to the plant so she could use the car. She'd have the kids off to school and time to tidy up before driving to the Perrys'. Tomorrow would be her first day on the job. She was a little nervous about it. She hadn't worked in twelve years . . . since young Jim was born. But if there was one thing she knew, it was how to keep a house shining.

She emerged from the warmth of the theater into the biting cold of the raw March evening. Shivering, she turned right and began walking briskly. Tiny pellets of sleet mixed with snow bit at her face and she huddled into the worn fur collar of her coat.

The car was in the parking lot behind the theater. Thank God they'd decided to spend the money and have it fixed. It was eight years old but the body still looked all right, and as Jim said, better to spend the four hundred dollars to get it shipshape than use the same money to buy another man's troubles.

Marian had walked so fast she was ahead of most of the movie crowd. Expectantly, she hurried into the parking area. Jim had promised to have supper ready and she was hungry.

But it had done her good to get out. He'd sensed her depression and said, "Three bucks won't make or break us and I'll take care of the kids. Enjoy yourself, Babe, and forget the bills."

His words echoed in Marian's ears as she slowed and frowned. She was sure that she'd parked the car over here to the right. She remembered that she'd been able to see the ad in the bank window, the one about "we want to say *yes* to your loan." Bid deal, she thought. *Yes* if you don't need it, *no* if your guts are hanging out for it.

She *had* parked the car over here. She *had*. She could see the bank window, lighted up now, the ad prominent even through the snow.

Ten minutes later, Marian called Jim from the police station. Choking back the angry, despairing tears that crowded her throat, she sobbed, "Jim . . . Jim . . . no . . . I'm all right . . . but Jim, some . . . some *bastard* stole our car."

12

As he drove through the thickening snow, he reviewed his timetable. Just about now this car should be missed. The woman would probably walk around a bit to be sure she hadn't made a mistake about where she'd left it. Then she'd start screaming for the police or call home. By the time the dispatcher put out a radio bulletin to squad cars, he'd be far away from the nosy Connecticut cops.

Not that anybody would look very hard for this heap. The cops would just roll their eyes when they heard an APB for a stolen car worth a couple of hundred bucks.

To have Sharon Martin in his possession! Excitement made his skin glisten. He remembered the rush of warmth he felt when he tied her up. Her body was so slender but her thighs and hips were curved and soft. He could feel that even through her heavy wool skirt. She had acted hostile and scared when he carried her to the car, but he was sure that she deliberately nuzzled her head against his side.

He had taken the Connecticut Turnpike to the Hutchinson River Parkway south to the Cross County to the Henry Hudson Parkway. He felt safe on the heavily traveled roads. But by the time he was approaching the West Side Highway into downtown Manhattan, he was behind schedule. Suppose, just suppose they *were* already watching for this car!

The other drivers were crawling along. Fools. Afraid of slippery roads, afraid to take a chance, delaying him, making problems. The pulse in his cheekbone started to throb. He felt the quickening, pressed one finger on it. He'd expected to go through the terminal by seven at the latest before the commuter rush was over. They'd be less noticeable then.

It was ten past seven when he exited from the West Side Highway at Forty-sixth Street. He drove a half block east, then made a quick right turn into a driveway that wound behind a warehouse. There were no guards here . . . and he only needed a minute.

Stopping the car, he turned off the lights. Fine, powdery snow stung his eyes and face when he opened the door. Cold. It was so damn cold.

With intense concentration, his eyes darted around the darkened parking area. Satisfied, he reached into the back of the car and lifted the coat he'd thrown over Sharon. He felt her eyes blazing up at him. Laughing softly, he pulled out a tiny camera and snapped her picture. The sudden flash made her blink. Now he extracted a pencil-thin flashlight from his inside pocket. He waited until his hand was deep in the car to flip it on.

Deliberately he shone the narrow beam of light in

Sharon's eyes, moving it back and forth slowly, an inch from her face, until she squeezed her eyes shut and tried to turn her head.

It felt good to tease her. With a short, soundless laugh, he grabbed her shoulders and forced her to lie on her stomach. Quick strokes of the knife sliced the cords on her ankles and wrists. A faint sigh, muffled by the gag, a shuddering movement of her body . . .

"Feels pretty good, don't it, Sharon?" he whispered. "Now I'm going to take that gag off. If one scream comes out of you, the boy dies. Understand?"

He did not wait for the affirmative nod before he cut the knotted cloth at the back of her head. Sharon spat out the wad of gauze in her mouth. Desperately she tried not to moan. "Neil . . . please . . ." Her whisper was almost inaudible. "He'll suffocate . . ."

"That's up to you." The stranger pulled her up, stood her on her feet next to the car. Vaguely, Sharon felt the snow on her face. She was so dizzy. The muscles in her arms and legs were frantic with cramps. She staggered, was roughly grabbed.

"Put this on." The voice was different now . . . urgent.

She reached out, felt greasy, rough material . . . the coat that he'd thrown over her. She raised her arm. The man pulled the coat around her. Her other arm was thrust into it.

"Put this scarf on."

It felt so dirty. She tried to fold it. It was so big, woolly. Somehow her fingers managed to knot it under her chin.

"Get back in the car. The faster we move, the faster the boy has that gag off." Roughly, he pushed her into the front seat. The khaki bag was on the floor. She stumbled, trying to keep her boots from hitting it. Leaning down, she ran her hands over the bag, felt the outline of Neil's head.

73

She realized that the drawstring wasn't tied. At least Neil was getting air—"Neil, Neil, I'm here. We'll be all right, Neil . . ."

Did she feel him moving? Oh God, don't let him strangle.

The stranger darted around the car, was in the driver's seat, turned the key in the engine. The car moved cautiously forward.

We're in midtown! The realization shocked Sharon, helped her to focus. She had to be calm. She had to do whatever this man ordered. The car approached Broadway. She saw the Times Square billboard clock: 7:20 . . . it was only 7:20.

At this time last night, she'd just gotten home from Washington. She'd showered and put chops on and sipped Chablis while they broiled. She'd been tired and uptight and trying to unwind before writing her column.

And she'd thought about Steve, how missing him had become a steady ache over the three weeks they'd been apart.

He'd phoned. The sound of his voice brought a peculiar combination of pleasure and anxiety. But he'd kept the conversation brief, almost impersonal. "Hi . . . just wanted to be sure you got in all right. Understand Washington has lousy weather and it's heading our way. I'll see you at the studio." Then he'd paused and added, "I've missed you. Don't forget you're staying with us tomorrow night."

She'd hung up, her need to see him intensified by talking with him and yet she'd somehow felt letdown and worried. What did she want, anyhow? What would he think when he got home and found them missing? Oh, Steve!

They stopped for a red light on Sixth Avenue. A patrol car drew up beside them. Sharon watched as the young driver pushed his peaked uniform hat back on his forehead. He glanced out the window and their eyes locked. Sharon felt the car begin to move. She kept her eyes directly on the policeman, willing him to keep looking at her, to sense something wrong.

She felt a sharp prodding against her side and looked down. The stranger had the knife in his hand. "If we get followed now, you get it first," he said. "I'll still have plenty of time for the boy."

There was icy matter-of-factness in his tone. The patrol car was directly behind them. Its dome light began flashing. Its siren began blasting. "No! Please . . ." In a burst of speed the police car sped around them and disappeared down the block.

They were turning south on Fifth Avenue. Pedestrian traffic was almost non-existent. It was too stormy, too icy to walk around New York.

The car made a quick left onto Forty-fourth Street. Where was he taking them? Forty-fourth wasn't a through street. It was blocked by Grand Central Station. Didn't he know that?

The stranger drove the two blocks to Vanderbilt Avenue and turned right. He parked near the entrance to the Biltmore Hotel, directly opposite the terminal.

"We're getting out," he said, his voice low. "We're going into the terminal. Walk next to me. Don't try anything. I'll be carrying the bag and if anybody pays any attention to us, the boys gets the knife." He looked down at Sharon. His eyes were glittering again. A pulse throbbed in his cheek. "Understand?"

She nodded. Could Neil hear him?

"Wait a minute." He was staring at her. Reaching past her into the glove compartment, he pulled out dark glasses. "Put these on."

He pushed the door open, looked around, and stepped out quickly. The street was deserted. Only a few cabs were lined up in the enclosed driveway at the terminal. There was no one to see them or care . . .

He's taking us on a train, Sharon thought. We'll be miles away before anyone even begins to look for us!

She became aware of a stinging in her left hand. The ring! The antique moonstone ring Steve had given her for Christmas . . . it had turned sideways when her hands were tied. The raised gold setting had been cutting her. Almost without thinking, Sharon slipped the ring off. She just had time to force it partly down into the seat cushion before the car door opened.

Unsteadily, she got out and onto the slippery sidewalk. The man gripped her wrist with his hand and looked carefully around inside the car. He quickly leaned down and picked up the gag that had been on her mouth, the cords he had cut when releasing her. Sharon held her breath. But he didn't notice the ring.

He bent down and picked up the duffel bag, pulled the drawstring tight and knotted the ends. Neil could suffocate with that bag closed.

"Look." She stared at the blade in his hand that was nearly concealed by his loose overcoat sleeve. "This is pointed right at the kid's heart. You try anything and he gets it."

"Come on!" His other hand was at her elbow. He was forcing her to walk in step with him across the street. They were a man and woman hurrying out of the cold into the terminal, nondescript in every way, anonymous in their cheap clothes with duffel bag instead of suitcase.

Even behind the dark glasses, the brightly lit terminal made Sharon blink. They stood on the concourse overlooking the main terminal. There was a newsstand a few feet to their left. The vendor looked at them indifferently. They started down the steps to the first landing. The huge Kodak display caught Sharon's eye. It read, "Capture beauty where you find it . . ."

An hysterical laugh threatened to escape her lips. *Capture? Capture?* The clock. The famous clock over the center of the Information Booth in the middle of the terminal. It was harder to see now that the investment office counter had been built in front of it. Sharon had read somewhere that when the six red lights around the clock's base were flashing, it signaled an emergency to Grand Central's private police force. What would they think if they knew what was happening now?

It was 7:29. Steve. *Steve was catching the 7:30.* He was here right now . . . in a train in this terminal, a train that in a minute would be taking him away. Steve, she wanted to shriek . . . Steve . . .

Steely fingers bit into her arm. "Down here." He was forcing her to go down the stairs to the lower terminal. The rush hour was over. There weren't many people in the main terminal . . . there were even fewer going down the stairs. Should she try to fall . . . draw attention to them? No . . . she couldn't take the chance, not with that burly arm encircling the duffel bag, that knife ready to plunge into Neil . . .

They were on the lower level. Over to the right she could see the entrance to the Oyster Bar. She and Steve had met there for a quick lunch last month. They'd sat at the counter and had steaming bowls of oyster stew . . . Steve, find us, help us . . .

She was being pushed toward the left. "We're going down there . . . not so fast . . ." Track 112. The sign said "Mount Vernon—8:10." A train must have just left. Why would he go there?

To the left of the ramp leading down to the tracks Sharon saw a shabby old woman carrying a shopping bag.

She was bundled in a man's jacket over a ragged woolen skirt. Thick cotton stockings drooped on her legs. The woman was staring at her. Did she realize something was wrong?

"Keep moving . . ."

They were going down the ramp on the 112 platform. Their footsteps echoed, a pinging sound on metal steps. The murmur of voices receded, the warmth of the terminal was vanquished by a clammy, cold draft.

The platform was deserted.

"Around here." He was forcing her to move faster now, around the end of the platform where the track terminated, down another ramp. Water was trickling nearby. Where were they going? The dark glasses made it hard to see here. A rhythmic, throbbing sound . . . a pump . . . a pneumatic pump . . . they were going down into the depths of the terminal . . . far underground. What was he going to do to them? She could hear the rumbling sounds of trains . . . there must be a tunnel nearby . . .

The concrete floor was still sloping down. The passage widened. They were in an area half the size of a football field; an area of thick pipes and shafts and rumbling motors. To the left, about twenty feet, there was a narrow staircase.

"Over there . . . hurry up!" Now his breath was coming in harsh gasps. She could hear him puffing as he followed her. She scrambled up the staircase, unconsciously counting the steps . . . ten . . . eleven . . . twelve. She was on a narrow landing, facing a thick metal door.

"Move over." She felt the heaviness of his body against her and shrank away. He set down the duffel bag, glanced at her quickly. In the dim light she saw shiny beads of perspiration glistening on his forehead. He pulled out a key, put it in the lock. A grating sound and the handle turned. He pushed the door open, thrust her in before him. She heard him grunt as he picked up the duffel bag again. The door closed behind them. Through the clammy darkness she heard the snap of a switch.

A half-second delay and then dusty overhead fluorescent lights blinked on.

Sharon looked around at the filthy, damp room, at rusty sinks, a boarded-up shaft, a sagging cot. an overturned crate, an old black suitcase on the floor.

"Where are we? What do you want with us?" Her voice was a near-whisper but took on an echo sound in this dungeon-like room.

Her abductor didn't answer. Pushing her forward, he hurried toward the cot. He laid the duffel bag on it, then flexed his arms. Dropping to her knees. Sharon fumbled with the drawstring on the bag.

At last she had it untied, was pulling it apart, pulling the bag down, reaching for the small, crumbled figure. She freed Neil's head. Frantically, she tugged at the gag, pulling it down over his chin.

Neil gasped, clawing for air, his breath harsh and sobbing. She heard the wheeze in his breath, felt the jerking of his chest. Supporting his head with her arm, she began to tug at the blindfold.

"Let that alone!" The order was sharp, violent.

"Please," she cried, "he's sick . . . he's having an asthma attack. Help him."

She looked up, then bit her lips to force back a scream.

Over the army cot, three enormous pictures were taped to the wall.

A young woman running, hands outstretched, looking back over her shoulder, terror stamped on her face . . . her mouth a twisted, screaming arc.

A blond woman lying by a car, her legs jackknifed under her.

79

A dark-haired teenager with one hand raised to her throat, a look of puzzled detachment settling into her staring eyes.

13

LONG AGO LALLY HAD BEEN A SCHOOLTEACHER in Nebraska. Finally retired, alone, she had come to New York for a visit. She never went back home.

The night she'd arrived in Grand Central Station was the turning point. Bewildered and awed, she'd carried her one suitcase across the enormous Concourse, looked up, and stopped. She was one of the few to realize immediately that the sky on the great vaulted ceiling had been painted on backward. The eastern stars were in the west.

She'd laughed aloud. Her lips parted, revealing two enormous front teeth. People glanced her way, then hurried along. Their reaction had delighted her. At home if Lally were seen looking up and laughing by herself, it would be all over town the next day.

She checked her suitcase in a locker, and washed up in

the main-floor ladies' room, smoothing her shapeless brown wool skirt, buttoning the thick cardigan sweater. Finally she combed the short gray hair, plastering it damply around her broad, chinless face.

For the next six hours Lally had toured the terminal, taking a childish delight in the bustling, rushing crowds. She ate at a counter in one of the small, cheap lunchstands, windowshopped in the corridors leading to the hotels, and finally returned to settle down in the main waiting room.

Fascinated, she watched a young mother breastfeed a screaming baby, stared at a young couple passionately embracing, followed the progress of a card game four men were playing.

The crowds thinned, swelled, thinned out again under the signs of the zodiac. It was nearly midnight when she noticed that one group had stayed a long time, six men and a tiny, birdlike woman who were clustered together, talking with the easy camaraderie of old friends.

The woman seemed to notice her watching them and came over to her. "You new here?" Her voice was raspy but kind. Earlier Lally had seen this woman take a newspaper from a disposal bin.

"Yes," she said.

"Got any place to go?"

Lally had a reservation at the Y but some instinct made her lie. "No."

"Just arrived here?"

"Yes."

"Got any money?"

"Not much." Another lie.

"Well, don't worry. We'll show you around. We're the regulars." Her arm jerked backward toward the group.

"You live near here then?" Lally asked.

A smile quirked the woman's eyes, revealed decaying teeth. "No, we live *here*. I'm Rosie Bidwell."

In all her cheerless sixty-two years, Lally had never had a close friend. Rosie Bidwell changed that. Soon Lally was accepted as one of the regulars. She got rid of the suitcase and like Rosie, kept all her possessions in shopping bags. She learned the routine . . . dawdling over cheap meals in the Automat, occasional showers in the public bath house in the Village, sleeping in flop houses, dollar a night hotels, or at the Salvation Army center.

Or . . . in her own room in Grand Central.

That was the one secret Lally kept from Rosie. A tireless explorer, she's become familiar with every inch of her terminal. She climbed the stairs behind the orange doors on the platforms and wandered around the gloomy cavernous area between the floor of the upper level and the ceiling of the lower level. She found the hidden staircase that connected the two ladies rooms and when the downstairs one was closed for repairs, she often slipped down that staircase and spent the night there with no one the wiser.

She even walked along the tracks of the tunnel that yawned under Park Avenue, flattening herself against the concrete wall when a train thundered by and sharing scraps of food with the hungry cats that prowled the tunnel.

But she was especially fascinated by the area right in the depths of the station that the guards called Sing-Sing. With its pumps and vents and airshafts and generators throbbing and creaking and groaning it was like being part of the very heartbeat of her station. The unmarked door at the head of a narrow staircase in Sing-Sing intrigued her. Cautiously, she'd mentioned it to one of the security guards who became a good friend. Rusty said that was only the miserable hole where they used to wash dishes for the Oyster Bar and she had no business in that area. But she'd worn him down until he took her to see the room.

She'd been delighted with it. The musty, peeling walls and ceilings didn't bother her at all. The room was large. The lights and sinks worked. There was even the tiny cubbyhole with the toilet. She'd known immediately that this place would fill her one remaining need, for occasional, absolute privacy.

"Room and bath," she said. "Rusty, let me sleep here."

He'd looked shocked. "No way! It'd cost me my job." But she'd worn him down on that, too, and every once in a while he'd let her spend a night there. Then one day she managed to borrow his key for a few hours and secretly had another one made from it. When Rusty retired she made the room her own.

Little by little, Lally carried objects up the steps, a dilapidated canvas army cot, a lumpy mattress, an orange crate.

She began to stay there regularly. That was what she liked best of all, to sleep in the womblike darkness, tucked in the very depth of her station, to hear the faint roar and rumble of trains that became less and less frequent as the night grew late, then accelerated again into the morning frenzy.

Sometimes lying there, she thought about teaching *Phantom of the Opera* to her classes. "And under that beautiful, gilded opera house, there was another world," she'd told them, "a world dark and mysterious, a world of alleys and sewers and dampness where a man could hide away from everyone."

The only cloud on her horizon was the awful, gnawing fear that someday they'd tear her station down. When the Committee to Save Grand Central held the rally, she'd been there, unobtrusively in a corner, but applauding loudly when all the celebrities like Jackie Onassis said that Grand Central Terminal was a part of the tradition of New York and should never be destroyed.

But even though they had managed to get it designated as an historical landmark, Lally knew there were still plenty of people trying to get it pulled down. No, God, please, not my station!

She never used her room during the winter. It was too cold and damp. But from May till September she stayed there about twice a week, just infrequently enough so the cops didn't catch her, so Rosie didn't get curious.

Six years passed, the best six years of Lally's life. She came to know all the guards, the paper vendors, the countermen. She recognized the faces of commuters, knew which ones took which trains, at what time. She even grew to know the faces of the drinkers who usually caught the late trains home, hurrying unsteadily to their platforms.

That Monday evening, Lally was meeting Rosie in the main waiting room. She'd had severe arthritis over the winter. That was the only thing that had kept her from going to her room. But it had been six months now and suddenly she felt she couldn't wait any longer to use it again. "I'll just go down and see how it looks," she thought. Maybe if it wasn't too cold, she'd even sleep there tonight. But probably not.

She walked heavily down the stairs to the lower terminal. There weren't many people there. Carefully, she moseyed around, watching for the policemen. She couldn't take a chance of being spotted going to the room. They'd never let her stay there, not even the nice guys.

She noticed a family with three young children. Nice-looking, all of them. She liked children and she'd been a

85

good teacher, too. After the class finished making fun of her homeliness, she usually got along well with her pupils. Not that she'd want those days back, not for anything.

She was about to drift down the ramp to track 112 when her attention was caught by a tattered, scarlet lining drooping below an old gray coat.

Lally recognized the coat. She'd tried it on in a Second Avenue thrift shop the week before. There couldn't be two like that, not with that lining. Her curiosity peaked, she studied the face of the woman wearing the coat and was surprised to see how young and pretty she was behind the scarf and dark glasses.

The man she was with . . . he was someone Lally had seen around the station lately. Lally noticed the expensive leather boots the girl was wearing; the kind the people wore who traveled the Connecticut line.

Funny combination, she thought. A thrift coat and those boots. Now fully interested, she watched the couple cross the terminal. The bag the man was carrying seemed pretty heavy. She frowned when she saw them go down to track 112. There wouldn't be a train for another forty minutes. Crazy, she thought. Why wait on the platform? It's cold and damp.

She shrugged. That settled that. She couldn't go to her room with them on the platform to see her. She'd have to wait until tomorrow.

Philosophically dismissing her disappointment, Lally headed for the main waiting room in search of Rosie.

14

"TALK, RON, TALK, DAMN YOU!" The dark-haired attorney depressed the "record" button. The cassette player was on the bunk between the two seated young men.

"No!" Ron Thompson got up, walked restlessly across the narrow cell and stared out through the barred window. Quickly he turned away. "Even snow looks dirty here," he said, "dirty and gray and cold. Do you want to record that?"

"No, I don't." Bob Kurner stood up and put his arms on the boy's shoulders. "Ron, please . . ."

"What good? What good?" The nineteen-year-old's lip quivered. His expression changed, became young and defenseless. Quickly he bit his lip, brushed a hand across his eyes. "Bob, you did your best . . . I know you did. But there's nothing anyone can do now."

"Nothing except give the Governor a reason why she should grant executive clemency . . . even a stay . . . even a stay, Ron."

"But you've tried . . . that writer Sharon Martin . . . if she couldn't with all the important signatures she got . . ."

"Damn that stinking Sharon Martin to hell!" Bob Kurner clenched his hands into fists. "Damn all these do-gooders who don't know their way out of a paper bag. She loused you up, Ron. We had a petition going, a *real* one from people who know you, people who know you're incapable of hurting anyone, and she goes screaming all over the country that of course you're guilty but you shouldn't die. She made it impossible for the Governor to commute your sentence—*impossible*."

"Then why waste your time? If it's no use, if it's hopeless, I don't want to talk about it anymore!"

"You've got to!" Bob Kurner's voice softened as he looked into the younger man's eyes. There was a compelling directness and honesty in them. Bob thought of himself at nineteen. Ten years ago he'd been a sophomore at Villanova. Ron had been planning to go to college . . . instead he was going to die in the electric chair. Even the two years in prison hadn't made his muscular body flabby. Ron exercised regularly in his cell, he was such a disciplined kid. But he'd lost twenty pounds and his face was chalk white.

"Look," Bob said, "there's got to be something somewhere that I missed . . ."

"You didn't miss anything."

"Ron, I defended you but you *didn't* kill Nina Peterson and you *were* convicted. If we can just find one piece of evidence to take to the Governor . . . one valid reason to make it possible for her to grant you a stay. We've got forty-two hours . . . only forty-two hours."

"You just said she won't commute my sentence."

Bob Kurner bent down and snapped off the cassette player. "Ron, maybe I shouldn't tell you this. God knows it's a long shot. But listen to me. When you were convicted of Nina Peterson's murder, a lot of people felt that you were guilty of committing those two other unsolved murders. You know that."

"They asked me enough about them . . ."

"You went to school with the Carfolli girl. You'd shoveled snow for Mrs. Weiss. It made sense to ask. That's just normal procedure. Then after you were arrested there weren't any more murders—*till now*. Ron, there have been two more murders of young women in Fairfield County in the last month. If we can just introduce something, some doubt, come up with something that might suggest a link between Nina Peterson's death and the others."

He put his arms around the boy. "Ron, I know how lousy this is for you. I can only guess what you're going through. But you've told me how often you go over that day in your mind. Maybe there's something . . . something that didn't seem important, some detail. If you'd just *talk*."

Ron pulled himself away, walked over to the bunk and sat down. He depressed the "record" button on the cassette player and turned his head so that his voice would be picked up clearly. Frowning in concentration, his voice halting, he began to speak.

"I was working that afternoon after school in Timberly's Market. Mrs. Peterson was in shopping. Mr. Timberly had just told me that he was going to fire me because of the time I needed off for baseball practice. She heard him. When I helped her to the car with the groceries, she said . . ."

89

15

THE TRAIN PULLED INTO THE CARLEY STATION at nine
o'clock. By then Steve's frantic impatience had settled into
deep, gnawing worry. He should have phoned the doctor.
If Neil were sick Sharon might have taken him for an
injection. Maybe that was why there was no answer.

Sharon had come. He was sure of that. She simply
wouldn't have changed her mind without calling him.

Maybe it was just that the phones were going fluky.
And if he'd missed this train, God knows when the next
one would get in. The conductor said something about the
tracks freezing.

Something was wrong. He felt it. He knew it.

But maybe it was the execution coming up that had him
so rattled, so apprehensive. God, the paper tonight had
rehashed the whole mess. Nina's picture on the front page.

The caption "Youth to die for brutal murder of young Connecticut mother."

Thompson's picture next to hers. A nice-looking kid. Hard to believe he'd been capable of cold-blooded murder.

Nina's picture. Over and over on the long train ride, Steve found himself staring down at it. The reporters had all clamored for a photograph at the time of the murder, but he cursed himself for letting them make copies of this one. It had been his favorite; a snapshot he'd taken of her with the breeze blowing the dark curls around her face, and the small straight nose wrinkled a little the way it always had when she laughed. And the scarf tied loosely around her neck. It was only afterward that he'd realized that was the scarf Thompson had used to strangle her.

Oh Christ!

Steve was the first one waiting to rush out when the train finally arrived at Carley forty minutes late. Racing down the slippery platform stairs, he hurried into the parking lot and attempted to brush the snow from the windshield of his car. A thin, ice-crusted layer resisted his efforts. Impatiently, he opened the trunk and reached for the de-icer and scraper.

The last time he'd seen Nina alive she'd driven him to the train. He'd noticed that the balding spare tire was on her right front wheel. Then she'd admitted that she had a flat the night before and was riding around without a spare.

He'd been ticked off and exploded at her. "You shouldn't be riding on that lousy tire. Damn it, honey, your carelessness will get you killed."

Will get you killed!

She'd promised to pick up the other tire right away. At the station, he'd started to get out of the car without kissing her goodbye. But she'd leaned over and her kiss had brushed his cheek, and with that familiar ripple of laughter in her voice, she'd said, "Have a good day, Grouchy. I love you."

He hadn't answered her, or looked back at her, just run for his train. He'd debated about calling her from the office but told himself that he wanted her to think he was really upset with her. He worried about her. She was careless in ways that mattered. A couple of nights, when he'd worked late, he'd come home to find her and Neil asleep and the door unlocked.

And so he hadn't called, hadn't made up with her. And when he got off the 5:30 train that night, Roger Perry was waiting for him at the station, waiting to ride home with him and tell him that Nina was dead.

And then nearly two years of bleak pain until that morning six months ago when he'd been introduced to the other guest on the *Today* show, Sharon Martin.

The windshield was clear enough. Steve got in the car, turned the key, and barely giving the engine time to catch, put his foot on the gas. He wanted to get home and find Neil all right. He wanted to make Neil happy again. He wanted to put his arms around Sharon and hold her. Tonight he wanted to hear her moving around in the guest room, know that she was near. They'd have to work it out. Nothing could be allowed to spoil it between them.

The five-minute drive took fifteen minutes. The roads were a sheet of ice. At one "stop" sign he put his foot on the brake and the car just slid onto the intersection. Thank God there was no one coming.

At last he turned onto Driftwood Lane. It seemed uncommonly dark to him. It was *his* place—the lights were off! A shock of fear tensed his body. Ignoring the slippery road, he floored the accelerator and the car shot forward, careened down the block. He turned into his driveway and jammed to a halt behind Sharon's car. Racing up the

93

stairs, he thrust his key in the lock and pushed the front door open. "Sharon . . . Neil," he called. "Sharon . . . Neil . . ."

Chilling silence offset the warmth of the foyer, made his hands clammy. "Sharon . . . Neil," he called again.

He looked into the living room. Papers were scattered on the floor. Neil must have been doing cutouts; there were scissors and scraps on one open page. An untouched cup of cocoa and a glass of sherry were on the small end table near the fireplace. Hurrying over, Steve felt the cup. The cocoa was cold. He rushed into the kitchen, noticed the saucepan in the sink, then ran down the hall to the den. The sense of danger was overwhelming, stifling. The den was empty too. A fire was flickering in the hearth. He'd asked Bill to make one before he left.

Not knowing what he was looking for, Steve raced from the den back to the foyer and noticed Sharon's overnight bag and purse. He opened the door of the guest closet. Her cape was there! What would make her rush out without it? Neil! Neil must have had one of those violent attacks, the kind that come on so suddenly, that almost suffocated him.

Steve raced to the phone on the kitchen wall. The emergency numbers—hospital, police, fire, their own doctor—were clearly listed. He called the doctor's office first. The nurse was still there. "No, Mr. Peterson, we didn't get a call about Neil. Is there anything . . ."

He hung up without explaining.

He called the emergency room at the hospital. "We have no record . . ."

Where were they? What happened to them? His breath was coming in hard gasps. He looked at the wall clock. Nine-twenty. Nearly two hours since he'd tried to phone home. They'd been gone at least that long. The Perrys!

Maybe they'd gone across the street to the Perrys. Sharon might have rushed over there with Neil if he started to get sick.

Steve reached for the phone again. Please God, please let them be at the Perrys. Let them be all right.

And then he saw it. The message on the memo board. Printed in chalk. Thick, uneven lettering.

"If you want your kid and girlfriend alive, wait for instructions." The next three words were heavily underlined. "*Don't call police.*" The message was signed "Foxy."

16

IN THE MIDTOWN MANHATTAN OFFICE OF THE FBI, Hugh Taylor sighed as he closed the top drawer of his desk. God, it would be good to get home, he thought. Nearly 9:30, so traffic should be okay. But the storm would botch up the West Side Highway and the bridge was probably a mess by now.

He stood up and stretched. His shoulders and neck were tense and stiff. Pushing fifty and feel like I'm eighty, he thought. It had been a rotten day. Another attempted bank robbery, this time the Chase Bank at Forty-eighth and Madison. A teller had managed to sound the alarm and they'd rounded up the perpetrators, but not until the guard had been shot. Poor guy was in critical condition and probably wouldn't make it.

Hugh's face hardened. Criminals who could do that should be locked up for good.

But not executed. Hugh reached for his coat. That was one of the reasons he'd been so depressed today. That Thompson kid. He couldn't get him out of his mind: the Peterson case two years ago. Hugh had been in charge of the investigation. With his squad, he'd traced Thompson to the motel in Virginia where they'd nabbed him.

The kid had so persistently denied he'd murdered Nina Peterson. Even when he knew the only chance to save his skin was by throwing himself at the mercy of the court, he'd still denied the murder.

Hugh shrugged. It was out of his hands. That was for sure. And day after tomorrow Ronald Thompson would be electrocuted.

Hugh walked down the hall, pushed the button for the elevator.

Bone-tired. He really was bone-tired.

Half a minute later a car stopped at his floor. The door slid open. He stepped in, pushed the "M" button.

He heard his named being shouted. Automatically he reached out and held the door, keeping it from closing. Running feet raced to the elevator. His arm was grabbed by Hank Lamont, one of the younger agents.

"Hugh," he was out of breath. "Steve Peterson is on the phone . . . you know . . . Nina Peterson's husband . . . the Thompson kid . . ."

"I know who he is," Hugh snapped. "What does he want?"

"It's his son, he says his son and that writer, Sharon Martin, have been kidnapped."

17

"WHO TOOK THOSE PICTURES?" Sharon heard the shrill fear in her voice, knew it was a mistake. She met his eye and saw that her tone had startled him. His lips narrowed, the pulse in his cheek quickened. Intuitively she said, "I mean, they're so realistic."

Something of the rigidity eased. "Maybe I found them."

She remembered the flash that had blinded her in the car.

"Or maybe you took them." There was a hint of a compliment.

"Maybe."

She felt his hand touch her hair, linger on her cheek. Don't act afraid, she thought frantically. She was still supporting Neil's head against her arm. He began to tremble. Sobs broke under the harsh asthmatic wheezing.

"Neil, don't cry," she implored. "You'll choke yourself."
She looked up at their captor. "He's so frightened. Cut him
loose."

"Will you like me if I do?" His leg was pressing against
her side as she knelt by the cot.

"Of course I'll like you, but *please*." Her fingers
smoothed damp, sandy ringlets from the small forehead.

"Don't touch that blindfold!" His hand, steely on hers,
pulling it away from Neil's face.

"I won't." Her voice was placating.

"All right. For a little while. But just his hands. First, you
lay down."

She stiffened. "Why?"

"I can't let both of you untied. Let go of the boy."

There was nothing to do except obey. This time he tied
her legs together from knees to ankles, then pulled her
to a sitting position on the cot. "I won't tie your hands
until I'm ready to go, Sharon." It was a concession. His
voice lingered over her name.

Ready to go? Was he going to leave them here alone?
He was bending over Neil, cutting the cords on his wrists.
Neil pulled his hands apart. They flailed the air. His gasps
were staccato-paced; the wheeze a constant, rising pitch.

Sharon pulled him on her lap. She was still wearing the
gray coat. She wrapped him inside it with her. The shaking
body struggled, trying to pull away.

"Neil, stop that! Calm down!" Her voice was firm. "Remember what your dad told you to do when you get
asthma. Be very still and breathe very slowly." She looked
up. "Please, will you get him a drink of water?"

In the uneven, dusty lighting, his shadow, dark and
blotchy against the concrete wall, seemed fragmented by
the peeling paint. He nodded and went over to the rusty
sink. The dripping faucet sputtered in an uneven gurgling.

While his back was turned, Sharon looked up at the posters. Two of those women were dead or dying; the other was trying to run from something or someone. Had he done that to them? What kind of madman was he? Why had he kidnapped her and Neil? It had taken daring to walk through the terminal with them. This man had planned this carefully. Why?

Neil's breath caught, choked. He began to cough a harsh, racking sound.

The abductor turned from the sink, a paper cup in his hand. The choking sound seemed to agitate him. When he handed Sharon the cup, his hand trembled. "Make him stop that," he said.

Sharon held the cup to Neil's lips. "Neil, sip this." He gulped the water. "No, slowly, Neil. Now lean back." The boy finished the water, sighed. She felt a faint relaxing of the slight body. "That's it."

The captor was leaning over her. "You're a very kind person, Sharon," he said. "That's why I fell in love with you. Because you're not frightened of me, are you?"

"No, of course not. I know you don't want to hurt us." Her tone was easy, conversational. "But why did you bring us here?"

Without answering, he walked over to the black suitcase, lifted it carefully and set it on the ground a few feet from the door. Crouching over the bag, he opened it.

"What is in there?" Sharon asked.

"Just something I have to make before I go."

"Where are you going to go?"

"Don't ask me so many questions, Sharon."

"I was just interested in your plans." She watched as his fingers moved among the contents of the suitcase. The fingers had a life of their own now, an existence in which they expertly handled wires and powder.

"I can't talk when I'm working like this. You have to be careful with nitroglycerin, even I do."

Sharon's arms tightened around Neil. This insane man was handling explosives a few feet away from them. If he made a mistake, if he jarred something . . . She remembered the story of the brownstone in Greenwich Village that had exploded. She'd been in New York on a school break that day and shopping a few blocks away when the deafening sound came. She thought of the mass of rubble, of the piles of broken stone and splintered wood. Those people thought they knew how to handle explosives too.

Prayerfully, she watched as he worked with painstaking care, watched as the circulation in her legs stopped, as the dampness penetrated her skin, as her ear became attuned to the faint rumbling sound of trains. The wheezing in Neil's chest developed a rhythm; fast, gasping, but not quite so frantic.

Finally the man straightened up. "It's all right." He sounded satisfied.

"What are you going to do with that?"

"It's your babysitter."

"What do you mean?"

"I have to leave you until morning. I can't take any chance of losing you, can I?"

"How can you lose us, if we're tied up alone here?"

"One in a million, one in ten million, someone tries to get in this room while I'm out . . ."

"How long are you going to keep us here?"

"Until Wednesday. Sharon, don't ask me questions. I'll tell you what I want you to know."

"I'm sorry. It's just that I don't understand."

"I can't let anyone find you. But I have to be away. So if the door is wired and someone tries to come in . . ."

She was not here. She was not hearing this. This could not be.

"Don't worry, Sharon. Tomorrow night Steve Peterson is going to give me eighty-two thousand dollars, and this will be all over."

"Eighty-two thousand dollars?"

"Yes. And then Wednesday morning you and I will go away and I'll leave word where they can find the boy." Somewhere far off there was a faint echo of a roar, a silence, another roar.

He came across the room. "I'm sorry, Sharon." In a sudden movement, he yanked Neil from her arms, dropped him on the cot. Before she could move, he pulled her hands behind her. He let the coat slide off before he tied her wrists together.

He reached for Neil. "Don't gag Neal, please," she begged. "If he chokes . . . you may not be able to get the money . . . you may have to prove he's alive. Please . . . I . . . I . . . like you. Because you're so smart."

He was watching her, considering.

"You . . . you know my name but you haven't even told me your name. I'd like to be thinking about you."

His hands turned her face to him. They were calloused, rough. Impossible to think they were so dextrous with delicate wires. He bent down over her. His breath was stale, hot. She suffered his kiss, harsh on her lips, moist, lingering on her cheek and ear. "My name is Foxy," he said huskily. "Say my name, Sharon."

"Foxy."

He tied Neil's wrists and pulled him beside her. There was barely room for both of them lying sideways on the narrow cot. Sharon's hands were squeezed against the rough concrete wall. He covered them with the soiled gray coat,

103

then stood over them. He looked from them to the boarded-up dumbwaiter.

"No." He looked dissatisfied, uncertain. "I can't take the chance that someone might hear you."

The gags were around their mouths again, but not quite so tight this time. She dared not protest any more. The nervousness was building up in him again.

And then she knew why. Because slowly, with agonizing care, he was fastening a slender wire to something in the suitcase and trailing it from the suitcase to the door. He was going to attach that wire to the door. Then if anyone happened to come in here, the bomb would be triggered!

She heard the snap of the switch, and the dust-shrouded lights flickered away. The door opened and closed noiselessly. For an instant he was silhouetted against the outside gloom, and then he was gone.

The room was desperately dark now and the cavernous silence was broken only by Neil's labored breathing and the occasional muted rumble of a train entering the tunnel.

18

ROGER AND GLENDA PERRY decided to watch the eleven o'clock news in bed. She had already bathed and offered to make a hot toddy for him while he showered.

"Sounds good, but don't start puttering around." He checked the lock on the kitchen door and went upstairs. The shower was hot, needlesharp, infinitely satisfying. Quickly he got into blue-striped pajamas, folded back the heavy spread from the king-sized bed, and turned on the reading lights that beamed on both pillows.

Just before getting into bed, he walked over to the front window. Even in weather like this, he and Glenda enjoyed the feel of fresh night air in the room. Automatically he glanced over at the Peterson house. It was lighted now, outside and in. Through the granular snow he could see cars parked in the driveway.

Glenda came into the bedroom carrying a steaming cup. "Roger, whatever are you looking at?"

He turned, sheepishly. "Nothing. But you don't have to worry about Steve's lights being off. His place is bright as a Christmas tree now."

"He must have company. Well, thank heaven we're not out tonight." She put the cup down on his night table, slipped off her robe and got into bed. "Oh, I am tired." Her expression changed, became thoughtful. Her body stilled.

"A pain?"

"Yes."

"Lie still. I'll get you a pill." With fingers that tried not to fumble, he reached for the ever-present bottle of nitro-glycerin tablets. He watched as she slipped one under her tongue and closed her eyes. A minute later, she sighed, "Oh, that was a pretty bad one. But it's all right now."

The phone rang. Roger reached for it, angrily. "If it's for you, I'll say you're asleep," he muttered. "Some people . . ." He picked up the receiver. His "yes" was curt.

Immediately his tone changed, became concerned. "Steve . . . is something wrong? No. No. Nothing. Of course. Oh, dear God! I'll be right over."

As Glenda stared, he replaced the receiver and reached for her hands. "Something's wrong at Steve's," he said carefully "Neil and Sharon Martin are . . . missing. I'm going over there, but I'll be back as fast as I possibly can."

"Roger . . ."

"Please, Glenda. For my sake, stay calm. You know how you've been feeling lately. Please!"

He pulled a heavy sweater and slacks over his pajamas and stuffed his feet into moccasins.

He was just closing the front door when he heard the telephone ring again. Knowing Glenda would pick it up, Roger ran out into the swirling snow. He cut diagonally across his lawn, down the street, up the Peterson driveway. He was barely aware of the cold that chilled his bare ankles, that made his breath come harsh and uneven.

He was panting heavily, his heart racing when he hurried up the steps. The door was opened by a trim-looking man with bold features and graying hair. "Mr. Perry. I'm Hugh Taylor, FBI. We met two years ago . . ."

Roger thought of that day when Glenda had been knocked down by Ronald Thompson as he ran from this house, when she'd rushed in to find Nina's body.

"I remember." Shaking his head, he went into the living room. Steve was standing by the fireplace, his hands gripped together. Red-eyed and sobbing, Dora Lufts was seated on the couch. Beside her, Bill Lufts hunched forward helplessly.

Roger went directly to Steve and gripped his shoulders. "Steve, my God, I don't know what to say."

"Roger, thanks for coming so fast."

"How long have they been gone?"

"We're not sure. It happened sometime between six and seven-thirty."

"Sharon and Neil were alone here?"

"Yes. They . . ." Steve's voice broke. Quickly he recovered. "They were alone."

"Mr. Perry," Huge Taylor interrupted. "Is there anything you can tell us? Did you notice any strangers in the neighborhood, strange cars or vans or trucks—anything? Can you think of anything unusual?"

Roger sat down heavily. Think. There *was* something. What was it? Yes. "Your outside lights!"

Steve turned to him, his expression intense. "Bill is positive they were on when he and Dora went out. They were off when I got home. What did you notice about them?"

Roger's analytical mind offered a precise timetable of his

evening activities. He'd left the office at ten past five, driven into his garage at twenty of six. "Your lights must have been on when I got home at about twenty of six," he told Steve. "Otherwise I'd have noticed. Glenda made a cocktail. It wasn't more than fifteen minutes later that we were looking out our front window and she remarked that your place was dark."

He frowned. "As a matter of fact, the clock was chiming shortly before that so it must have been about five past six." He paused. "Glenda said something about a car coming from your driveway."

"A car! What kind of car?" Huge Taylor snapped.

"I don't know. Glenda mentioned it to me. I had turned my back to the window."

"You're sure of the time?"

Roger looked directly at the FBI agent. "I'm positive." He realized that he was having difficulty making sense out of what he was hearing. Had Glenda actually watched a car drive away with Neil and Sharon in it? Neil and Sharon being abducted! Shouldn't some instinct have warned them that something was wrong? But it had. He remembered the feeling of alarm Glenda had at the window, how she'd wanted him to walk over here. And he'd cautioned her about overreacting.

Glenda!

How much could he tell her. He looked at Hugh Taylor. "My wife will be terribly upset."

Hugh nodded. "I understand. And Mr. Peterson feels she can be trusted to know the truth. But it is absolutely vital that there be no publicity about this. We don't want to scare the abductor or abductors off."

"I understand."

"Two lives depend on all of you acting as normally as possible."

"Two lives . . ." Dora Lufts broke into dry, racking sobs. "My little Neil . . . and that pretty girl. I can't believe this, not after Mrs. Peterson . . ."

"Dora, keep quiet." Bill Lufts' voice was a whiny plea.

Roger watched as Steve's face contorted into a spasm of pain.

"Mr. Perry, do you know Miss Martin?" Hugh Taylor asked.

"Yes. I've met Sharon several times both here and at my home. Now may I please go over for my wife?"

"Certainly. We want to speak with her about the car she saw. I have another agent with me. I can send him."

"No. I'd prefer to go myself. She's not well and Neil means a great deal to her."

Roger thought, I am making conversation. I don't believe this. I don't. Steve. How can Steve stand this? He looked at the younger man compassionately. Steve was outwardly calm but the bleak look of suffering that had been etched in his face, that had only begun to lighten in these last months, was there again in the gray pallor, in the suddenly deepened creases in his forehead, the taut lines around his mouth. "Why don't you have a drink or some coffee, Steve," he suggested. "You look pretty shaken."

"Maybe coffee . . ."

Dora looked up eagerly. "I'l make it, and some sandwiches. Oh my God, when I think . . . Neil . . . Why did I have to go to the movies tonight? If anything has happened to that boy, I can't take it. I can't take it!"

Bill Lufts put his hand over his wife's mouth. "For once in your life, shut up!" he barked. "Shut up!" There was ferocity, bitterness in his voice. Roger realized that Hugh Taylor was studying the couple intensely.

The Lufts? Could he suspect them? No. Never. Impossible.

He was in the foyer when the chimes began to peal frantically. They all jumped as an agent, who'd been in the kitchen, covered the length of the foyer in seconds, raced past Roger and pulled the door open.

Glenda stood in the doorway. Her hair and face were wet with snow. Her feet were in open satin slippers. Her pink wool dressing gown was her only protection against the sharp, wet wind. Her face was marble-white. The pupils of her eyes were dilated and staring. In her hand she was clutching a sheet of notepaper. She was trembling violently.

Roger ran to her, caught her just before she collapsed. He held her against him.

"Roger, the call, the phonecall . . ." She was sobbing now. "He made me write it down. He made me read it back to him. He said, get it right or . . . or . . . Neil . . ."

Hugh snatched the paper from her hand and read it aloud. "Tell Steven Peterson if he wants his son and girlfriend back to be in the telephone booth of the Exxon station at exit 22 of the Merritt Parkway tomorrow morning at eight o'clock. He'll get instructions for the ransom."

Hugh frowned. The last word was indistinguishable. "What is this word, Mrs. Perry?" he demanded.

"He made me read it back . . . I could hardly write . . . he was so impatient . . . it's 'Foxy.' That's it. He repeated it." Glenda's voice rose in pitch. Her face twisted in pain. She pulled away from Roger, clutching her chest. "He . . . he was trying to disguise his voice . . . but when he repeated that name . . . Roger, *I've heard that voice*. That man is someone I know."

19

Before he left Somers State Prison, Bob Kurner phoned Kathy Moore and asked her to meet him in her office.

Kathy was an assistant prosecutor in Bridgeport assigned to Juvenile Court, and they'd met when he was serving as Public Defender there. They'd been going together for three months and Kathy had become deeply involved in his fight to save Ron Thompson.

She was waiting for him in the reception area with the typist he'd requested. "Marge said she'll stay all night if necessary. How much have you got?"

"A lot," Bob said. "I made him go over the story four times. There's a good two hours' worth."

Marge Evans stretched out her hand. "Just give it to me." Her tone was businesslike. She set the recorder on her desk, squeezed her massive body onto the swivel chair, inserted the cassette labeled "1" in the machine and ran it back to the beginning. Ron Thompson's voice, halting and low, began to speak: "I was working that afternoon after school in Timberly's Market . . ."

Marge snapped the "off" button and said, "Okay, you two get to something else. I'll take care of this."

"Thanks, Marge." Bob turned to Kathy. "Did you get those files?"

"Yes, they're inside." He followed her into her small crammed cubbyhole of an office. The desk was bare except for four manila folders labeled "Carfolli," "Weiss," "Ambrose," "Callahan."

"The police reports are right on top. Les Brooks wouldn't appreciate this, Bob. In fact, he'll probably fire me if he finds out about it."

Les Brooks was the prosecutor. Bob sat down at the desk and reached for the first file. Before he opened it he looked up at Kathy. She was wearing dungarees and a heavy sweater. Her dark hair was held back by a rubberband at the nape of her neck. She looked more like an eighteen-year-old co-ed than a twenty-five-year-old lawyer. But after the first time he'd been pitted against her in court Bob never made the mistake of underestimating Kathy. She was a good lawyer with a keen, analytical mind and a passion for justice.

"I know the chance you're taking, Kath. But if we can only find some thread between these murders and Nina Peterson's . . . Our one hope for Ron now is new evidence."

Kathy pulled a chair to the other side of the desk and reached for two of the files. "Well, God knows, if we can find any connection between these cases, Les will forget the irregularity in your seeing our files. The newspapers are really on his back. As of this morning they're calling these last two the 'Citizen Band Murders.' "

"How come?"

"Both the Callahan girl and Mrs. Ambrose had C.B. radios and had called for assistance. Mrs. Ambrose was lost and almost out of gas and Barbara Callahan had had a blowout.

"And two years ago Mrs. Weiss and Jean Carfolli were killed while driving alone at night on lonely roads."

"But that doesn't prove any connection. When Jean and Mrs. Weiss were killed the papers had started to write about the 'Highwayman Murders.' It's all catch phrases to make headlines."

"What do *you* think?"

"I don't know what I think. After Ron Thompson was arrested for the Peterson murder, we didn't have another woman killed in Fairfield County until last month. Now we have two unsolved deaths. But there have been other C.B.-related murders around the country. Those radios are great to have but it's insanity for a woman to get on the air and say she's alone on a deserted road and her car has broken down. It's an open invitation to every kook in the area who's listening to head straight to her. My God, they had a case in Long Island last year of a fifteen-year-old kid who used to listen to the police channel and head for trouble spots. They finally got him when he knifed a woman who'd called for assistance."

"I still say there's a connection between these four cases and that somehow Nina Peterson's case is linked with them," Bob said. "Call it a hunch. Call it grasping at straws. Call it anything. But help me."

"I want to. How do we go about it?"

"We'll start with a list: place, time, cause of death, weapon used, weather condition, kind of car, family background, witnesses' testimony. where victims were going, where they'd been that evening. In the last two cases, we'll measure the time elapsed between the message they sent out on the C.B. and the finding of the body. When we're finished, we'll compare everything with the circumstances of Mrs. Peterson's death. If there's nothing there, we'll start from another angle."

They began at ten past eight. At midnight, Marge came in with four sets of papers. "All finished," she said. 'I typed them triple-spaced to make it easier to pick up discrepancies in any of the versions. You know, listening to that boy is enough to break your heart. I've been a legal stenographer for twenty years and I've heard an awful lot of stuff but I know the ring of truth when I hear it and that kid's telling the truth."

Bob smiled wearily. "I wish to God you were the Governor, Marge," he said. "Thanks so much."

"How're you two doing?"

Kathy shook her head. "Nothing. Absolutely nothing."

"Well, maybe these will show something. Why don't I get you some coffee. Bet neither one of you had dinner."

When she came back ten minutes later, Bob and Kathy were sitting with two sets of papers in front of each of them. Bob was reading aloud. They were making line by line comparisons of the transcripts.

Marge set the coffee down and left silently. A security guard let her out of the building. As she huddled into the warmth of her heavy stormcoat, bracing herself for the long walk across the snow-blown parking lot, she realized she was praying. "Please God, if there's anything there to find that will help that boy, let those kids find it."

Bob and Kathy worked until dawn. Then she said, "We've got to quit. I have to go home and shower and dress. I'm due in court at eight o'clock. And anyhow, I don't want anyone to see you here."

Bob nodded. The words he was reading were blurring in his mind now. Over and over they'd compared the four versions of Ron's account of his activities the day of the murder. They'd concentrated on the time Nina Peterson talked to him in Timberly's Market until he ran panic-stricken from her home. There wasn't a single meaningful discrepancy they could pick up. "There's got to be something here," Bob said stubbornly. "I'll take these home with me, and let me have the lists we made on the other four cases."

"I can't let you take the files."

"I know that. But maybe we missed some factor in comparing the cases."

"We didn't, Bob." Kathy's voice was gentle.

He stood up. "I'll go right to my office and start again. I'll compare these with the trial transcript now."

Kathy helped him to put the material in his briefcase. "Don't forget the recorder and the cassettes," she said.

"I won't." He reached his arm out and encircled her. For an instant she leaned against him. "Love you, Kath."

"Love you."

"If we only had more time," he cried. "It's this damn capital punishment. How the hell can twelve people have come in and said that kid has to die. When, and if, they get the real killer it will be too late for Ron."

Kathy rubbed her forehead. "At first, I was glad when capital punishment was reinstated. I'm sorry for victims, a lot sorrier for them than for perpetrators. But yesterday we had a kid in Juvenile. He's fourteen and looks about eleven; a skinny, small kid. Both parents are hopeless alcoholics. They signed a complaint against him as an incorrigible when he was seven years old, *seven years old*. He's been in and out of children's homes since then. He keeps running away. This time the mother signed the complaint and the father is fighting it. They're separated and he wants the kid with him."

"What happened?"

"I won, if you can call it that. I insisted that he be sent back to a juvenile home and the judge agreed. The father's so disoriented from booze that he's not much more than a vegetable. The boy tried to run out of the courtroom; the sheriff's officer had to tackle him to catch him He got hysterical and kept screaming, 'I hate everybody. Why can't I have a home like other kids?' Psychologically, he's so damaged that it's probably already too late to save him. If in five or six years he kills someone, will we burn him? Should we?" Weary tears glistened in her eyes.

"I know, Kath. Why'd we get into law, anyhow? Maybe we should have been smarter. This tears your guts out." He bent down and kissed her forehead. "Talk to you later."

In his office, Bob put the kettle, brimming with water, on the hotplate. Four cups of Nescafé, strong and black, cleared the sensation of fogginess. He splashed cold water on his face and sat down at the long table in his office. Neatly, he laid out the rows of papers. He glanced at the clock over his desk. It was 7:30. He had just twenty-eight hours till the execution. That was why his heart was pounding, why his throat felt so constricted.

No. It was more than the frantic sense of urgency. Something was hammering at his consciousness. *There is something we have missed*, he thought.

This time it was not a hunch. It was certainty.

20

LONG AFTER THE PEREYS WENT HOME and the Lufts retired, Steve and Hugh Taylor sat at the dining-room table.

Quietly and efficiently, other agents had dusted the house for fingerprints and searched house and grounds for signs of the abductor. But the scrawled message was the only evidence to be found.

"The prints on the glass and cup will probably match the ones on Sharon Martin's purse," Huge told Steve.

Steve nodded. His mouth felt dry and brackish. Four cups of coffee. Endless cigarettes. He'd given up smoking when he turned thirty. Then when Nina died he'd started again. It was Hugh Taylor who gave him the first one. Something like a smile, grim and humorless, tugged at the corners of his mouth. "You're the one who got me back on these weeds," he said as he lit another one.

Hugh nodded. If ever a guy needed a cigarette that last time, it was Steve Peterson. And now his child! Hugh remembered how he was sitting with Steve at this table when some crackpot mystic phoned to say Nina had a message for him. The message was, "Tell my husband to beware. My son is in danger." That was the morning of Nina's funeral.

Remembering the incident, Hugh flinched. He hoped Steve wasn't thinking about that. He studied the methodical notes he had made. "There's a pay telephone in an outside booth at that Exxon station," he told Steve. "We're putting a tap on it as well as on this house and the Perrys' line. The thing to remember when you talk to Foxy is to try to keep him on the phone. That'll give us a chance to run a trace and record his voice. Our big break may be that Mrs. Perry will be able to remember who he is if she hears him again."

"Do you really think it's possible that she isn't just imagining she recognized the voice? You saw how upset she was."

"Anything's possible. But she seems like a level-headed woman to me and she's so *positive*. Anyhow, cooperate. Tell Foxy you want proof that Sharon and Neil are alive and unharmed, that you must have a message from them on a cassette or tape. Whatever money he asks for, promise to get it, but insist that you'll pay it only when you receive the proof."

"That won't antagonize him?" Steve wondered that he could sound so detached.

"No. But it will help insure that he won't panic and . . ." Abruptly Hugh clamped his lips together. But he knew Steve had gotten his meaning. He picked up his notebook.

"Let's start all over again. How many people knew the schedule of this house tonight, that the Lufts were planning to go out, that Sharon was coming up?"

"I don't know."

"The Perrys?"

"No. I hadn't seen them over the last week except to wave hello."

"Then it was just the Lufts and Sharon Martin and yourself?"

"And Neil."

"That's right. Is there any chance that Neil would have talked about Sharon's coming to other people, to his friends or his teachers at school?"

"It's possible."

"How serious is your friendship with Sharon? Sorry, but I have to ask."

"Very serious. I'm planning to ask her to marry me."

"I understand that you and Miss Martin were on the *Today* show this morning and that you disagreed strongly about the capital punishment issue and specifically that she was terribly upset about the Thompson execution."

"You work fast."

"We have to. Mr. Peterson. How much did that disagreement affect your personal relationship?"

"What's that supposed to mean?"

"Only this. As you know, Sharon Martin has been desperately trying to save Ronald Thompson's life. She's been in the Perry home and could have made a note of the phone number. Don't forget it's unlisted. Do you think there's a possibility that this kidnapping is a hoax, that she's hoping somehow to delay the execution?"

"No . . . no . . . no! Hugh, I understand you have to look at that angle, but please, for God's sake, don't waste your time on it. Whoever wrote that message could have copied the Perrys' number. It's right on that blackboard with the doctor's. Sharon would be incapable of doing this to me, incapable."

Hugh looked unconvinced. "Mr. Peterson, we've had some mighty unusual people breaking the law in the name of causes these last ten years. I only offer this thought, if Sharon Martin engineered this, your child is safe."

A tiny flicker of hope flared in Steve. This morning Sharon saying to him, "How can you be so positive, so sure, so relentless?" If that was the way she thought of him, could she . . .? The hope died. "No," he said flatly. "That's impossible."

"Very well. We'll leave it at that for the moment. What about your mail—any threats, hate letters, anything at all?"

"Quite a few hate letters because of my editorial stand on capital punishment, especially with the Thompson execution so near. But that isn't surprising."

"You've received no direct threats?"

"No." Steve frowned.

"What are you thinking?" Hugh asked quickly.

"Just that Ronald Thompson's mother stopped me last week. I take Neil for antihistamine shots every Saturday morning. She was in the parking lot of the medical building when we came out. She asked me to beg the Governor to spare Thompson."

"What did you tell her?"

"I said I couldn't do anything. I was anxious to get Neil away. Naturally I didn't want him to be aware about Wednesday. I wanted to get him inside the car as quickly as possible so he wouldn't hear us talking and so I turned my back to her. But she seemed to think I was ignoring her. She said something like, 'How would you feel if it was your only son, how would you feel?' And then she walked away."

Hugh made a note in his book. "We'll check her out." Standing up, he flexed his shoulders, vaguely aware that hours ago he'd been looking forward to going to bed. "Mr.

Peterson," he said, "try to hang on to the thought that our record of recovering kidnapping victims is a very good one and everything possible will be done. Now, I'd suggest that you try to get a few hours' sleep."

"Sleep?" Steve looked at him incredulously.

"Then rest. Go up to your room and lie down. We'll be right here and we'll call you if there's any reason. If the phone rings, you pick it up. We've got a tap on it now. But I don't think you'll get any further word from the abductor tonight."

"All right." Wearily, Steve walked out of the dining room. He stopped in the kitchen to get a glass of water and was sorry he had. The mug of cocoa and glass of sherry, smeared now with sooty powder, were on the kitchen table.

Sharon. Only a few hours ago she had been here in this house with Neil. He hadn't realized just how much he wanted Neil to trust and like Sharon until these last three weeks when she'd been away and he'd missed her so terribly.

Silently he left the kitchen, went into the foyer, up the stairs, down the hallway past Neil's room and the guest room to the master bedroom. Overhead, he could hear footsteps. The Lufts were walking around their third-floor room. Obviously they couldn't sleep either.

He switched on the light and stood near the door, studying the room. After Nina died, he'd refurnished it. He hadn't wanted to be around the antique white furniture she'd loved so much. He'd replaced the double bed with a twin-size brass fourposter, selected a color scheme of brown-and-white tweed. A man's room, the decorating shop had assured him.

He'd never cared for it. It was lonely and barren and impersonal, like a motel room. The whole house was like that. They'd bought it because they wanted waterfront property. Nina had said, "The house has real possibilities. Just wait and see. Give me six months with it." She'd had two weeks . . .

The last time he'd been in Sharon's apartment, he'd daydreamed about redoing this room, this house with her. She knew how to make a home charming and restful and inviting, too. It was the colors she used and the uncluttered look. And it was her presence.

Pulling off his shoes, he lay heavily across the bed. The room felt cool and he reached for the folded coverlet and drew it up. He touched the switch that turned off the overhead light.

The room was completely dark. Outside the wind was slapping branches of the dogwood trees against the house. The snow made a furry, pelting sound against the windows.

Steve dozed off into a light, uneasy sleep. He began to dream. Sharon, Neil. They wanted him to help them. He was running through a thick fog . . . running down a long hallway. There was a room at the end of it. He was trying to get into the room. He *had* to get into the room. He reached it and threw the door open. And the fog cleared. The fog was gone. And Neil and Sharon were lying on the floor, scarves knotted around their throats and iridescent chalk marks outlining their bodies.

21

IT WAS MUCH TOO DANGEROUS to be seen coming up from the Mount Vernon tracks alone late in the evening. The guards in the lower terminal had eyes for details like that. That was why he left Sharon and the boy at two minutes of eleven. Because at exactly eleven a train chugged into the station and he was able to go up the ramp and stairs with the eight or ten people who got off it.

He drifted near three of them who went to the Vanderbilt Avenue exit. He knew that to anyone watching he was one of a group of four people. He slipped away from the others when they turned left on Vanderbilt Avenue. He turned right, glanced across the street and stopped short. A police tow truck was there. Clanging chains were being attached to a shabby brown Chevrolet. They were just about to tow the car away!

Hugely amused, he started uptown. He was planning to make the phonecall from a booth in front of Bloomingdale's. The fifteen-block walk up Lexington Avenue chilled him and reduced some of the pulsing desire he'd experienced when he kissed Sharon. And she wanted him just as much. He could feel it.

He might have made love to Sharon then except for the boy. Even with the blindfold the eyes were there. Maybe the boy could see through the blindfold. The thought made him shiver.

The snow had tapered off some but the sky was still dark and heavy. He frowned, remembering how important it would be for the roads to be clear when he picked up the money.

He was planning to phone the Perrys and if they weren't home he'd call the Peterson house directly. But that could be risky.

He was lucky. Mrs. Perry picked up the phone on the first ring. He could tell by her voice that she was extremely nervous. Probably Peterson had called over there when he found the boy and Sharon missing. He gave Mrs. Perry the message in the low, gruff voice he'd practiced. It was only when she couldn't get the name that he exploded and raised his tone. Careless of him! Stupid! But she probably was too upset to notice.

Gently replacing the phone, he smiled. If the FBI had been called, they'd tap the phone in the Exxon station. That was why in the morning when he called Peterson on that phone, he'd tell him to go right to the booth in the next service station. They wouldn't have time to put a tracer on it.

He left the phonebooth feeling exhilarated, brilliant. A girl was standing in the doorway of a small dress shop. In spite of the cold she was wearing a miniskirt. White boots and a white fur jacket completed an outfit he thought very attractive. She smiled at him. Her hair was thick and curly around her face. She was young, not more than eighteen or nineteen and she liked him. He could tell. Her eyes were smiling at him and he started walking toward her.

But then he stopped. She was undoubtedly a prostitute and even though she was sincere about liking him, just suppose the police were watching and arrested them both? He looked around fearfully. He'd read about great plans being ruined by a small mistake.

Stoically passing the girl, he permitted her a brief, skeletal smile before he put his head down into the frigid wind and hurried to the Biltmore.

The same sneering night clerk gave him his key. He hadn't had dinner and was very hungry. And he'd order two or three bottles of beer from room service too. Around this time he always got thirsty for beer. Habit, maybe.

While he waited for the two hamburgers and french fries and apple pie, he soaked in the tub. It had felt so musty and cold and dirty in the room. After drying himself, he put on the pajamas he'd bought for this trip and examined his suit carefully. But it wasn't soiled.

He tipped the room service waiter generously. They always did that in the movies. The first bottle of beer he gulped down. The second he had with the hamburgers. The third he sipped listening to the midnight news. There was more about that Thompson kid. "The last possibility of a reprieve from death for Ronald Thompson was ended yesterday. Plans are being made to carry out the execution at 11:30 A.M. tomorrow as scheduled. . . ." But not a whisper about Neil or Sharon. Publicity was the one thing that he feared. Because someone might start putting two and two together.

The girls last month had been a mistake. It was just that

he couldn't help it. He never went cruising around anymore. Too dangerous. But when he heard them on the C.B., something made him go to them.

The thought of the girls made him churn up inside. Restlessly, he switched off the radio. He really shouldn't ... it might excite him.

He *had* to.

From his coat pocket he took out the expensive miniature recorder and the cassettes he always carried with him. Selecting one, he slipped it in the recorder, got into bed and turned out the light. He snuggled under the covers, appreciating the clean, crisp sheets, the warm blanket and coverlet. He and Sharon would stay in many hotels together.

Putting the earplug in his right ear, he cautiously deflected the "play" button of the machine. For several minutes there was only the sound of a car engine, then the faint squeal of brakes, a door opening and his own voice friendly and helpful as he got out of the Volks.

He let the cassette run until he got to the best part. That he kept replaying over and over again. Finally he had heard enough. He turned off the recorder, pulled out the earplug, and fell into deep sleep, the sound of Jean Carfolli's sobbing scream, "Don't ... please don't ..." ringing in his ears.

22

Marian and Jim Vogler talked far into the night. Despite Jim's efforts to console her, something like despair had seeped into Marian's soul.

"I wouldn't mind so much if we hadn't just spent all that money! *Four hundred dollars!* If someone had to steal the car why didn't they take it last week before we fixed it? And it was running so well. Arty did such a good job on it. And now how can I get to the Perrys? I'll lose that job!"

"Babe, you won't have to give up the job. I'll get somebody to lend me a couple of hundred bucks and I'll look around for another jalopy tomorrow."

"Oh, Jim, would you?" Marian knew how Jim hated borrowing from friends, but if he would do it just this once . . .

It was too dark for Jim to see her face but he felt the

faint relaxing of her body. "Babe," he reassured her, "someday we'll laugh about these lousy bills. Before you know it, we'll get caught up."

"I guess so," Marian agreed. Suddenly she felt desperately tired. Her eyes began to close.

They were just drifting off to sleep when the phone rang. Its jangle startled them. Marian pulled herself up on one elbow as Jim fumbled for the lamp on the night table and reached for the phone.

"Hello. Yeah, this is Jim—James Vogler. Tonight. That's right. Oh, that's good! Where? When can I get it? You're kidding. *You're kidding.* If that don't beat! All right . . . Thirty-sixth Street and Twelfth Avenue. I know. Right. Thanks." He hung up the phone.

"The car," Marian cried. "They found our car!"

"Yeah, in New York City. It was parked illegally in midtown and the cops towed it away. We can get it in the morning. The cop said it was probably heisted by some fool kids joyriding."

"Oh, Jim, that's wonderful!"

"There's a hitch."

"What is it?"

Jim Vogler's eyes crinkled. His lips twitched. "Babe, can you believe . . . we're stuck with the fifteen-buck parking ticket and the sixty-buck tow charge?"

Marian gasped. "That's my first week's pay!" She began to laugh helplessly with him.

In the morning Jim took the 6:15 train to New York and was back with the car at five of nine. Marian was ready to leave. Promptly at nine o'clock she turned into Driftwood Lane. The car was none the worse for its unauthorized trip into New York and she was grateful for the new snow tires. You sure needed them in this weather.

A Mercury was parked in the Perrys' driveway. It looked

like the one she'd noticed in front of the house across the street when she'd come for the interview last week. The Perrys must have company.

Somewhat uncertainly she pulled up beside the Mercury taking care that her car didn't block access to the garage. Then she lingered a moment before opening the door. She was a little nervous . . . all that excitement with the car just when she was starting a job. Well, just get yourself together, she thought. Count your blessings. The car was back. Affectionately, she patted the seat beside her with her gloved hand.

Her hand stopped moving. One of the fingers had touched something hard. She looked down, and with two fingers tugged a shiny object from where it was wedged between the cushion and the backrest.

Why, it was a ring. She inspected it closely. How pretty—a pale, pink moonstone in a lovely raised antique gold setting. Whoever stole the car must have lost it.

Well, it was a cinch they wouldn't come around to claim it. As far as she was concerned the ring was hers. It made up for the seventy-five dollars Jim laid out for the ticket and towing fee. She pulled off her glove and slipped the ring on her finger. It fit perfectly.

It was a good omen. Wait until Jim found out about this. Suddenly confident, Marian opened the door of the car, stepped out into the snow, and walked briskly around to the kitchen door of the Perry home.

23

THE PHONE IN THE OUTSIDE BOOTH of the Exxon station rang promptly at eight o'clock. Swallowing over the convulsion of his throat muscles, the sudden, absolute dryness in his mouth, Steve picked up the receiver. "Hello."

"Peterson?" A voice so muffled, so low, he had to strain to hear it.

"Yes."

"In ten minutes I'll call you at the payphone of the service station just past exit twenty-one."

The connection was broken.

"Wait . . . wait . . ." A buzzing sound assaulted his ear.

Desperately he looked over to the service island. Hugh had driven into the station a few minutes before him. The hood of his car was up and he was standing outside with the attendant, pointing at one of the tires. Steve knew he was watching him. Shaking his head, he got back in his own car and careened onto the parkway. Before he turned, he caught a glimpse of Hugh, jumping into his car.

The traffic was creeping cautiously down the slippery road. Steve clenched the wheel. He'd never make it to the next station in ten minutes. Twisting the wheel, he rode down the right-hand shoulder of the parkway.

The voice. He could hardly hear it. The FBI wouldn't have a prayer of tracing the call.

This time he'd try to keep Foxy on the phone longer. Maybe it was a voice he'd recognize too. He felt for the pad and paper in his pocket. He had to write down everything Foxy said. In the rearview mirror, he could see a green car behind him, Hugh's car.

It was eleven minutes past eight when Steve pulled into the next service station. The public phone was ringing insistently. He raced into the booth, grabbed the receiver.

"Peterson?"

This time the caller spoke so softly that he had to cover his other ear to block out the highway sounds. "Yes."

"I want eighty-two thousand dollars in tens, twenties and fifties. *No new bills.* At two o'clock tomorrow morning be at the payphone on the southwest corner of Fifty-ninth and Lexington in Manhattan. Drive in your own car. Be alone. You'll be told where to leave the money."

"Eighty-two thousand dollars . . ." Steve began to repeat the instructions. The voice, he thought frantically. Listen to the intonation, try to memorize it, be able to mimic it.

"Hurry up, Peterson."

"I'm writing this down. I'll get the money. I'll be there. But how do I know my son and Sharon are still alive? How do I know that you have them? I need proof."

"Proof? What kind of proof?" The whisper was angry now.

"A tape . . . or a cassette . . . something with them talking."

"A *cassette*!"

Was that muffled sound a laugh? Was the caller *laughing*? "I must have it," Steve insisted Oh God, he prayed, don't let this be a mistake.

"You'll get your cassette, Peterson." The receiver on the other end was slammed down.

"Wait!" Steve shouted. "Wait!"

Silence. The dial tone. He hung up slowly.

As they'd arranged, he drove directly to the Perrys' and waited for Hugh. Too restless to stay in the car, he got out and stood in the driveway. The icy, moisture-filled wind made him shiver. Oh God, was this happening? Was this nightmare real?

Hugh drove down the block, parked. "What'd he say?"

Steve pulled out the pad, read the instructions. The sense of unreality deepened.

"How about the voice?" Hugh asked.

"Disguised I think, very low. I don't think anybody could possibly identify it even if you had been able to tap that second phone." He stared unseeingly across the street, groped for comfort, found a slender thread.

"He promised the cassette. That means they're probably still alive."

"I'm sure of it." Hugh did not voice the gnawing worry that it would be virtually impossible for a cassette to reach Steve before he paid the ransom. There wasn't time to mail it even special delivery. A messenger service would be too easy to trace. The abductor didn't want the kidnapping publicized so he'd hardly leave a cassette at a newspaper or radio station. "How about the ransom?" he asked Steve. "Can you raise eighty-two thousand dollars today?"

"I couldn't raise five cents myself," Steve said. "I've

invested so much in the magazine that I'm absolutely strapped. Second mortgage, you name it. But thanks to Neil's mother, I can get that much money."

"Neil's mother?"

"She inherited seventy-five thousand dollars from her grandmother just before she died. I put it in a trust fund for Neil for college. It's in a bank in New York. With the interest it comes to just over eighty-two thousand."

"*Just over eighty-two thousand.* Mr. Peterson, how many people are aware of that trust?"

"I don't know. Nobody except my lawyer and accountant. You don't go around talking about that."

"What about Sharon Martin?"

"I don't remember mentioning it to her."

"But it is possible you told her?"

"I don't think I did."

Hugh started to go up the porch steps. "Mr. Peterson," he said carefully, "you have got to go over in your own mind everyone who knows about that money. That and the possibility that Mrs. Perry can identify the kidnapper's voice are our only leads."

When they rang the front doorbell, Roger answered quickly. He put a finger to his lips as they came in. His face was pale and strained, his shoulders sagging. "The doctor just left. He's given Glenda a sedative. She refuses to go to the hospital but he thinks she's on the verge of another coronary."

"Mr. Perry, I'm sorry. But we have to ask her to listen to a recording of the first call the kidnapper made this morning."

"She can't! Not now! This is killing her. It's killing her!" Clenching his fists, he swallowed, "Steve, I'm sorry . . . what happened?"

Mechanically, Steve explained. He still had the feeling of unreality, of being an observer, watching a tragedy being acted out without power to interfere.

There was a long pause, then Roger said slowly, "Glenda refused to go to the hospital because she knew you'd need her to hear that tape. The doctor gave her a strong tranquilizer. If she just slept for a little while . . . Can you bring it over later? She absolutely can't get out of bed."

"Of course." Hugh said.

Chimes were an intrusion. "That's the back door," Roger said. "Who on earth . . .? Oh my God, the new housekeeper. I forgot all about her."

"How long will she be here?" Hugh asked quickly.

"Four hours."

"No good. She might overhear something. Introduce me as the doctor. When we leave, send her home. Say you'll call her in a day or two. Where is she from anyhow?"

"Carley."

The chimes sounded again.

"She been in this house before?"

"Last week "

"We may want to check her out."

"All right." Roger hurried to the back door and returned with Marian. Hugh studied the pleasant-looking woman carefully.

"I've explained to Mrs. Vogler that my wife is ill," Roger said. "Mrs. Vogler, my neighbor, Mr. Peterson, and err . . . Doctor Taylor."

"How do you do?" Her voice was warm, a little shy. "Oh, Mr. Peterson, is that Mercury your car?"

"Yes."

"Then that must be your little boy. He's the dearest thing. He was out front when I came here last week and he pointed out this house to me. He was so polite. You must be very proud of him." Marian was peeling off her glove, reaching out her hand to Steve.

"I . . . am proud of Neil." Abruptly Steve turned his back to her and reached for the knob of the front door. Blinding tears stung his eyes. "Oh God, please . . ."

Hugh jumped into the breach, shaking Marian's hand, careful not to squeeze the unusual ring she was wearing. Pretty fancy to do housework in, he thought. His expression had changed subtly. "I think it's a very good idea Mrs. Vogler is here, Mr. Perry," he said. "You know how concerned your wife gets about the house. I'd have her start today just as you originally planned."

"Oh . . . I see . . . very well." Roger stared at Hugh, understanding the implication. Did Hugh think this woman might be tied to Neil's disappearance?

Bewildered, Marian looked past Hugh and Roger and watched Steve open the front door. Maybe he thought she was too forward offering to shake hands. Maybe she should apologize. She'd better remember she was the housekeeper here. She started to touch his shoulder, thought better of it, and silently held the door open for Hugh. Embarrassed, she closed it quietly behind them and as she did the moonstone ring made a faint clinking sound on the knob.

24

HE DIDN'T WANT TO BE A CRYBABY. He tried so hard not to cry but it was like when the asthma came. He couldn't stop it. He'd get that gulpy feeling in his throat and his nose would start running and big baby tears would get his face all wet. He cried a lot in school. He knew the other kids thought he was a baby and the teacher did, too, even though she wasn't mean about it.

It was just that there was something inside him that kept bothering him all the time, some scared, worried feeling. It all began that day when Mommy got hurt and went to heaven. He'd been playing with his trains. He never played with them anymore.

The thought of that day made Neil's breath come faster. He couldn't breathe through his mouth because of the rag over it. His chest began to heave. He gulped and a piece of the rag went into his mouth. It tasted thick and raspy on his tongue. He tried to say, "I can't breathe." The rag went back further in his mouth. He was gagging. He was going to start crying . . .

"Neil, stop that." Sharon's voice sounded funny and low and hoarse like she was talking from somewhere down in her throat. But her face was right next to his and through some kind of cloth he could feel her face move when she talked. She must have something around her mouth too.

Where were they? It was so cold and so smelly here. There was something over him, a smelly blanket, he guessed. His eyes were so squeezed together and it was so dark.

The man had opened the door and knocked him down. He had tied them up and he'd taken Sharon away. Then he'd come back and Neil had felt himself being picked up and squished into some kind of bag. Once, over at Sandy's, they'd played hide-and-seek and he'd hidden in a big leaf bag that he found in the garage. It had felt like that. He didn't remember anything after the man put him in the bag, not until Sharon was pulling him out of it. He wondered why he didn't remember. It was like when Mommy fell.

He didn't want to think about that. Sharon was saying, "Breathe slowly, Neil. Don't cry, Neil, you're brave."

She probably thought he was a crybaby too. Tonight he'd been crying when she came. It was just that when he didn't eat the toast and tea Mrs. Lufts made for him she said, "Looks like we'll have to take you to Florida when we go, Neil. Got to fatten you up somehow."

See. That proved it. If Daddy married Sharon it was like Sandy said. Nobody wanted sick kids and they'd make him go with the Lufts.

And he'd started to cry.

But Sharon didn't seem to be mad that he was sick now. In that funny voice she was saying, "in . . . out . . . slowly breathe through your nose . . ." He tried to obey, in . . . out . . . "You're brave, Neil, think about when you tell all this to your friends."

Sometimes Sandy asked him about the day Mommy got hurt. Sandy said, "If anybody started to hurt my mother, I'd make them stop."

Maybe he should have been able to make the man stop. He wanted to ask Daddy about that but he never had. Daddy always told him not to think about that day anymore.

But sometimes he couldn't help it.

In . . . out . . . Sharon's hair was on his cheek. She didn't seem to mind that he was all squished against her. Why had that man brought them here? He knew who he was. He'd seen him a couple of weeks ago when Mr. Lufts took him to where the man worked.

He'd been getting a lot of bad dreams since that day. He'd started to tell Daddy about them but Mrs. Lufts came in and he felt stupid and didn't say anymore. Mrs. Lufts always asked so many dumb questions: "Did you brush your teeth? Did you keep your scarf on at lunch? Do you feel all right? Did you sleep well? Did you eat all your lunch? Did you get your feet wet? Did you hang up your clothes?" And she never let him answer really. She'd just rummage through his lunchbox to see if he'd eaten or make him open his mouth so she could look down his throat.

It was different when Mommy was there. Mrs. Lufts came in just one day every week to clean. It was after Mommy went to heaven that she and Mr. Lufts moved in upstairs and that was when everything changed.

Thinking about all that, listening to Sharon, had made the tears go away by themselves. He was scared now but it wasn't like that day when Mommy fell and he'd been alone. It wasn't like that . . .

The man . . .

His breathing got fast again, chokey. "Neil," now Sharon was rubbing her face against his. "Try to think about when we get out of here. Your dad will be so glad to see us. I bet he'll take us out. You know, I'd like to go ice-skating with you. You didn't come with us that time your dad came down to New York. And afterwards we were going to take you to the zoo next to the rink . . ."

He listened. Sharon sounded as though she really meant it. He'd been planning to go down that day, but when he told Sandy he was going, Sandy said that Sharon probably didn't want him but was just trying to make his father feel good by asking him along too.

"Your dad tells me that he wants to start taking you to football games at Princeton next fall," she said. "I used to go to Dartmouth games all the time when I was in college. Every year they played Princeton, but your dad had graduated by then. I went to a girl's college, Mount Holyoke. It was just two hours from Dartmouth and a whole bunch of us used to go up some weekends, especially in football season . . ."

Her voice sounded so funny, like a growly whisper, Neil decided.

"Lots of men bring their families to the games. Your dad's so proud of you. He says you're so brave when you get the asthma shots. He said most kids would be carrying on about having to have a shot every single week, but you never complain or cry. That's pretty brave."

It was so hard to talk. She tried to swallow.

"Neil, plan now. That's what I do when I'm scared or

sick. I plan something nice that I know will be fun. Last year when I was in Lebanon—that's a country about five thousand miles from here—I was writing a story about the war they'd had, and I was staying in this ratty place, and one night I was so sick. I had flu and a fever and I was by myself and everything ached, my arms and legs, just the way they hurt now all tied up, and I made myself think of something nice that I'd do when I got home. And I remembered a painting that I wanted to buy. It was of a harbor with sailboats. And I promised myself that as soon as I got home, I'd treat myself to that picture. And I did."

Her voice was getting lower. He had to listen hard to catch every word.

"And I think we should plan a treat for you, a real treat. You know your dad says that the Lufts are really anxious to move to Florida now."

Neil felt a giant fist squeeze his chest.

"Easy Neil! Remember, in . . . out . . . breathe slowly. Well, when your dad showed me your house and I saw the Lufts' room and looked out the window, it was just like my painting. Because you can see all over the harbor and the boats and the Sound and the island. And if I were you, when the Lufts move to Florida, I'd take that room for myself. I'd put bookcases in it and shelves for your games and a desk. The alcove is so big you could really put tracks all over it for your trains. Your dad said you loved your trains. I had them when I was little too. In fact, I've got some great Lionel trains that used to be *my* dad's. That's how old they are. I'd like you to have them."

When the Lufts move to Florida . . . when the Lufts move to Florida . . . Sharon didn't expect him to go with them. Sharon thought he should have their room.

"And I'm scared now and I'm uncomfortable and I wish I was out of here but I'm glad you're with me and I'm

141

going to tell your dad how brave you were and how careful you were to breathe slowly and not get all chokey."

The heavy, black stone that always seemed to be lying on Neil's chest moved a little. Just the way he could wiggle a baby tooth when it got loose, Sharon's voice was moving the stone back and forth. Suddenly Neil felt desperately sleepy. His hands were tied but he could move his fingers and slide them along Sharon's arm until he found what he wanted, a piece of her sleeve that he could hold. Wrapping his fingers around the soft wool, he drifted into sleep.

The harsh, raspy breathing assumed an even pattern. Apprehensively, Sharon listened to the thick wheeze, felt the labored movement of Neil's chest. This room was so freezing, so damp, and Neil already had a cold. But at least lying this close together meant their shared body heat gave some warmth.

What time was it? They'd gotten to this place just past seven-thirty. The man . . . Foxy . . . had stayed at least a few hours with them. How long had he been gone? It must be past midnight. It was Tuesday now. Foxy had said that they'd be here till Wednesday. Where would Steve get eighty-two thousand dollars ransom money in one day? And why that crazy figure? Would he try to get in touch with her parents? It would be hard, with them living in Iran now. When Neil woke up, she'd tell him about that and about how her father was an engineer.

"Wednesday morning you and I are going away and I'll leave word where to find the boy." She explored the promise. She would have to act as though she wanted to go with him. As soon as Neil was safe and only she and the kidnapper were in the terminal, she'd start screaming. No matter what he might do to her, she'd have to take the chance.

Why in God's name had he kidnapped them? There was something about the way he looked at Neil. As though he hated him and was . . . frightened of him. But that was impossible.

Had he kept the blindfold on Neil because he was afraid Neil might recognize him? Maybe he was someone from around Carley. If that were true, how could he let Neil live? Neil had seen him when he pushed his way into the house. Neil had *stared* at him. Neil would recognize this man if he saw him again. She was sure of it. He must realize that too. Was he planning to kill Neil as soon as he had the money?

Yes he was.

Even if he brought her out of this place, it might be too late for Neil.

A passion of fear and anger made her press closer to Neil, bend her legs against his, attempt to enfold him in the woman's arc of her body.

Tomorrow. Wednesday.

This must be the way Mrs. Thompson was feeling now, this minute. This sense of rage and fear and helplessness, this primal need to protect one's young. Neil was Steve's son and Steve had suffered so much already. Steve must be frantic. He and Mrs. Thompson were going through identical agony.

She didn't blame Mrs. Thompson for lashing out at her. She didn't mean what she said; she couldn't. Ron was guilty; there was no hope of anyone believing anything else. That was what Mrs. Thompson didn't understand; that the only possible hope of saving him was to have a massive outcry against the execution.

At least she, Sharon, had tried to help him. Steve, oh Steve, she cried silently, now do you understand? Now do you see?

She tried to rub her wrists against the wall. The cinder-blocks were rough and jagged but the way the cords were tied, the knuckles and sides of her hand were taking the brunt of the contact.

When Foxy came back, she'd tell him she had to use the bathroom. He'd have to untie her. Maybe then, somehow . . .

Those pictures. He had killed those women. Only a madman would take pictures as he murdered and blow them up to that size.

He had taken *her* picture.

That bomb. Suppose someone did come near this room? If that bomb went off, she and Neil and how many others? How powerful was it?

She tried to pray, could only say over and over again, "Please, let Steve find us in time, please don't take his son from him."

That must be Mrs. Thompson's prayer. "Spare my son."

I blame you, Miss Martin . . .

Time moved agonizingly past. Her arms and legs subsided from pain into sudden numbness. Miraculously, Neil slept. Sometimes he'd moan and his breath would catch and he'd gasp, but then he'd sink back into fitful sleep.

It must be getting toward morning. The train sounds were becoming more frequent. What time did the station open? Five o'clock? It must be that now.

By eight this terminal would be swarming with people. Suppose that bomb went off?

Neil stirred restlessly. He muttered something. She couldn't make it out. He was waking up.

Neil tried to open his eyes and could not. He had to go to the bathroom. His arms and legs hurt. It was hard to breathe. Then he remembered what had happened. He'd run to the door and said, "Oh, that's all right," and opened it. Why had he said that?

He remembered.

He felt the rock moving back and forth in his chest. He felt Sharon's breath on his face. There was a far-off train sound.

A train sound.

And Mommy. He'd run downstairs.

And the man let Mommy drop and turned to him.

And then the man was bending over Mommy, looking all sweaty and scared.

No.

The man who pushed the door in last night, who stood over him and looked down at him; he'd done that before.

He'd come at him. He'd let Mommy drop and come at him. He'd put his hands out and looked right down at him.

And something happened.

The chimes. The chimes from the front door.

The man had run away. Neil had watched him run away.

That was why he couldn't stop dreaming about that day. Because of the part he forgot . . . the scary part when the man came to him and had his hands out and reached down to him . . .

The man . . .

The man who'd been talking to Mr. Lufts.

And last night had come pushing into the house and stood over him.

"Sharon," Neil's voice was muffled and hoarse as he struggled to speak through the thick wheeze . . .

"Yes, Neil. I'm here."

"Sharon, that man, the bad man who tied us up . . ."

"Yes, dear, don't be afraid, I'll take care of you."

"Sharon, that's the man who killed my Mommy."

25

THE ROOM. Lally *had* to go to her room. It didn't matter how cold it was. Newspapers between her two blankets would keep her warm enough. She missed it so much. The Tenth Avenue flop she and Rosie and some of the others had slept in most of the winter was too crowded. She needed her alone time. She needed her place to dream.

Years ago when she was young, after she read the Louella Parsons and Hedda Hopper columns, Lally would lull herself to sleep pretending that instead of being a homely spinster schoolteacher, she was a movie star coming into Grand Central Station with all the reporters and photographers waiting.

Sometimes she'd be in white fox when she stepped off the *Twentieth Century Limited*; or she'd be wearing a tailored silk suit, holding sable skins, and her secretary would be carrying the dressing case with her jewels.

Once she fantasized that she was already in an evening gown because she was going directly to the premier of her movie on Broadway, wearing that ball gown Ginger Rogers wore in *Top Hat*.

After a while the dreams faded and she became used to life as it was; dreary, monotonous, lonely. But when she arrived in New York and began to spend all her time in Grand Central, it was as though she really was remembering her heyday as a star; not pretending at all.

Then when Rusty gave her the key to the room and she could sleep nestled in her station, listening to the faint sound of her trains coming and going, it made everything perfect.

At 8:30 Tuesday morning, armed with her shopping bags, she was heading toward the lower terminal to the Mount Vernon track. Her plan was to mosey down the ramp with the people who were taking the 8:50 and then slip around to her room. On the way she stopped at the Nedicks in the corridor leading from the Biltmore and ordered coffee and donuts. She had already finished the *Times* and *News*, which she had gotten out of a receptacle.

The man ahead of her at the takeout counter looked vaguely familiar. Why, he was the one who spoiled her plans last night by going down to the Mount Vernon platform with the girl in the gray coat! Resentfully, she heard him order two coffees and rolls and milk. With hostile eyes she watched him pay his bill and pick up his package. She wondered if he worked around here. Somehow she didn't think so.

After leaving Nedicks, she deliberately dawdled through the terminal so the cops who knew her wouldn't think she was doing anything out of the ordinary. But at last she was at the ramp to the Mount Vernon track. The train was loading. People were hurrying now. Delighted, Lally fell into step with them, moving down the platform. As the others rushed into the train, she slipped around the last car and turned right. In an instant she'd be out of sight.

And then she saw him. The man who'd just bought the coffee and milk and rolls. The man who'd come down here last night. His back was to her. He was hurrying now, disappearing into the gloom of the throbbing depths of the terminal.

There was only one place where he could be going. *Her room.*

He had found it! That was why he went down on the platform last night. He wasn't waiting for the train. He had gone to her room with the girl.

And he had two coffees and milk and four rolls. So the girl must be there now.

Bitter, disappointed tears welled up in Lally's eyes. They had taken over her room! Then her lifelong ability to cope rescued her. She could handle this. She'd get rid of them! She'd watch and when she was sure he was out, she'd go into the room and warn the girl that the cops knew they were there and were coming to arrest them. That'd scare her off fast enough. He was a mean-looking one, but the girl wasn't the kind to be hanging around stations. Probably thought it was some kind of game being there. She'd probably clear out fast and take him with her.

Grimly satisfied at the prospect of tricking the interlopers, Lally turned around and headed for the upstairs waiting room. Her imagination leaped to the girl who was probably right now lying on *her* cot waiting for her boyfriend to bring in breakfast. "Don't get too comfortable in there, missy," she thought, "you're going to have company real soon."

26

STEVE, HUGH, THE LUFTS AND AGENT HANK LAMONT sat at the dining-room table. Dora Lufts had just brought a pot of coffee and freshly baked corn muffins to the table. Steve looked at them without interest. His chin was resting on his hand. Just the other night Neil had said to him, "You're always telling me not to put my elbows on the table and you always sit like that, Daddy."

He blinked away the thought. No use. No use. Keep concentrating on what could be done. Carefully, he studied Bill Lufts. Undoubtedly Bill had consoled himself with booze during the night. His eyes were bloodshot and his hands were shaking.

They had just heard the nineteen-word tape of the first phonecall. Muffled, indistinct, it was impossible to recognize the voice as familiar. Hugh played it three times, then snapped it off. "All right. We'll take it over to Mrs. Perry, as soon as Mr. Perry calls us, and see what she says about it. Now it's very, very important that we get a few things straight."

He consulted the list in front of him. "First, there'll be an agent here 'round the clock till this is settled. I think the man who calls himself Foxy is too clever to call this phone or the Perrys'. He'll guess that we have taps on them. But there's always the chance . . .

"Mr. Peterson has to go down to New York, so if the phone rings, Mrs. Lufts, you must answer it immediately. Agent Lamont will be on the extension and we'll be recording it as well. But if the abductor does call, you must not get rattled. You must try to keep him on the phone as long as possible. Can you do that?"

"I'll try." Dora quavered.

"What about Neil's school? Did you phone and report him ill?"

"Yes. Right at eight-thirty, just as you told me."

"Fine." Hugh turned to Steve. "Did you reach your office, Mr. Peterson?"

"Yes. The publisher had suggested I take Neil away for a few days until after the Thompson execution tomorrow. I left word I was doing that."

Hugh turned to Bill Lufts. "Mr. Lufts, I'd like you to stay right here in the house for today at least. Would anyone find that unusual?"

His wife laughed mirthlessly. "Only the regulars at the Mill Tavern," she said.

"All right, thank you both." Hugh's tone dismissed the Lufts. They got up and went into the kitchen, partially closing the door behind them.

Hugh leaned over and closed it with a decided thud.

He raised one eyebrow to Steve. "I don't think the Lufts miss very much of what's said in this house, Mr. Peterson," he commented.

Steve shrugged. "I know. But ever since Bill retired the first of the year, they've really been staying on as a favor to me. They're very anxious to get to Florida."

"You said they've been here two years?"

"A little longer than that. Dora was our cleaning woman. She came in one day a week since before Neil was born. Our other house was only six blocks from here, you know. They were saving money for their retirement. When Nina was killed we'd just moved in here and I had to have someone to take care of Neil. I suggested that they take that large third-floor room. That way they could save the overhead they'd been paying, and I paid Dora as much as she was getting for all her cleaning jobs."

"How has it worked out?"

"Reasonably well. They're both very fond of Neil and she looks after him very carefully, too carefully maybe. She's always fussing over him. But since Bill's been hanging around with nothing to do, he's been into a lot of drinking. Frankly, I'll be glad when they do make the move."

"What's been holding them back?" Hugh asked sharply. "Money?"

"No. I don't think so. Dora would love to see me remarried so that Neil would have a mother again. Dora's really an awfully good soul."

"And you've been getting close to that with Sharon Martin?"

Steve's smile was wintry. "I hope so." Restlessly, he stood up and walked to the window. The snow was falling again, effortlessly, noiselessly. It seemed to him that he had as much control over his life as one of those snowflakes had over its ultimate destination . . . to fall, land on shrub or grass or street, to melt or freeze on contact, to be swept away, driven over, crunched down by boots.

He was getting fanciful, lightheaded. Deliberately he pulled his mind back to the present. He could not be helpless, waiting here immobilized. He had to *do* something.

"I'll get the bankbook and start down to New York," he told Hugh.

"Just a minute, Mr. Peterson. There are a few things we need to discuss."

Steve waited.

"What happens if you don't get a tape of your son and Sharon?"

"He *promised* . . ."

"He may not be able to deliver. How would he get it to you, assuming he makes it? The point is, are you prepared to pay the money without the proof?"

Steve considered. "Yes. I won't take the chance of antagonizing him. Maybe he'll leave a tape or cassette somewhere expecting it to be found, and then if I don't follow through . . ."

"All right. We'll face that later. If it hasn't come by two A.M. when he calls you at the Fifty-ninth Street payphone, you can consider stalling. Tell him you didn't get it. If he claims he left it somewhere, it's easy enough to pick it up.

"Now the next consideration. Do you want to give him real cash? We could get counterfeit money that would be easy to trace."

"I simply won't take that chance. The money in the trust is for Neil's education. If anything happens to him . . ."

"All right. So you'll get the money from your account and take it down to the Federal Reserve Bank. Get a cashier's check. Our men will be there photographing the ransom bills. That way at least we'll have some record."

154

Steve interrupted. "I don't want the money marked."

"I'm not talking about *marking* it. There's no way the abductor can possibly know if we've *photographed* it. But that will take time. Eighty-two thousand dollars in tens, twenties and fifties is a lot of bills to handle."

"I know."

"Mr. Peterson, there are several precautions I'm going to urge you to take. One, let us rig cameras into your car. That way we may have some kind of lead to follow after you make contact with the abductor. We may be able to get a picture of him or pick up the license number of the car he's driving. We'd also like to install a beeper device in your car so that we can follow you from a distance. I promise you they'll be impossible to detect. Last, and this is entirely up to you, we'd like to conceal an electronic tracer in the suitcase with the money."

"Suppose it's found. The abductor will know I brought you in."

"Suppose you *don't* put it in and you don't hear another word. You've paid the money and you don't have your child or Sharon. Believe me, Mr. Peterson, our first concern is to get them back safely. After that we'll pull out all the stops to find the perpetrators. But it's up to you."

"What would you do if it were your son and your . . . wife?"

"Mr. Peterson, we're not dealing with honorable people. It's not as simple as pay the money and you get them back. Maybe they'll release them. *Maybe.* But maybe they'll just abandon them somewhere unable to free themselves. That has to be considered. At least the area may be narrowed down if we can follow the kidnapper's trail electronically."

Steve shrugged helplessly. "Do what you have to. I'll take Bill's car to New York."

"No. I'd like to suggest that you take your own car and

park it in the lot near the station as usual. It's very possible your movements are being watched. We'll have a loose tail on you, an agent following you from a distance. Leave your keys on the floor. We'll pick the car up and get the equipment installed and have it there when you come back. Now here's where you go with the money . . ."

Steve caught the 10:40 train to Grand Central Station. It was ten minutes behind schedule and he arrived at the terminal at 11:50. Electing to walk up Park Avenue, he carried a large, empty suitcase in his hand.

His sense of futility and misery deepened as he trudged the blocks between the terminal and Fifty-first Street. On this, the second day of the snowstorm, New Yorkers, exhibiting their customary resiliency, were out on the streets as usual. There was even a buoyancy about the way they stepped over icy curbs, maneuvered around drifts. Yesterday morning he and Sharon had stood in the falling snow a few blocks from here and he'd held her face in his hands and kissed her goodbye. Her lips had been unresponsive just as he'd been unresponsive when Nina kissed him goodbye that last day.

He arrived at the bank. The news that he wanted to withdraw all but two hundred dollars from Neil's account was greeted with a lifted eyebrow. The teller left her cage and consulted with a senior vice-president, who hurried over to Steve.

"Mr. Peterson," he asked, "is there any problem?"

"No, Mr. Strauss. I simply wish to make a withdrawal."

"I'll have to ask you to fill out state and federal forms. It's required for any withdrawal that large. I hope there has been no dissatisfaction with our handling of your son's account."

Steve struggled to keep his tone and expression even. "None at all."

156

"Very well." The vice-president's tone became coolly professional. "You can fill out the necessary forms at my desk. Follow me, please."

Mechanically, Steve scrawled the required information. By the time he was finished, the teller had brought the cashier's check to the desk.

Mr. Strauss quickly signed it, handed it to him and stood up. The man's face had become thoughtful. "I don't mean to intrude, but there isn't any trouble, is there, Mr. Peterson? Perhaps something we can help with?

Steve stood up. "No, no, thank you, Mr. Strauss." To his own ears, he sounded strained, unconvincing.

"I hope not. We value you very much, as a client of this bank and, I hope, as a friend. If there *is* a problem and if we can help, please give us the chance." He held out his hand.

Steve grasped it. "You're very kind but it's quite all right, I assure you."

Carrying the suitcase, he went out, hailed a cab and directed it to the Federal Reserve Bank. There he was taken to a room where grim-faced FBI agents were busily counting and photographing the money he would exchange for the check he was carrying. Bleakly he watched them.

"The king was in the counting house, counting up his money." The nursery rhyme ran through his head. Nina used to singsong it to Neil when she was getting him ready for bed.

He returned to Grand Central just in time to miss the 3:05 train. The next train wouldn't leave for an hour. He called home. Dora answered and agent Lamont spoke from the extension. No further news. No sign of a cassette. Hugh Taylor would be back by the time he arrived.

The prospect of the hour to kill appalled Steve. His head was aching; a slow, burning ache that began in the center of his forehead and traveled back on each side like an ever tightening vise. He realized he'd eaten nothing since yesterday's lunch.

The Oyster Bar. He'd go down there and order a plate of oyster stew and a drink. He passed the phone he'd used last night when he tried to call Sharon. That had been the beginning of this nightmare. When he didn't get an answer, he'd known that something was wrong. That was only twenty hours ago. It seemed a lifetime.

Twenty hours. Where were Sharon and Neil? Had they been given anything to eat? It was so cold out. Were they in a place with heat? If there was any way possible, Sharon would take care of Neil, he knew that. Suppose Sharon had answered the phone when he'd called last night. Suppose the three of them had spent the evening together as they'd planned. After Neil went to bed, he was going to say, "You won't be getting much, Sharon. You probably could do a lot better if you waited, but don't wait. Marry me. We're good together."

She probably would have turned him down. She despised his position on capital punishment. Well, he'd been sure enough of it, relentless about it, positive he was right.

Was this the way Ronald Thompson's mother was feeling right this minute? Even when it was over for that boy, she'd go on suffering the rest of her life.

As he would, if anything happened to Sharon and Neil.

The pace of this terminal was beginning to quicken. Executives leaving early to avoid the commuter rush walked briskly to the New Haven trains that would take them to Westchester and Connecticut. Women in for a day of shopping crossed the terminal, consulting timetables, anxious to be home in time to start dinner.

Steve descended the stairs to the lower level and went into the Oyster Bar. It was nearly empty. The lunch rush was long since over. It was too early for the cocktail and dinner crowd. He sat at the bar and ordered, carefully keeping the suitcase right under his foot.

Last month he and Sharon had met here for lunch. She'd been exhilarated because of the overwhelming response to her campaign to have Thompson's sentence commuted to life imprisonment. "We're going to make it, Steve," she said confidently. She'd been so happy; she cared so much. She'd talked about her forthcoming trip to raise more support.

"I'll miss you," he'd said.

"I'll miss you, too."

I love you, Sharon. I love you. Sharon. I love you, Sharon. Had he said it then?

He gulped the martini the bartender put in front of him.

He sat in the Oyster Bar, the steaming, bubbling stew untouched, until at five minutes of four he paid his bill and went to the upper terminal and the Carley train. He didn't notice that as he made his way to the smoking car, a man seated in the rear of the car he entered, buried his face behind a newspaper. It was only after he had passed that the newspaper was lowered slightly and glittering eyes followed his progress through the coach with the heavy suitcase.

That same passenger got off at Carley, but carefully waited on the platform until Steve had entered the parking lot and driven away in the car which now had powerful cameras hidden in the headlights and behind the rear-view mirror.

27

GLENDA PERRY SLEPT UNTIL ONE O'CLOCK. It was the sound of Marian's car pulling out of the driveway that brought her to full wakefulness. Before she opened her eyes she lay perfectly still, waiting. But the pain that often accompanied that first stirring did not come. It had been so bad during the night, worse than she had let on to Roger. Except he probably guessed, and she knew the doctor was concerned about the cardiogram.

She was *not* going to the hospital. They'd sedate her so much there that she'd be useless. She wouldn't let it happen. She knew why the pains had been so frequent lately. It was the Thompson boy. He was so young and her testimony had helped condemn him.

"He knocked you down, Mrs. Perry . . ."

"Yes, he was running from the house."

"It was dark, Mrs. Perry. Can you be sure it wasn't some-one else running away?"

"Positive. He hesitated in the doorway before he collided into me. The kitchen light was on."

And now Neil and Sharon. Oh God, let me remember. She bit her lip . . . a flicker of pain . . . no, don't get upset. That won't do any good. For God sake, *think*. She slipped a nitro under her tongue. That would ward off the pain before it became acute. Foxy. The way he said it. What was the association? It wasn't that long ago, either.

The door opened a crack and she saw Roger looking in at her. "It's all right, dear, I'm awake."

"How do you feel?" He hurried over to the bed, touched her hand.

"Not bad. How long have I been asleep?"

"Over four hours."

"Whose car just left?"

"That was Mrs. Vogler."

"Oh, I forgot. What did she do?"

"She seemed to keep herself pretty busy in the kitchen. Was on the stepladder taking things from the top shelves."

"Thank heaven. I've been afraid to stretch up there and they're so dusty. Roger, what happened? Did Steve talk to . . . Foxy?"

Roger explained—" . . . so they only have a few words. Are you up to listening to them?"

"Yes."

Fifteen minutes later, propped up on pillows, a cup of tea in her hand, Glenda watched Hugh Taylor enter her bedroom.

"This is good of you, Mrs. Perry. I understand that it's a strain for you."

She waved away his concern. "Mr. Taylor, I'm just

ashamed I ve wasted the whole morning. Please turn that on."

She listened intently as Hugh ran the cassette.

"Oh, it's so low. It's impossible . . ."

The terse expectancy slid from Hugh's face. His tone was emotionless as he said, "Well. thank you very much for listening, Mrs. Perry. We're going to analyze this for voice pattern. It isn't admissible evidence, but when we get the abductor it may help to confirm the identification." He picked up the recorder.

"No . . . wait!" Glenda put her hand on the machine. "Is this your only record of the call?"

"No. We ran both a tape and cassette during the wire-tap."

"Will you leave this with me?"

"Why?"

"Because I *know* the person I spoke to last night. I know him. I'm going to try now to retrace every single thing I've done in the last few weeks. Maybe something will come to me. And I'd like to be able to hear that tape again."

"Mrs. Perry, if you could only remember . . . " Hugh bit his lip as Roger Perry shot a warning glance at him. Quickly he left the room, followed by Roger.

When they were downstairs, Roger asked, "Why did you have me keep Mrs. Vogler here today? Surely you don't suspect . . . ?"

"We can't let any possibility pass. But she seems all right. Good character, good family situation, well-liked. It's just coincidence that she talked about Neil this morning. And anyhow, she's got the best alibi of anyone last night and so does her husband."

"Why is that?"

"She was seen by the cashier both entering and leaving

163

the movie. Her husband was seen by his neighbors at home with their kids. And shortly after seven o'clock they were in the police station reporting a stolen car."

"Oh yes. She did mention that. Lucky she got it back."

"Yeah. She gets a lousy eight-year-old car back and we haven't got a trace of two kidnap victims. Mr. Perry, what *is* your impression of Sharon Martin? Do you think she's capable of planning this?"

Roger considered. "Every instinct says no."

"How do you size up her relationship with Mr. Peterson?"

Roger thought of the last time Sharon and Steve had been over. She'd seemed a little depressed and Glenda asked her if anything was wrong. Steve had gone into the kitchen for ice and she'd said, "Oh, it's just that Neil shuts me out so." Then when Steve came back, he'd ruffled her hair as he passed her. Roger remembered the expression on both their faces. "I think they were . . . are . . . very much in love, more than either one of them realizes. I think Sharon has been troubled by Neil's rejection, and of course Steve is worried about it too. Then he's been pretty strapped financially. He sank everything he had into *Events*. I'm sure it will pay off, but that's had him concerned. He's said as much to me."

"And there was the Thompson execution."

"Yes. Glenda and I both hoped that Sharon would succeed in saving him. Glenda is heartsick over her role in that case."

"Did Sharon want Mr. Peterson to intercede with the Governor?"

"I think she realized that he wouldn't do it and that the Governor would only resent a purely emotional appeal. Don't forget, she's been bitterly criticized for the two stays she's already granted Thompson."

"Mr. Perry, what do you think of the Lufts? Is it possible that they might be part of this? They're trying to save money; they've had access to your private number. They could have known about the trust fund."

Roger shook his head. "Not a chance. If Dora ever picks up anything for Glenda at the store, she spends twenty minutes making sure she's given her the exact change. He's like that too. Sometimes he takes my car to be serviced and always brags about how much he saves me. Neither one of them has the capacity to be anything except painfully honest."

"Okay. I know you'll call us at the Peterson's immediately if Mrs. Perry has anything to tell us."

Hank Lamont was waiting for Hugh. Something in his manner telegraphed the fact that he had news. Hugh didn't waste time on preliminaries. "What have you got?"

"Mrs. Thompson . . . "

"What about her?"

"Last night. She talked to Sharon Martin!"

"She *what*?"

"The Thompson kid told us. Don and Stan interviewed him in his cell. Said there'd been some threats against the Peterson boy and warned him that if his friends were pulling something, we'd better get their names before they got into deep trouble."

"They didn't admit Neil and Sharon were kidnapped?"

"Of course not."

"What did he say?"

"He's clean. The only visitors he's had in the last year are his mother, his lawyer and the parish priest. His closest friends from high school are in college now. He gave us their names. Everyone of them is away. But he did tell us that Sharon called his mother."

"Did they talk to the mother?"

"Yes. She's staying at a motel near the prison. They found her."

"In the motel?"

"No, in church. God help her, Hugh, she's just kneeling there praying. Won't believe the kid's going to be executed tomorrow. Won't believe it. She says Sharon called her a few minutes before six. Wanted to know if she could do anything. Admitted she blew up at her, blamed her for running around the country saying the boy is guilty. Threatened that she wouldn't know what she'd do to Sharon if the boy dies. What do you make of it?"

"Let's try this," Hugh said. "Sharon Martin is upset by the phonecall, maybe even thinks there's some validity in what the mother said. She's desperate and calls someone to come for her and the boy. She's planning a grandstand stunt, make it look like a bona fide kidnapping and then make Neil a hostage for Thompson's life."

"It's a possibility," Hank said.

Hugh's face hardened. "I think it's more than a possibility. I think that poor guy, Peterson, is having his guts torn out and Mrs. Perry is verging on a coronary because Sharon Martin thinks she can manipulate justice."

"What do we do now?"

"Continue to treat this as a real snatch. And dig up everything we can about Sharon Martin's associates, particularly anyone she knows in this area. If only Mrs. Perry can remember where she heard that voice, we'll crack this wide open."

In her room, Glenda was playing the cassette over and over. ("Peterson? In ten minutes I'll call you at the payphone of the service station just past exit twenty-one.") Helplessly, she shook her head and turned off the machine.

166

That wasn't the way to do it. Start retracing this last couple of weeks. *But what was it about that cassette?*

Yesterday she hadn't gone out at all. She'd talked on the phone to the drugstore, and to Agnes and then to Julie about the hospital benefit. Chip and Maria had called from California and put the baby on. That was the last time she was on the phone yesterday until Foxy called.

Sunday she and Roger drove to New York right after church and had brunch in the Pierre and went to Carnegie Hall to hear Serkin. She hadn't spoken to anyone on the phone at all.

Saturday, she'd been at the decorator's about the slip-covers. And she'd had her hair done, or was that Friday? She shook her head impatiently. This wasn't the way to go about it at all. Getting out of bed, she walked slowly over to her desk and reached for her appointment book. She'd ask Roger to bring up the calender from the kitchen wall too. Sometimes she jotted notes on it. And her charge slips. She kept them together. They were all dated. They'd help her to remember where she'd stopped. And her checkbook. She pulled the checkbook out of a compartment, the charge slips out of a drawer.

Carrying the items, she got back into bed, sighing as a constriction began in her chest and mounted into sharp pain. As she reached for a nitroglycerin pill she pushed the button of the recorder and began running the cassette. Once again, the muffled, throaty whisper filled her ears. "Peterson? In ten minutes I'll call you at the payphone of the service station just past exit twenty-one."

28

WALKING BACK FROM THE PHONEBOOTH, he thought about the cassette. After he recorded Sharon and the boy, should he do it?

Why not?

He went directly to Grand Central. Better to go to them while there was still some commuter activity. Those guards had a sixth sense about people who didn't belong in the terminal.

Sharon and the kid probably hadn't had any dinner last night. They'd be hungry. He didn't want her to be hungry. But she probably wouldn't eat if he didn't feed the boy too. Thinking of the boy always made him nervous. A couple of weeks ago, he'd almost panicked when he'd looked out and seen the boy staring at him from the car. Just the way he did in the dream, those round brown eyes, pupils so wide they looked black, accusing, always accusing.

Tomorrow it would all be over. He'd have to buy Sharon a ticket on the plane. He didn't have enough money now but after tonight he would. He could make a reservation. But what name would he use? He'd have to make up a name for her.

Yesterday on the *Today* show, she'd been introduced as the author and columnist. She was very well known and very popular. That's why it was so wonderful that she was so much in love with him.

She was very well known.

She'd been on the *Today* show.

Lots of people would recognize her.

Frowning, he stopped short, was jostled by the woman hurrying along behind him. He glowered at her and she said, "Oh, excuse me," and hurried past him down the street. He softened. She hadn't meant to be rude. In fact, she had smiled at him, really smiled at him. Lots of women would smile at him when they knew how wealthy he was.

Slowly he resumed the walk along Lexington Avenue. Buses had ground the fallen snow into filthy slush. Even that was freezing except what was directly in the path of buses and cars. He wished he were going to the Biltmore. That room was so comfortable. He'd never been in a place quite like that.

He'd stay with Sharon and the child until this afternoon. Then he'd take the train up to Carley. He'd go over to his place and see if there were any messages. No point in having people wondering why he wasn't around. He struggled to think of where he could leave the cassette. Maybe Peterson wouldn't pay if he didn't get it.

He had to have the money. It was too dangerous for him to stay in Fairfield County now. And he had a good reason to leave. Everyone expected him to leave.

"Any unexpected departures in this area?" the cops might start asking.

"Him? No. He's been complaining about losing the place; begged the old man to renew his lease.'

But that was before the last two girls. "The C.B. Murderer," the papers were calling him. If they only knew . . .

He had even gone to the Callahan funeral service. The funeral service!

Suddenly he knew where to leave the cassette, where he could be sure it would be found that evening and delivered.

Satisfied, he walked briskly into Nedicks, ordered coffee, milk and rolls. He'd be staying a while so they might as well have some food right away and some later before he left. He didn't want Sharon to think he was unkind.

When he left the area of the Mount Vernon track he had an odd sense of being watched. His instinct was very good about that. He stopped and listened. He thought he heard something and tiptoed back. But it was just one of those shopping bag ladies making her way up the ramp to the terminal. She'd probably been sleeping on the platform.

With infinite care he released the sliver of wire that was taped to the door of the room. Gingerly, he took out his key and inserted it in the lock. Opening the door a hairsbreadth at a time to keep from jerking the wire, he slipped into the room and closed the door.

He switched on the fluorescent lights and grunted in satisfaction. Sharon and the boy were just as he left them. The boy couldn't see him because of the blindfold of course, but behind him, Sharon lifted her head. Setting down the package, he hurried over to her and yanked the gag from her mouth.

"It wasn't very tight this time," he told her. He thought that he'd seen a kind of reproach in her eyes.

171

"No." She was very nervous, nervous in a different way. Her eyes were very scared now. He didn't want her to be scared of him.

"Are you afraid, Sharon?" His voice was horribly gentle.

"Oh, no . . . not at all."

"I brought you some food."

"Oh, I'm glad, but won't you please take the gag off Neil? And please, won't you untie us, even just our hands, like before?"

His eyes narrowed. There was something different about her. "Certainly, Sharon." He nuzzled his nose against her face. His fingers were very strong. He could untie the knots very quickly. In a minute her hands were free and he reached for the boy.

The child shrank against Sharon. "It's all right, Neil," she said, "remember what we talked about."

"What did you talk about, Sharon?"

"Just that Neil's dad would give you the money you want and that tomorrow you'd tell his dad where to find him. I said that I was going away with you but that his dad would be here very soon after we left. Isn't that right?"

The voice was thoughtful, the glittering eyes speculative. "You're sure you want to go, Sharon?"

"Oh yes, very much. I . . . I like you, Foxy."

"I brought some rolls and coffee and some milk for the boy."

"That's very nice of you." She was flexing her fingers. He watched as she began to rub Neil's wrists, as she smoothed his hair back from his forehead. The way she was pressing the boy's hands, like a signal, like a secret pact.

He pulled over the orange crate and deposited the bag on it. He gave Sharon a container of coffee.

"Thank you." She put the container down without sipping from it. "Where is Neil's milk?"

He handed it to her, watched as she put it in Neil's hands. "There it is; hold onto it, Neil. Drink slowly." The boy's raspy breathing was irritating, worrisome, evoked memories.

He brought out the rolls. He'd had them thickly buttered the way he liked them. Sharon broke off a piece of one of them and handed it to the boy. "Here, Neil, it's a roll." Her voice was soothing. It was like she and the boy were in a conspiracy against him. Sullenly, he watched them eat. He gulped his own coffee, barely tasting it. They both ate one roll, finished the coffee and milk.

He hadn't taken his coat off. It was so cold in here and anyhow he didn't want to take the chance of getting his new suit dirty. He cleared off the orange crate, putting the bag with the remaining rolls on the floor, sat down on the crate and stared at them.

When they were finished eating, Sharon pulled Neil over on her lap. The boy's breathing was loud and strained. The sound irritated Foxy, jangled his nerves. Sharon didn't look at him at all. She just kept rubbing the boy's back, talking to him softly, telling him to try to sleep. Foxy watched as she kissed Neil's forehead, then pressed his head down on her shoulder.

She was a very loving girl, Foxy thought, and probably was just trying to be nice to the boy. Maybe he should get rid of the boy right now and let her start being nice like that to him. The expression in his eyes changed, a little smile played on his lips as he began thinking about the ways Sharon could be nice to him. Anticipation flooded his body with warmth. He realized that Sharon was staring at him now and he watched as her arms tightened around the boy. He wanted to have those arms around *him*.

He started to get up to go over to the cot. His foot struck the recorder. The recorder! The cassette Peterson had demanded. It was too soon to get rid of the boy. Disappointed and angry, he sat down again. "You're going to make a recording for Peterson now," he told Sharon.

"A recording?" Sharon's voice was quick and nervous. A second ago she'd have sworn that he was planning to do something to them; there was something about the way he was looking at them, the expression on his face. She tried to think. Was there a chance, was there any way? Ever since Neil had told her that this man murdered his mother, she'd been even more frantic to find a way to get out of here. Tomorrow might be too late for Ronald Thompson as well as for Neil. She didn't know what time Foxy was planning to come for her. *If* he came for her. He was cunning. He'd surely realize that sooner or later she'd be recognized. The memory of her quest to save Ronald tortured and mocked her. His mother had been right. By insisting on his guilt, she had helped condemn him. Nothing mattered except to save Neil's life, to save Ronald's life. Whatever happened to her, she deserved. And she had been the one to tell Steve *he* was trying to play God.

Foxy had a gun. It was in the pocket of his coat. If she could get him to put his arms around her, she could reach for it.

If she had a chance, could she kill him?

She looked down at Neil, thought of the condemned boy in the prison cell. Yes, she could kill this man.

She watched as he expertly handled the recorder, inserted the cassette. It was a TWX cassette, the most common kind. They'd never be able to trace it. He pulled the crate over to the cot.

"Here, Sharon, you read this." He had a message written down. "Steve, pay the ransom if you want us back. The money must be in tens, twenties and fifties. Eighty-two thousand dollars. Don't fail to have it; don't let it be marked. Go to the phonebooth at Fifty-ninth and Lexington at two A.M. in your car. Be alone. Don't call the police."

She looked up at him. "Can I add anything? I mean, we had a quarrel. We broke off. Maybe maybe he wouldn't pay money for me, if I don't apologize. You see. he's very stubborn. Maybe he'll only pay half the money. for Neil, because he knows I don't love him. But we'll need all the money, won't we?"

"What do you want to say, Sharon?" Was he toying with her? Did he believe her?

"Just an apology, that's all." She tried to smile. She slid Neil off her lap, reached over and stroked Foxy's hand.

"No tricks, Sharon."

"Why would I trick you? What do you want Neil to say?"

"Just that he wants to come home. Nothing else." His finger was poised over the "record" button. "When I push this down, start talking. The mike is built in."

She swallowed, waited until the cassette began to wind. "Steve . . ." she read the message slowly, trying to buy time, trying to phrase what she would say next. She finished reading the message ". . . . don't call the police." She paused.

He was looking at her intently.

"Steve," she had to begin, "Steve, Neil is going to talk to you now. But first, I was wrong, I hope you'll forgive me . . ." The recorder clicked off. She was about to say, "I made a terrible mistake . . ."

"That's enough, Sharon. That's enough apology." He pointed at Neil. She put her arm around the child.

"All right, Neil, now talk to your dad."

The wheezing was accentuated by his effort to speak. "Dad, I'm all right. Sharon is taking care of me. But Mommy wouldn't want me to be here, Dad."

The recorder stopped. *Neil had tried to give Steve a mes-*

sage, had tried to connect their kidnapping to his mother's death.

The man rewound the cassette, played it back. He smiled at Sharon. "Very nice. I'd pay to get you two back if I was Peterson."

"That's good. I'm glad if you're satisfied." Was he deliberately baiting her?

"Sharon." Neil groped for her sleeve, tugged it. "I have to . . ."

"You want to go to the john, kid?" Foxy's voice was matter of fact. "Guess you have to by now." He went over to Neil, picked him up and walked into the toilet with him, closing the door. Sharon froze, waiting, but almost immediately he was back, carrying Neil under his arm. She noticed that he had Neil's face turned away from him, almost as though he were afraid that Neil could see through the blindfold. He dropped Neil on the cot. The boy was trembling. "Sharon."

"I'm here." She moved her hand against his back.

"Sharon, you want to?" The captor nodded his head toward the toilet.

"Yes."

He took her by the arm and half-carried her into the musty cubbywhole. The cords bit through her legs and ankles making her wince with pain. "There's a bolt up there, Sharon," he said. "I'll even let you put it on, if you want while you're here, 'cause otherwise the door don't stay shut. But you better come right out." His hand caressed her cheek. "Because if you don't and I get mad, the boy gets it now." He stepped out, pulling the door closed behind him.

Quickly she slid the bolt and looked around. In the darkness inside the small compartment, she ran her hands down the walls, along the tank. Maybe there was something here, some piece of piping, something sharp. She felt along the floor.

"Hurry up, Sharon."

"All right."

When she started to open the door, the handle felt loose in her hand. Instantly she tried to twist it completely around. Maybe if she could get it off, she could slip it in the deep pocket of her skirt. It might have a sharp edge. But she couldn't wrest it free.

"Come out of there!" His voice was edgy now. Quickly she opened the door, tried to hobble out, stumbled, grabbed the metal frame of the doorway. He came over to her. Deliberately she put her arms around his neck. Forcing back revulsion, she kissed his cheek, his lips. His arms tightened. She felt the sudden racing of his heart. Oh, God, please . . .

She slid her arms down around his shoulders, his back. Her fingers made soft, petting motions on his neck. Her right hand moved forward, slipped into his coat pocket, felt steel.

He shoved her backward. She slammed onto the concrete floor, her tightly bound legs buckling under her. Blinding, shocking pain shot through her right ankle.

"You're like the rest, Sharon," he screamed. He was standing over her. From the floor, through the waves of pain that were causing the food she'd just eaten to gag her, she could see him. His face seemed disembodied as he leaned over her. The pulse under his eye was throbbing. Red spots accentuated the sharp lines of his cheeks. His eyes were black narrow pits spewing over with rage. "You bitch," he said, "you bitch."

Yanking her up, he threw her on the cot and slapped her arms behind her. Pain made great foggy blackness close over her. "My ankle." Was that her voice?

"Sharon, Sharon, what happened?" Neil's voice was terrified.

With a tremendous effort, she bit back a moan. "I fell."

"Like all the others . . . pretending . . . but worse . . . trying to trick me. I could tell you were fooling, lying, I could tell . . ." She felt hands close on her throat. Oh God! Powerful fingers were pressing into her neck . . . God . . . help . . .

"No." The pressure vanished. Her neck fell backward.

"Sharon, Sharon," Neil was crying, his voice agitated, choking.

Gulping in air, she moved her face to his. Her eyelids felt so heavy. She forced them open. Foxy was at the rusty sink, splashing water in his face. The water must be freezing. Fearfully, she watched. He was trying to calm himself. He'd been about to kill her. What stopped him? Maybe he was afraid he'd still need her.

She bit her lip against the pain. There was no way out, no way. Tomorrow when he got the money he'd kill her and Neil. And Ronald Thompson would die for a crime he didn't commit. She and Neil were the only ones who could prove his innocence. Her ankle was swelling, pressing out against the leather boot. The cords were biting into it. Oh, God, please. Pain made her shiver even while it brought perspiration to her face.

She watched as he dried his face with a handkerchief. He came over and methodically retied Neil's hands, put tight gags on both of them. He adjusted the wire from the suitcase to the door. "I'm leaving, Sharon," he said. "I'll be back tomorrow. I'll be back just once more . . ."

He hadn't planned to leave this early but he knew if he stayed any longer, he'd kill her. And he might need her again. They might demand more proof that she and the boy were alive. He had to have the money. He couldn't take the chance of killing her yet.

There was a train coming in from Mount Vernon at eleven o'clock. He'd just have to wait a few minutes before it arrived. He stayed near the entrance to the tunnel. It was dark there.

Footsteps. He shrank against the wall, peered out cautiously. A guard! The man looked around carefully, walked up and down the area, stared curiously at the pipes and valves, glanced up at the stairs leading to the room, and then walked slowly back onto the Mount Vernon platform.

He felt the freezing sweat drip all over his body. His luck was running out. He could feel it. He had to finish all this and get away. There was a rumbling sound, the squealing of brakes. Carefully he slipped around the ventilating shafts, the sewer pumps, to the ramp, gratefully melting in with the disembarking passengers.

It was just eleven o'clock. He didn't want to sit in the hotel room. He was too restless. Walking west across Forty-second Street, he went into a movie. For four and a half hours he stared fascinated as three porno films titillated his senses, satisfied his needs. At 4:05 he was on the train to Carley.

He did not see Steve Peterson until he was already seated on the train. He happened to look up as Peterson was passing. Fortunately, he already was buried behind the papers, a precaution against being recognized and having someone he knew sit beside him.

Steve was carrying a heavy suitcase.

It was the money! He knew it! And tonight he'd have it. The sensation of impending disaster left him. It was with high confidence and good humor that he left the Carley station after he was sure Steve had driven away. He walked briskly through the snow the eight blocks to his place, a shabby garage on a dead-end street. The sign said "A. R. Taggert—Auto Repairs."

Unlocking the door, he went inside quickly. There were no messages shoved under the door. Good. Nobody had come looking for him. But even if someone had, it wouldn't be unusual not to find him. He often fixed people's cars right in their own driveways.

The garage looked cold and dirty, not much better than the place in Grand Central. He'd certainly always worked in stinking holes.

His car was there, ready to go. He'd filled it with gas from the pump in the corner. Installing that pump had been the best idea he'd ever had. Handy for the customers; they loved that touch of having their cars all gassed up. Handy for him too. Easy to go around cruising the highways at night. "You're out of gas, ma'am? Why, I've got some right in my trunk. Cars are my business . . ."

The car was already equipped with an old set of license plates he'd changed for a customer a couple of years ago; just in case any prying eyes jotted down a number tonight.

He'd unhooked the C.B. radio and it was crated on the front seat.

He'd gotten rid of all the other license plates he'd accumulated over the last six years and the extra sets of car keys he'd made. They'd been tossed in a dump near Poughkeepsie.

There were some odd tools and parts on the shelves, some tires stacked in the corner. Let old man Montgomery worry about getting rid of them. He was going to tear down this place anyhow. He'd have plenty of crap to haul away.

This was his last time here ever. Just as well. He hadn't

been able to work much the past couple of months. He'd gotten too nervous. Lucky he'd had that big job on the Vogler car. Just tided him over.

That's that.

He went into the small shabby room in the rear, took a battered suitcase out from under the single bed. From an unsteady old maple dresser he extracted his meager collection of underwear and socks and placed them in the suitcase.

A badly cut fraying red sports jacket and plaid pants were lifted off a hook on the back of the door and folded into the suitcase. His overalls, thick with grease, he tossed onto the bed. He'd leave them here. With all the money he wouldn't need them again.

He took his recorder from his coat pocket and listened again to the cassette he had made with Sharon and Neil. His other recorder, the Sony, was on top of the dresser. He put it on the bed, rummaged through his cassettes, selected one, and put it on. He just needed the beginning part.

That was it.

Again he played the cassette with Sharon and Neil, letting it run just past the trailing off of Neil's voice. Then he pressed the "record" button. On the other machine, the Sony, he deflected the 'play" button.

It only took a minute. When he was finished, he re-ran the revised cassette he was sending to Peterson. Perfect. Perfect. He wrapped it in a piece of brown paper, fastened it with Scotch tape. With a red magic marker, he wrote a message across the front of the package.

The other cassettes and the two recording machines were placed in the suitcase between his folded clothes. The suitcase was closed, locked, and carried to the car. He'd have enough to manage the suitcase with the money in the cabin of the plane. This one and his C.B. could go in the baggage compartment.

He opened the garage door, got into the car and turned on the engine. As it idled, he smiled, a musing, secret smile. "Now for a visit to church and a beer," he said.

29

"I DON'T BELIEVE IT," Steve told Hugh flatly, "and you are endangering the lives of Neil and Sharon if you treat this as a hoax."

Just back from New York, he was pacing the living room, his hands thrust in his pockets. Hugh watched him with a mixture of compassion and irritation. The poor guy had himself in such iron control but he'd aged ten years in as many hours. Even since morning, Hugh could see new lines of anguish around Steve's eyes and mouth.

"Mr. Peterson," he said crisply, "I assure you we are presuming this is a bona fide kidnapping. However, we are beginning to believe that Sharon and Neil's . . . disappearance is going to be directly tied into an attempt to bargain for clemency for Ronald Thompson."

"And I say it won't! There's been no word from Glenda?"

"I'm afraid not."

"And no sign of a tape or cassette from Foxy?"

"I'm sorry."

"Then we can only wait."

"Yes. You'd better plan to leave for New York by midnight."

"The phonecall isn't till two."

"The road conditions, Mr. Peterson, are pretty grim."

"Do you think that Foxy might be afraid to meet me, afraid of not being able to make a getaway?"

Hugh shook his head. "Your guess is as good as mine. We've put a tap on the phone at Fifty-ninth Street, of course. But I suspect that he'll direct you immediately to another phonebooth just as he did before. We can't risk putting a mike in your car because for all we know he might plan to get in your car with you. We'll have agents in surrounding buildings who will be able to follow your progress. We'll have the area covered with cars which will keep you in sight and then radio other cars to pick you up. Don't worry, we won't give the appearance of following you. The beeper in the suitcase will let us track you within a few blocks."

Dora put her head into the living room. "Excuse me." Her voice was different. Something in Hugh's steely manner intimidated her. She didn't like the way he kept studying her and Bill. Just because Bill liked his liquor didn't mean he wasn't a good man. The strain of the past twenty-four hours was too much for her. Mr. Peterson would get Neil and Sharon back safely. She had to believe that; he was too good a man to suffer any more than he had these two years.

Then she and Bill were going to leave. It was time to go to Florida. She was getting too old, too tired to take care of a child and this house. Neil needed someone young, someone he could talk to. She knew she fussed over him too much. It doesn't do a child good to be jumping every time he sniffles.

Oh, Neil. He used to be such a happy little boy when his mother was alive. He never had asthma then and hardly ever a cold and those big brown eyes were always twinkling, not lost and sad the way they looked now.

Mr. Peterson should get married again soon; if not to Sharon, to someone who would make this a real home.

Dora realized that Steve was looking at her questioningly, that she'd spoken to him. It was just that she couldn't function with this kind of worry; she hadn't closed her eyes all night. What did she want to say to him? Oh, yes, "I know you don't want much," she said, "but couldn't I just fix a club steak for you and Mr. Taylor?"

"Not for me, thank you, Dora. Maybe, Mr. Taylor . . ."

"Put on steaks for both of us if you don't mind, Mrs. Lufts." Hugh put his hand on Steve's arm. "Look, you haven't eaten anything since yesterday. You'll be up all night. You need to be alert and able to drive and follow directions."

"I guess you're right."

They were barely at the dining-room table when the bell rang. Hugh jumped up. "I'll get it."

Steve wadded the napkin he'd been about to put on his lap. Was it the proof he had demanded? Would he hear Neil's voice, Sharon's voice?

Hugh was coming back, followed by a young, dark-haired man. He was familiar—of course, it was Ronald Thompson's defense attorney. Kurner. That was his name,

Robert Kurner. He looked agitated, somehow unkempt. His coat was open, his suit was rumpled as though he'd slept in it. Hugh's face was inscrutable.

Bob did not apologize for interrupting their dinner. "Mr. Peterson," he said, "I've got to talk about your son."

"My son?" Steve felt the warning glance Hugh shot at him. Under the table he clenched his hands into fists. "What about my son?"

"Mr. Peterson, I defended Ron Thompson. I did a lousy job."

"It isn't your fault Ronald Thompson was convicted," Steve said. He did not look at the young man. Instead he stared down at the steak, watching the bubbling strip of fat at the edge begin to congeal. He pushed it away. Was Hugh right? Was the kidnapping a hoax after all?

"Mr. Peterson, Ron did not kill your wife. He was convicted because most of those jurors, consciously or unconsciously, thought he also killed the Carfolli girl and Mrs. Weiss."

"He had a record . . ."

"A *juvenile* record, a single occurrence."

"He attacked a girl before, was choking her . . ."

"Mr. Peterson, he was a fifteen-year-old kid at a party. He got into a beer drinking contest. What kid doesn't do that at some point in high school? When he was absolutely out of it, somebody slipped him cocaine. He didn't know what he was doing. He had absolutely no memory of putting his hands on that girl. We all know what a combination of drugs and alcohol can do to the mind. Ron was a kid with the lousy, hard luck to get in serious trouble the first and only time he ever got drunk. He never even had a beer for the next two years. And he had the incredibly bad luck to come into your house right after your wife was murdered."

Bob's voice was trembling now; his words rushing out. "Mr. Peterson, I've been studying the trial transcript. Then yesterday I had Ron repeat over and over again every single thing he said or did between the time he spoke to Mrs. Peterson in Timberly's Market and when he found her body. And I realized a mistake I made.

"Mr. Peterson, your son, Neil, told about coming downstairs when he heard your wife gasping, seeing a man strangle her and then seeing the man's face . . ."

"Ron Thompson's face."

"No! No! Don't you see. Here, look at the transcript." Bob slammed his briefcase on the table, pulled out a thick sheaf of legal-sized papers, raced through them until he came to a page near the center. "Here it is. The prosecutor asked Neil why he was so sure it was Ron. And Neil said, *'It got light so I'm sure'*

"I missed that. I missed it. Because when Ron was going over and over his testimony yesterday, he said that he rang the front doorbell. Then he waited a couple of minutes and rang it again. Neil didn't say one word about hearing chimes, not one word."

"That proves nothing," Hugh interrupted. "Neil was upstairs playing with his trains. He was probably quite absorbed and the trains were noisy."

"No, no. Because he said, *'It got light.'* Mr. Peterson, this is my point. Ron rang the front doorbell. He waited, rang it again, walked around the house. He gave the killer time to escape. That's why the back door was open.

"Ron turned on the kitchen light. Don't you see? The reason Neil saw Ron's face clearly was because the light was coming in from the kitchen. Mr. Peterson, a little boy comes running downstairs and sees his mother being strangled. The living room was dark. Remember that. Only the foyer light was on. Isn't it possible that he went into some kind of shock, that he maybe even passed out? Adults have been known to do that. Then when he comes to, he sees. *Sees*, because now the light is coming from the kitchen through to the living room. Neil sees someone bending over his mother, someone tugging at her throat. Ron was trying to get the scarf off. But it was impossible. It was knotted so tightly. And he realized she was dead and how it would look for him. So he panicked and ran.

"If he were a killer would he have left an eyewitness like Neil? Would he have left Mrs. Perry alive knowing she probably recognized him? She shops in Timberly's. A killer doesn't leave witnesses, Mr. Peterson."

Hugh shook his head. "It doesn't wash. It's all conjecture. There isn't a scrap of proof in this."

"But Neil can give us the proof," Bob begged. "Mr. Peterson, would you consent to his being hypnotized? I've spoken today to several doctors. They say if he's suppressing something it might very well be revealed through hypnosis."

"That's impossible!" Steve bit his lip. He'd been about to blurt out that you can't hypnotize a kidnapped child. "Get out," he said, "just get out of here."

"No, I won't get out!" Bob hesitated, then reached into his briefcase again. "I'm sorry to show these to you, Mr. Peterson. I didn't want to. I've been studying them. They're the pictures taken of this house after the murder."

"Are you nuts?" Hugh grabbed for the photos. "Where the hell did you get them? They're state's evidence."

"Never mind where I got them. Look at this one. See? The kitchen. The globe isn't on the ceiling fixture. That means the light might have been unusually strong."

Bob thrust open the kitchen door almost knocking down Dora and Bill Lufts who were standing right behind it. Ignoring them, he dragged a chair over to the light fixture, jumped up on it, quickly unscrewed the globe. The room brightened measurably. He ran back into the dining room, snapped off the light. He hurried into the foyer and turned that light on. Finally he switched off the living room lamps.

"Look, look into the living room. Now it's perfectly possible to see into it. Now wait." He rushed back into the kitchen and turned off the light. Steve and Hugh sat mesmerized at the table watching him. Under Steve's hand was the photograph of Nina's body.

"Look," Bob pleaded. "With the kitchen light out, the living room is almost dark. Suppose you're a child coming down the stairs. Please, stand in the foyer on the landing. Look into the living room. What could Neil have seen? Not much more than a silhouette. Someone is attacking his mother. He passes out. He never heard the bell. Remember that, *he never heard the bell*. The killer escapes. By the time Ron had rung the bell, and waited and rung it again and walked around the house, the killer is gone. And Ron probably saved your child's life by coming here that day."

Is it possible? Steve wondered. Is it possible that boy is innocent? He stood in the foyer, staring into the living room. How much had Neil seen? Could he have blacked out for a few moments?

Hugh strode past him into the living room, snapped on a lamp. "It's not good enough," he said flatly. "It's conjecture, pure and simple conjecture. There's not a shred of evidence to back it up."

"Neil is the one who could give us the evidence. He's our only hope. Mr. Peterson, I beg you to let him be questioned. I've been on the phone with Dr. Michael Lane. He's willing to come up tonight to question Neil. He's on the staff of Mount Sinai. Mr. Peterson, please, give Ron that chance."

Steve looked at Hugh, saw the faint, negative movement of his head. If he admitted Neil had been kidnapped, this lawyer would grasp at the excuse to suggest that it was tied into Nina's death. It would mean publicity; it might mean the end of any hope of getting Neil and Sharon back safely.

"My son is away," he said. "There have been threats against me, because of my stand on capital punishment. I will not divulge his whereabouts to anyone."

"*You will not divulge his whereabouts!* Mr. Peterson, an innocent nineteen-year-old kid is going to die tomorrow morning for something he didn't do!"

"I can't help you." Steve's calm snapped. "Get out of here. Get out and take those cursed pictures with you!"

Bob knew it was hopeless. Striding into the dining room, he jammed the trial transcript into his briefcase and scooped up the pictures. He started to close the bag, then reached in and yanked out the copies of the statements Ron had made the day before. He slammed them on the table.

"Read these, Mr. Peterson," he said. "Read them and see if you can find a killer talking. Ron was sentenced to the electric chair because Fairfield County was shocked by the Carfolli and Weiss murders as well as your wife's. There have been two more murders of women alone in their cars on lonely roads in the last few weeks. You know that. I swear to God those four murders are linked and I swear that somehow your wife's murder is connected to them. They were strangled with their scarves or belts. Don't forget that. The only difference is that for some reason, the killer chose to come into your home. But every one of those five women died the same way."

He was gone, slamming the front door behind him. Steve looked at Hugh. "What about your theory, that the kidnapping is tied into the execution tomorrow?" he asked accusingly.

Hugh shook his head. "We only know that Kurner isn't part of any conspiracy, but we never suspected that he was."

"Is there any chance, any chance at all, that he's right about Nina's death?"

"He's grasping at straws. It's all 'maybe' and conjecture. He's a lawyer trying to save his client."

"If Neil were here I would have allowed that doctor to talk with him, to hypnotize him, if necessary. Neil has had recurring nightmares since that night. Just last week he started talking about it again."

"What did he say?"

"He said something about being scared and not being able to forget. I've actually spoken to a psychiatrist in New York who suggested that there may be some repression there. Hugh, tell me honestly, are you *convinced* Ronald Thompson killed my wife?"

Hugh shrugged. "Mr. Peterson, when the evidence is as clearcut as it is in this case, it's impossible to come to any other conclusion."

"You haven't answered my question."

"I've answered it the only way I can. Please, that steak's probably not worth eating by now, but have *something*."

They went into the dining room. Steve crumbled a piece of roll, reached for the coffee. The transcripts of Ron's statement were at his elbow. He picked up the top sheet, started to read it:

I was pretty down about losing the job, but I understood. Mr. Timberly needed someone who could work more hours. I knew that being on the varsity would help me get into college and maybe get a scholarship. So I couldn't work more. Mrs. Peterson heard Mr. Timberly. She said she was sorry and that I was always so nice about bringing her packages to the car. She asked me what kind of job I'd get. I said I'd done housepainting during the summer. That was when we were walking out to the car. She told me that they'd just moved and there was a lot of painting to do, inside and out, and asked me to come over and look at the house. I was putting her groceries in the trunk. I said I guess this is my lucky day and it's just like my mom's always saying, bad luck can turn into good luck. Then we joked because she said, "It's my lucky day that way too. At least there's room in the trunk for all these darn groceries." She said she really didn't like grocery shopping, that's why she always bought so much at one time. That was at four o'clock. Then . . .

Steve stopped reading. Nina's lucky day. *Lucky day!* He pushed the transcript away.

The phone rang. He and Hugh both jumped. He rushed to the kitchen phone. Hugh hurried to the extension in the den. "Steve Peterson?" His voice was guarded. Let it be good news, please.

"Mr. Peterson, this is Father Kennedy from St. Monica's Church. I'm afraid something quite unusual has happened."

Steve felt his throat muscles close. It was an effort to speak. "What is it, Father?"

"Twenty minutes ago when I went on the altar to offer the evening mass, I found a small package propped against the door of the sanctuary. Let me read exactly what it says. 'Deliver to Steve Peterson at once—life or death.' And your phone number. Could it possibly be some sort of joke?"

Steven heard the hoarseness in his voice, felt the clammy sweat in his hands. "No, it's not a joke. It may be important. I'll be right down for it, Father, and please, don't say anything about this to anyone."

"Of course, Mr. Peterson. I'll wait for you in the rectory."

When Steve got back to the house half an hour later, Hugh was waiting with the recorder. Grimly they leaned over the machine as the spool began to turn.

For an instant they heard just a muted, rasping sound, then Sharon's voice. Steve paled and Hugh gripped his arm. The message. She was repeating the message the kidnapper had given him. What did she mean about being wrong? What was he supposed to forgive her for? There was something so abrupt about the way she stopped. As though she'd been cut off. Neil. That was the rasping sound. Neil, choked with asthma. Steve listened to his son's halting voice. Sharon was caring for him. Why did he mention his mother? Why now?

He gripped his fists until his knuckles were white, held them to his lips to push back the sobs that he felt shaking his chest.

"That's it," Hugh said. He reached out his hand. "We'll run it through again."

But before he could press the "stop" button it came. A warm, bubbly voice, melodic, welcoming. "Why, how nice of you," it was saying, "do come in."

Steve jumped up as an anguished cry broke from his lips.

"What is it?" Hugh shouted. "Who is that?"

"Oh Christ . . . oh Christ," Steve cried, "that's my wife, that's Nina!"

30

Hank Lamont parked his car in front of Mill Tavern on Fairfield Avenue in Carley. The snow was falling hard again and sharp gusts of wind were slapping it against the windshield. His large innocent-looking blue eyes narrowed as he studied the dimly lit interior of the tavern. It seemed pretty empty. Probably the weather had kept people home, but that was just as well. He'd get more chance to talk to the bartender. Let's hope he was the kind who liked to chew the rag.

He stepped out of the car. God, it was cold. Lousy, lousy night. It would be hard to keep a tail on Peterson's car later on. There'd probably be so few cars on the road, the ones that were there would stick out like sore thumbs.

He pushed open the door and stepped inside the bar.

Warm air embraced him and a not unpleasant beer and food smell filled his nostrils. Blinking to clear his eyes of snow, he glanced at the bar. There were only four men at it. He ambled up, heaved his bulk onto a stool, and ordered a Michelob.

While he sipped it, his eyes flitted from side to side. Two of the patrons were watching a hockey game on television. Halfway down the bar, a well-dressed glassy-eyed executive-type with a fringe of white hair was sipping a martini. He caught Hank's gaze. "Do you agree with me, sir, that it's the mark of a sensible man not to drive ten miles in these adverse conditions; that it is far more expedient to call a cab?" He considered his own premise. "Especially with a snootful," he added unnecessarily.

"You're right, mister," Hank said heartily. "I just drove down from Peterboro and let me tell you these roads are *bad*." He swallowed a large gulp of beer.

The bartender was drying glasses. "You from Peterboro? Never seen you around here, have I?"

"No. Just passing through. Wanted to take a break and remembered my old buddy, Bill Lufts, says he's usually here about this time."

"Yeah, Bill's here just about every night," the bartender agreed. "But you might be out of luck. Last night he didn't make it 'cause he was taking his wife out for their anniversary; going to dinner and the movies. We figured he'd drop her off home and come on down for a nightcap, but he never did show up. Really surprising he's not here again tonight, unless she's giving him a lot of flak again. And if she does, we'll hear about it, right Arty?"

The other solitary drinker looked up from where he was hunched over a beer. "In one ear and out the other," he said, "who wants to listen to that stuff?"

Hank laughed. "Well, what's a bar for if not to get your beefs out of your system?"

The men watching the hockey game switched it off. "Lousy game," one of them commented.

"Stinks," the other agreed.

"This here's a friend of Bill Lufts," the bartender jerked his head toward Hank.

"Les Watkins," the taller man said.

"Pete Lerner," Hank lied.

"Joe Reynolds," the plump man volunteered. "What's your work, Pete?"

"Plumbing supply house in New Hampshire; on my way to New York to pick up some samples. Say, how about everyone having a beer on me?"

An hour passed. Hugh learned that Les and Joe were salesmen in the Modell discount house on Route 7. Arty repaired cars. The bald-headed executive, Allan Kroeger, worked in an advertising agency.

A number of the regulars weren't around, thanks to the weather. For instance, Bill Finelli hadn't been by tonight, neither had Don Brannigan. Charley Pincher usually drifted in, but he and his wife were active in the Little Theatre group and were probably rehearsing a new play.

Kroeger's cab arrived. Les was giving Joe a ride. They asked for their bill. Arty got up to go. The bartender waved away his money. "This one's on me," he said. "We'll miss you."

"That's right," Les said, "good luck, Arty. Let us know how you're doing."

"Thanks. If it don't work I'll come back and take the job at Shaw's. He's always bugging me to go with him."

"Why wouldn't he? He knows a good mechanic," Les said.

"Where'ye heading for?" Hank asked.

"Rhode Island—Providence."

"To bad you didn't get a chance to say goodbye to Bill," Joe commented.

Arty laughed cynically. "Rhode Island ain't Arizona," he said. "I'll be back. Well, better get some sleep. Want to get an early start in the morning."

Allan Kroeger wove unsteadily toward the door. "Arizona," he said, "home of the painted desert." The four men went out together, letting in a sharp blast of cold air.

Hank studied Arty's retreating back. "That Arty, he a particular friend of Bill Lufts'?"

The bartender shook his head. "Nah. Anybody who can *hear* is a friend of Bill's after he gets a couple of boilermakers. You should know that. The way the guys have it figured, Bill's wife yaks in his ear all day and he comes here at night and yaks in everyone else's ear."

"I see." Hank shoved his glass across the bar. "Have one yourself."

"Don't mind if I do. Don't usually if it's busy, but you could swing a cat around here. Lousy kind of night anyhow. Kind of gives you the creeps. Guess everybody feels that way. That Thompson kid, you know. His mother lives two blocks from me."

Hank's eyes narrowed. "That's what happens when you go around murdering people," he suggested.

The bartender shook his head. "Most of us can't imagine that kid murdering anyone. 'Course he did go off the deep end once before, so maybe it's possible. They say some of the most vicious killers are real ordinary on the surface."

"That's what I hear."

"You know Bill and his misses live at the house of the woman who was murdered—the Peterson house."

"Yeah, I did know that."

"They took it awful hard. Dora Lufts worked for the Petersons for years. Bill says the little kid is still like a ghost of himself, cries a lot, has nightmares."

"It's tough," Hank agreed.

"Bill and the missus really want to get down to Florida. They're hanging around hoping the kid's father will get married. He's going with some writer; good-looking, Bill says. She was coming up last night."

"Was she?"

"Yeah. The little kid is pretty cool about her, probably scared about having his mother replaced. Kids are like that."

"Guess so."

"The father's the editor of *Events* magazine, you know, that new one, just a couple of years old. Guess he sunk a lot of dough into it. Second mortgage, you name it. But it's coming along pretty well now. Well, guess I'll start closing up. It's a cinch nobody else is coming around here tonight. Want another?"

Hank considered. He needed answers. There was no more time to waste. He sat his glass down, reached for his wallet, flipped out his badge. "FBI," he said.

An hour later he was back at the Peterson house. After conferring with Hugh, he called FBI headquarters in Manhattan. Making sure the den door was securely closed, he spoke softly into the phone. "Hughie was right. Bill Lufts is a bigmouth. Everyone in the Mill Tavern has known for two weeks that he and Mrs. Lufts would be out last night, that Peterson had a late meeting and that Sharon Martin was expected up. The bartender gave me a list of ten regulars who are always talking to Bill. Some of them were there tonight. They all seemed okay. You might check on a Charley Pincher though, he and his wife are in theatricals; maybe one of them could mimic a voice they'd heard a couple of years ago. There's an Arty Taggert who'll be pulling out tomorrow for Rhode Island. Seems harmless. Two salesmen, Les Watkins and Joe Reynolds—wouldn't waste time on them. Here are the rest of the names . . .

When he'd concluded the list, he added, "Another thing. Bill Lufts told the whole bar about Neil's trust fund less than a month ago; overheard Peterson talking to his accountant. So everyone in the Mill Tavern and God knows where else knows about it. Okay. I'll start down with the cassette. Have you reached John Owens?"

He hung up the phone, walked thoughtfully past the living room. Hugh Taylor and Steve were talking in muted tones. Steve was just putting on his coat. It was nearly midnight and time for him to leave for the rendezvous with Foxy.

31

LALLY WAS SO UPSET OVER THE INTRUDERS that when she met Rosie in the main waiting room she blurted out the story to her and immediately was sorry. "It's kind of a special place for me," she finished lamely. Now what would she say if Rosie wanted to share it? She couldn't let her. She just couldn't.

She needn't have worried. "You mean you bed down in Sing Sing?" Rosie asked incredulously. "You couldn't get me near there with a ten-foot pole. You know how I hate cats."

Of course. She'd never thought. Rosie was frightened of cats, would walk across the street to avoid one.

"Well, you know me," Lally said. "I love them. Poor things get so hungry. There're more slithering around that tunnel than ever," she exaggerated. Rosie shuddered.

"So I figure the two of them are staying there," Lally concluded, "and I'll scare off the girl when he's out."

Rosie was deep in thought. "Suppose you make a mistake," she suggested. "Suppose he's there. You say he looks mean."

"More than mean. Maybe, maybe you could help me keep an eye on him."

Rosie loved intrigue. She smiled widely, revealing broken yellow teeth. "Sure."

They finished their coffee, carefully putting leftover pieces of the donuts in their shopping bags, and headed for the lower level.

"Might take a long time," Lally fretted.

"It don't matter, except Olendorf's on today," Rosie said.

He was one of the strictest guards. He didn't believe in letting the regulars hang around the station; he was always chasing them and watching to see they didn't panhandle or litter.

Somewhat nervously, they took up a position near the *Open Book* display windows. Time passed. They waited patiently, almost motionlessly. Lally had a story ready if Olendorf came over to them. She'd say she had a friend coming to New York and had promised to meet her right here.

But the guard ignored them. Lally's feet and legs began to throb. She was about to suggest to Rosie that they give up the vigil when a stream of people came up the steps of the Mount Vernon platform. One of them had dark hair, a stiff way of walking.

She grabbed Rosie's arm. "That's him," she cried. "See, he's going toward the stairs, brown coat, green pants."

Rosie's eyes narrowed. "Oh yeah, I see him."

"Now I can go down," Lally exulted.

Rosie looked doubtful. "Not with Olendorf around, I wouldn't. He just looked over here."

But Lally was not to be dissuaded. She waited until she saw Olendorf leave for his lunch break, then slipped down to the platform. The 12:10 was starting to load; she knew she wasn't too conspicuous. She disappeared around to the other side of the track, hurried down the ramp as fast as her arthritic knees would allow. She really didn't feel well. This had been the hardest winter ever. The arthritis was in her back now and in the soles of her feet. Her whole body was hurting a lot. She couldn't wait to lie down and have a rest on her own cot. She'd have the girl out of there in the next two minutes.

"Missy," she'd say, 'the cops are wise. They're on their way to arrest you. Get out and warn your boyfriend."

That would do it.

She shuffled past the generator, around the sewer pipes. The tunnel loomed dark and still at the far end of the area.

She looked up at the door of her room and smiled happily. Eight more shuffling movements and she was at the base of the steps leading to it. Shifting the handles of her shopping bag over one arm, she fished her key out of her jacket. With the other hand she gripped the railing and began to pull herself up the steep steps.

"Where do you think you're going, Lally?" The voice was sharp. Lally let out a frightened cry and almost tumbled over backward. She regained her balance, and fighting for time, turned around slowly to face the menacing form of Officer Olendorf. So he'd been keeping an eye on her, just like Rosie warned; he'd tried to trap her by pretending to go to lunch. She let the key slide into the shopping bag. Had he seen it?

"I asked, where are you going, Lally?"

Near her the generators throbbed. There was a rushing,

squealing sound as a train entered a platform somewhere overhead. She was silent, helpless.

A sudden, sharp spitting sound, a snarling yowl came from a shadowy corner and inspiration struck Lally. "The cats!" With a trembling hand she pointed to the moving, skeletal forms. "They're starving! I wanted to bring them something to eat. I was just getting it out." Eagerly, she yanked the crumbled napkin with the bits of donut from her shopping bag.

The guard examined the greasy napkin with distaste, but his tone was somewhat less hostile when he spoke. "I'm sorry for them too, but you've no business here, Lally. Throw that stuff to them and clear out." His glance passed her, eyed the steps, moved upward, lingered thoughtfully on the door of her room. Lally's heart beat wildly. She picked up her bag, hobbled over to the cats, tossed the meager scraps, watched as they fought over them.

"See how hungry they are." Her voice was placating. "You got cats home, Mr. Olendorf?" She was moving out of the area, willing him to follow her. Suppose he used his passkey and checked her room? If he found the girl there, they'd surely change the lock. Maybe padlock it.

He hesitated, shrugged, decided to follow her. "Used to, but my wife isn't much for cats anymore, not since we lost the one she was crazy about."

Safely back in the waiting room, Lally realized her heart was still beating wildly. That was that. She wouldn't go near her place again until tonight when Olendorf went home. Thanking her stars that the cats had staged their fight, she went over to a bin and plucked out a discarded copy of *People* magazine and the crumped first section of the *Village Voice*.

32

NEIL KNEW SHARON WAS HURT. She hadn't fooled him when she said she fell. The man must have pushed her down. He wanted to talk to Sharon but the rag on his mouth was so tight he couldn't. It was much tighter than before. He wanted to tell Sharon how brave she was to try to fight that man. He'd been too scared to fight him when he was hurting Mommy. But even Sharon, who was almost as tall as the man, wasn't strong enough to beat him.

Sharon had told him that she was going to try to get the man's gun. She had said, "Don't be scared if you hear me talking about leaving you. I won't leave you. But if I can get his gun, maybe we can make him take us out of here. We both made a mistake and we're the only ones who can save Ronald Thompson."

Her voice had been all funny and growly trying to talk and his had too, but somehow he'd been able to tell her about it . . . how Sandy said that he should have helped Mommy; how he kept dreaming about that day; how Sandy said the Lufts would probably take him to Florida; how the kids asked him if he wanted Ronald Thompson to fry.

Even though it was hard to talk with the gag on it was easier to breathe after he talked. He knew what Sharon meant. They were going to kill Ronald Thompson for hurting Mommy and he hadn't done it. But Neil said he had. Neil hadn't meant to lie. That was what he was trying to tell Daddy on the message.

Now he had to be careful to breathe very slowly through his nose and not get scared or cry because then he wouldn't be able to breathe.

It was cold and his arms and legs hurt so much. But even so, something inside him had stopped hurting. Sharon would figure a way to get them out of here away from the man so they could tell about Ronald. Or Daddy would come and get them. Neil was sure of that.

He could feel Sharon's breath on his cheek. His head was right under her chin. Sometimes she made a funny sound, like something was hurting her. But being squished against her made him feel better. It was like when he was a little kid and sometimes woke up in the middle of the night with a bad dream and used to get into bed with Mommy and Daddy. Mommy would pull him close and say, "stop wiggling" in a sleepy voice, and he'd go back to sleep all tucked against her.

Sharon and Daddy would take care of him. Neil wiggled a fraction closer to Sharon. He wished he could tell her not to worry about him. He'd take long, slow breaths through his nose. His arms hurt so much. Determinedly he pushed that thought away. He'd think about something nice . . . the room on the top floor and the Lionel trains Sharon would give him.

33

"FOR GOD SAKE, DEAR, it's nearly midnight. Give it up."
Roger watched helplessly as Glenda shook her head.
Alarmed, he saw that the vial of nitroglycerin tablets on her
night table was nearly empty. It had been full only this
morning.

"No. I'll get it. I know I will. Roger, here . . . let's try
this. I'll tell you everything I did over the past month.
I've been going back day by day but I still have missed
something. Maybe if I tell it to you . . ."

He knew it was useless to protest. Pulling up a chair
close to the bed, he prepared to concentrate. His head was
throbbing. The doctor had come back and been furious
that Glenda was upsetting herself so much. Of course they
hadn't been able to explain why she was so agitated.

The doctor wanted to give her a strong shot, but Roger

knew she'd never forgive him if he okayed it. Now, watching her ashen pallor and the telltale purplish-blue lips, he thought of that day when she'd had the coronary: . . . we're doing everything we can, Mr. Perry . . . it's touch and go . . . it might be wise to send for your sons . . .

But she'd pulled out of it. Oh God, if she knows anything let her remember, Roger prayed. Let me help her remember. If Neil and Sharon died and afterward Glenda felt she could have saved them, it would kill her too.

What was Steve feeling right now? It would soon be time for him to leave for New York with the ransom money.

Where was Ronald Thompson's mother now? What was she thinking? Did she know this same futile anguish? Of course she did.

What about Sharon and Neil? Were they terrified, had they been abused? Were they still alive or was it already too late?

And Ronald Thompson. At the trial, Roger had been able to think only of how much he resembled Chip and Doug at that age. At nineteen, his boys had been sophomores in college; Chip at Harvard, Doug at the University of Michigan. That's where nineteen-year-olds belong—in college, not in prison cells on Death Row.

"Roger." Glenda's voice was remarkably steady. "Maybe if you make a diagram of each day, nine o'clock, ten o'clock, that kind of thing, it will help to point up whatever I'm missing. There's a pad in my desk."

He walked over and got it. "All right," she said, "I'm sure of yesterday and Sunday, so we won't waste time on them. Let's start with last Saturday . . ."

34

"No questions, Mr. Peterson? You're sure you've got it straight?" Hugh and Steve were in the foyer. Steve had the heavy suitcase containing the ransom money gripped in his hand.

"I think so." Steve's voice was even, almost a monotone. Somewhere in the past hours, the fatigue had retreated; overwhelming numbness had anesthetized pain and worry. He could think clearly, almost abstractly. He was standing on a high hill overlooking a drama. He was viewer as well as participant.

"All right. Run it down for me." Hugh recognized the symptoms in the other man. Peterson was coming to the end of his emotional tether. Already he was in some kind of shock, of course. That business of imitating his wife's voice had been the limit. And the poor guy kept insisting it was her. What a cheap, clumsy way to try to link the abduction to Nina Peterson's death. There were a couple of other things Hugh had noticed; Sharon's request for Steve to forgive her. Neil saying, "Sharon is taking care of me." Wasn't that the tip-off that this was a fraud?

Was it?

Maybe John Owens could help them. They'd located him and he was meeting Hugh at headquarters in New York.

Steve said, "I go directly to the Fifty-ninth Street phone-booth. If I'm early, I sit and wait in the car until just before two A.M., then get out of the car and stand at the phone. I'll probably be directed to another phone. I go there. Then hopefully I make direct contact and turn the suitcase over to the abductor. After I leave him, I drive to FBI head-quarters on Sixty-ninth Street and Third Avenue. You'll be waiting to take the cameras out of the car and develop the film."

"That's it. We'll be trailing you from a distance. The beeper in your car will keep us informed of your move-ments. One of our men is waiting to follow you down the parkway now to make sure you don't get stuck or de-layed. Mr. Peterson . . ." Hugh reached out his hand, "good luck."

"Luck?" Steve said the word with wonderment as though he were hearing it for the first time. "I haven't been thinking of luck so much as I have of an old Wexford curse. Do you know it by any chance?"

"I don't think so."

"I can't quite remember all of it, but it's something like this, 'May the fox build his nest on your hearthstone. May the light fade from your eyes so you never see what you love. May the sweetest drink you take be the bitterest cup of sorrow . . .' There's more, but that pretty much sums it up. Rather appropriate, isn't it?"

Without waiting for an answer, Steve left. Hugh

watched the Mercury pull out of the driveway, turn left toward the parkway. *May the fox build his nest on your hearthstone.* God help that guy Peterson. Shaking his head to try to relieve the persistent sense of impending doom, Hugh grabbed his own coat. None of the FBI cars were in the driveway. He and the other agents were slipping out the back door, across the two acres of vacant woods next to Steve's place. Their cars were parked on the narrow road that had been made in the woods when sewer lines were laid. There they were invisible from the street.

Maybe John Owens could make something of the cassette the kidnapper had sent. A retired agent who'd gone blind from glaucoma twenty years before, John had developed his hearing so keenly that he could interpret background sounds on recordings with remarkable accuracy. They brought him in whenever this kind of evidence came into a case. Later on of course, they'd run the cassette through regular lab tests, but that would take days.

Without explaining his reason, Hugh had asked Steve about Nina's background: Philadelphia Main Line family, fourth generation. Nina had attended a Swiss boarding school, Bryn Mawr College. Her parents spent most of their time now in their home in Monte Carlo. Hugh remembered meeting them at Nina's funeral. They'd flown in for the service and internment; hardly spoken to Steve, a pair of cold potatoes if ever he saw them.

But the information would be enough for Owens to give a pretty accurate opinion whether that voice actually was Nina's or an impersonation. Hugh had little doubt about the outcome.

The Merritt Parkway had been sanded and even though fresh snow was still falling, the driving was better than

Steve had expected. He'd been fearful that the abductor might call off meeting him if the roads were hazardous. Now he was sure they'd somehow make contact.

He wondered why Hugh had queried him about Nina's background. He'd only wanted a few basic facts. "What college did your wife go to, Mr. Peterson? Where was she raised?"

"She went to Bryn Mawr." They'd met when they were both seniors. He was at Princeton. It was love at first sight. Corny but true.

"Her family is fourth generation Philadelphia Main Line." They were outraged about him. They wanted Nina to "marry her own kind," as they put it. Someone with good family and money and a preppie background. Not an impoverished student who waited table at the Nassau Inn to stretch his scholarship, who'd graduated from Christopher Columbus High School in the Bronx.

God, they'd been formidable when he and Nina were going around together. He'd said to Nina, "How did you ever get to be *their* daughter?" She was so funny, so bright, so unpretentious. They'd been married right after graduation. Then he'd gone into service, been commissioned and sent to Vietnam. They didn't see each other for two years. Finally he'd gotten an R and R and she'd met him in Hawaii. She'd been so beautiful, running down the steps of the plane, tumbling into his arms.

After he was discharged, he'd gone to Columbia for a Master's in Journalism. Then he got the job at *Time* and they moved up to Connecticut and she became pregnant with Neil.

He'd bought her the Karman Ghia when Neil was born, and you'd have thought it was a Rolls. Which, of course, was what her father had.

He'd sold Nina's car the week after the funeral. It was

impossible to see it parked next to his Mercury in the garage. That night when he'd come home to find her dead, he'd walked out to it, hoping against hope. "Your carelessness will get you killed!" But the new radial was back on the front wheel; the balding spare was in the trunk. If she hadn't bothered to have it changed that day, it would have meant that she didn't take his annoyance too seriously.

Nina, Nina, I'm sorry.

Sharon She'd made him come alive again. Because of her the numbness and pain had dissolved like ice gradually melting in a spring thaw. These six months had been so good. He'd started to believe that he'd been given a second chance at happiness.

You didn't fall in love the first time you met someone. He was thirty-four now, not twenty-two.

Or didn't you?

That first meeting on the *Today* show. After it was over they walked out of the studio together and stood talking in front of the building. He hadn't been even vaguely interested in any woman after Nina died, but that morning he'd found himself reluctant to let Sharon go. He was due at an early meeting and couldn't suggest having breakfast with her. Finally he'd blurted out, "Look, I have to run now but how about dinner tonight?"

Sharon said yes, quickly, almost as though she'd been hoping he'd ask. The whole day had seemed interminably long before he was finally at her apartment ringing her doorbell. At that time their debate over capital punishment was more ideological than personal. It was only when Sharon began to feel that she couldn't save Ronald Thompson that she started to turn on him.

He was on the Cross County Parkway. His hands were working independently, selecting the roads without his conscious awareness.

Sharon. It was so good to talk to someone again, over dinner, over a nightcap at her place. She understood the problems of launching a new magazine, the struggle to get advertisers, to get readership. The nearest thing to pillow-talk, he'd joked.

He'd left his job at *Time* to go with *Events* a few months before Nina died. It had been a real gamble. He was making important money at *Time*. Part of it had been pride. He was going to help create the best magazine in the country. He was going to be a rich, hotshot editor and show Nina's father. He'd make him eat his words.

Nina's parents blamed him for her death. "If she'd been in a properly staffed, properly secured house, this never would have happened," they said. They'd wanted to take Neil back with them to Europe. Neil, with those two!

Neil. The poor little kid. Like father, like son. Steve's mother had died when he was three. He didn't remember her at all. His father had never remarried. That was a mistake. Steve had grown up wanting a mother. He remembered when he was seven, there'd been a substitute teacher in his class and she'd had them draw Mother's Day cards.

At the end of the day she noticed that he didn't put his in his schoolbag. "You're not going to leave that here, are you?" she'd asked. "Your mother will be so pleased to have it Sunday."

He'd torn it up and run out of the room.

He didn't want that for Neil. He wanted Neil to grow up in a happy home, a home with brothers and sisters. He didn't want to live the way his father had, alone, making Steve his whole life, bragging to everybody in the post office about his son in Princeton. A lonely man in a lonely apartment. One morning he hadn't awakened. When he didn't show up for work, they'd investigated. And Steve had been called out of class.

Maybe that was why over the past years he'd taken the stand on capital punishment. Because he knew how elderly, poor people lived, how little they had. Because it sickened him to think of any of them being brutally murdered by thugs.

The suitcase was on the front seat next to him. Hugh had assured him the electronic device wouldn't be detected. Now he was glad that he'd let them put it in.

At 1:30 Steve pulled off the Fifty-seventh Street exit of the West Side Highway. At twenty of two, he was parked in front of the payphone outside Bloomingdale's. At ten of two he got out of the car and, unmindful of the wet, icy wind, stood in the booth.

At precisely 2:00 A.M. the phone rang. The same muffled, whispering voice instructed him to go immediately to a phone on Ninety-sixth Street and Lexington Avenue.

At 2:15 that phone rang. Steve was told to drive over the Triborough Bridge, take the Grand Central Parkway to the Brooklyn Queens Expressway exit. He was to drive on the BQE to Roosevelt Avenue, turn left to the end of the first block, and park immediately. He was to turn out his headlights and wait. "Be sure to have the money. Be alone."

Frantically, Steve scribbled, repeated the instructions. The abductor hung up.

At 2:35 he turned off the BQE onto Roosevelt Avenue. A large sedan was parked halfway down the block on the other side of the street. As he passed it, he twisted the wheel a fraction, hoping the hidden cameras might be able to pick up the make and license number; then he pulled over to the curb and waited.

It was a dark street. The doors and windows of the shabby old stores were protected with chains and bars; the elevated tracks helped cut off the street lights; the snow blocked remaining visibility.

Were the FBI agents able to trace his course through the beeper? Suppose it stopped working. He hadn't noticed any cars following him. But they'd said they wouldn't get too close.

There was a thump at the driver's door. Steven spun his head around, felt his mouth go dry. A gloved hand was gesturing for him to pull the window down. He switched the ignition key on, deflected the window button.

"Don't look at me, Peterson."

But he'd already glimpsed a brownish coat, a stocking mask. Something was dropped on his lap, some large canvas bag—a duffel bag. He felt a sick feeling in the pit of his stomach. This man was not going to take the suitcase with the tracer. He knew it.

"Open that suitcase and put the money in the bag. Hurry up."

He tried to stall for time. "How do I know that you'll return my son and Sharon unharmed?"

"*Fill that bag!*" He could hear the high-pitched under-current in the voice. The man was violently nervous. If he panicked and ran off without the money, he might kill Sharon and Neil. With fumbling hands, Steve wrenched the neat packets of money from the suitcase, jammed them into the duffel bag.

"Close it!"

He drew the strings tightly together, knotted them.

"Hand it over. Don't look at me."

He stared straight ahead. "What about my son and Sharon?"

Gloved hands reached in through the window, yanked the bag away from him. The gloves. He tried to notice them. Stiff-looking, cheap imitation leather, dark gray or brown, large. The sleeve of the coat was frayed; broken pieces of thread spidered out from it.

"You're being watched, Peterson." The abductor's voice was hurried, almost trembling. "Don't leave here for fifteen minutes; remember that, *fifteen minutes*. If I'm not followed and the money is all here, you'll be told where to pick up your son and Sharon at eleven-thirty this morning."

Eleven-thirty. The exact minute of Ronald Thompson's execution. "Did you have anything to do with my wife's death?" Steve burst out.

There was no answer. He waited, then cautiously turned his head. The abductor had slipped away. Across the street, a car started.

His watch said 2:38. The entire meeting had taken place in less than three minutes. Was he being watched? Was there an observer on the roof of one of those buildings ready to report if he moved? The FBI wouldn't get any signal of location change from the suitcase. Did he dare start sooner?

No.

At 2:53 Steve made a U turn and headed back toward Manhattan. At 3:10 he was at the FBI headquarters on Sixty-ninth Street and Third Avenue. Grim-faced agents rushed to his car and began unscrewing the headlights. A somber-looking Hugh listened to his explanation as they rode up to the twelfth floor. There he was introduced to a man with snow-white hair and a patient, intelligent expression that was not concealed by dark glasses.

"John has been listening to the cassette," Hugh explained. "From the quality of their voices and a certain echo, he concludes that Sharon and Neil are being kept in a nearly empty, cold room, about eleven by twenty-three feet in size. They may be in the basement of a freightyard; there's a continuing faint sound of trains pulling in and leaving from somewhere nearby."

Steve stared.

"I'll be able to be considerably more specific later," the blind agent said. "There's no magic to this. It's simply a case of listening with the same degree of intensity with which you'd study a specimen under a microscope."

A cold room, nearly empty. A freightyard. Steve looked accusingly at Hugh. "What does this do to your theory that Sharon may have planned this?"

"I don't know," Hugh replied simply.

"Mr. Peterson, about the last voice on the cassette," John Owens' manner was hesitant, "by any chance was your late wife's first tongue French rather than English?"

"No, not at all. She was raised in Philadelphia till she went to boarding school at ten. Why?"

"There's an intonation in that voice that to an expert definitely suggests that English was not the first language."

"Wait a minute! Nina did tell me that she'd had a French nurse, that as a young child she actually thought in French rather than English."

"That's exactly what I'm talking about. Then that was no imposter or mimic. You are correct in identifying your wife's voice."

"All right. I was wrong about that," Hugh said. "But John says that last voice was definitely added to the cassette after Neil and Sharon were recorded. Think, Mr. Peterson. Somebody who knows a great deal about your personal life has planned this. Where you ever at a party, maybe, where people were doing home movies, where someone might have recorded a voice track of your wife and excerpted those few words from it?"

It was so hard to think . . . Steve frowned. "The country club. When it was renovated and redecorated four years ago, they made a film for some charity. Nina was the narrator, going from room to room, explaining what had been done."

"Now we're getting somewhere," Hugh said. "Might she have used those words within the framework of that film?"

"Possibly."

The phone rang. Hugh grabbed it, identified himself, listened intently. "Good. Get right on it!" He slammed the receiver down; he had the look of a hunter on a fresh scent. "Things are beginning to break, Mr. Peterson," he said. "You got a clear picture of the car and license plate. We're tracing it now."

The first faint hope he'd been offered! Then why was the knot in his throat still choking him? It's too easy, something was saying; it's not going to work out.

John Owens stretched out his hand in the direction of Steve's voice. "Mr. Peterson, just one question. My impression is that, if that actually is your wife on the cassette, she spoke while she was in the process of opening a door. Are you aware by any chance of a particular door with a faint squealing sound when it opens, something like this—'eerkkk'?" He gave a startling imitation of a rusty hinge moving.

Hugh and Steve stared at each other. It is a mockery, Steve thought dully. It is a farce; it is already too late for everybody.

Hugh answered for him. "Yes, John." he said. "That's exactly the way Mr. Peterson's kitchen door sounds as it's being opened."

35

ARTY DROVE AWAY FROM THE MILL TAVERN, a nagging
worry sending out alarm signals through his body, dissolv-
ing the euphoric sense of infallibility he'd been enjoying.

He'd really counted on Bill Lufts being in the bar; it
would have been helpful to pump Bill. Oh, the boy's away?
Where is he? How's Mr. Peterson? Has he had any company?

He'd figured that Peterson wouldn't admit to the Lufts
that Neil and Sharon were missing. He'd figured Peterson
knew that the Lufts shot their mouths off about everything.

So if Bill wasn't there. it was because Peterson had called
the cops—, no. not the cops, the FBI.

That guy who called himself Pete Lerner, who asked so
many questions. He was an FBI agent. Arty knew it.

He steered the dark-green Beetle onto the Merritt Parkway south. Anxiety made perspiration ooze from his forehead and armpits and hands.

Twelve years slipped away. He was being grilled in FBI headquarters in Manhattan. "Come on, Arty, the news vendor saw you leave with that kid. Where'd you take her?"

"I put her in a cab. She said she was meeting some guy."

"What guy?"

"How do I know? I carried her bag out, that's all."

They couldn't prove anything. But they tried. God, they tried.

"How about the other girls, Arty. Take a look at these pictures. You're always hanging around the Port Authority. How many of them did you carry bags for?"

"I don't know what you mean."

They were coming too close. It was too dangerous. That was when he left New York, drifted up to Connecticut, got a job pumping gas. Six years ago he'd taken over the repair shop in Carley.

Arizona. That had been a bad mistake. Why did he say, "Rhode Island ain't Arizona"? Probably that guy who called himself Pete Lerner hadn't noticed, but even so it had been a mistake.

They had nothing on him unless they started checking way back, unless they came up with the time they questioned him about the kid from Texas. "Come on down to my place in the Village," he'd told her. "I have a lot of artist friends who can use a good-looking model."

But they didn't have proof then and they didn't have it now. Nothing. There hadn't been any slip-ups. He was sure of it.

"Is this your place," she'd asked, *"this dump?"*

The Merritt faded into the Hutchinson River Parkway. He followed the signs leading to the Throgs Neck Bridge.

His plan was ingenious. Stealing a car was dangerous. There was always the chance that the owner might come back in ten minutes; that the cops would have an alert before it was gone five miles. You shouldn't steal a car unless you're sure the owner is out of the way—like sitting, watching a thirty-year-old movie, or taking off on a plane.

The Throgs Neck Bridge had caution signs flashing. Ice. Wind. But that was all right. He was a good driver and tonight the chicken drivers would be staying home. That would make it easy for him to move around later.

At 11:20 he drove into LaGuardia Airport into parking lot five, the one with special rates for long-term parkers.

He took a ticket from the machine; the gate lifted and he drove slowly through the lot, taking care to get well away from the view of the cashier in the exit line next to the automatic check-in. He pulled into an empty space in section nine, between a Chrysler and a Cadillac, behind an Oldsmobile wagon. In the midst of them the Beetle was diminished and hidden.

He leaned back in the seat and waited. Forty minutes passed. Two cars came into the lot, one a flashy red, the other a yellow station wagon. Both too easy to spot. He was glad when they ignored the empty spaces near him and drove further down into the far-left section.

Another car drove slowly by. A dark-blue Pontiac that pulled into a spot three rows ahead. The lights went off. He watched as the driver got out, walked around to the trunk and extracted a large suitcase. This guy would be away for a while.

Slumped in the Volks, only the top of his head above the level of the windshield, he watched as the man slammed the trunk down, picked up the suitcase and made his way to the nearest bus shelter from which the courtesy airport bus would take him to the departure terminal.

The bus came in a few minutes. Foxy observed the silhouetted figure get on the vehicle. The bus pulled away.

Slowly, quietly, he got out of the Beetle and looked around. There were no headlights approaching. In quick strides he was at the side of the Pontiac. The second key he tried opened the door. He was in the car.

It was still comfortably warm. He put the key he was holding in the ignition. The engine turned over almost noiselessly; the tank was three-quarters full.

Perfect.

He'd have to wait. The guard would be suspicious if he collected on a ticket with less than a couple of hours' parking in this lot. But he had plenty of time and he wanted to think. He leaned back, closed his eyes, and Nina's image floated across his mind, the way she'd looked that first night . . .

He'd been cruising around, knowing he shouldn't be out, knowing it was too soon after Jean Carfolli and Mrs. Weiss, but not able to stay in. And he'd seen her. The Karmann Ghia pulled over on Route 7 in that quiet, lonely spot. The slender, small body caught up in his headlights. The dark hair. The little hands that were struggling with the jack. The enormous brown eyes that looked startled when he slowed down and pulled over. Probably hearing in her head all the talk about the highwayman murders.

"Can I help you, miss? That's rough work for you, but it's my job. I'm a mechanic."

The worried look disappeared. "Oh, great," she said. "I don't mind telling you that I'm a bit nervous . . . of all the crazy places to get a flat."

He never glanced at her; just at the tire, like she didn't exist, like she was nine hundred years old. "You've picked up some glass, no big deal." Quickly, effortlessly, he

226

changed it. Less than three minutes. No cars coming in either direction. He stood up.

"How much do I owe you?" Her purse open, her neck bent. Her breast rising and falling under the suede coat. Class. Something about her that showed it. Not a scared kid like Jean Carfolli, not an outraged old bitch like Weiss, just a beautiful young woman who was very grateful to him. He reached out his hand to touch her breast.

The light began on the tree across the road, swung around, illuminated the two of them. A cop car. He could see the dome. "It's three dollars to change the tire," he said briskly, "and I can fix your flat if you want." He had his hand in his pocket now. "I'm Arty Taggert, I have a repair shop in Carley on Monroe Street, about half a mile from Mill Tavern.".

The police car was coming up, pulling toward them. The trooper got out. "You all right, ma'am?" His look at Arty was very funny, very suspicious.

"Oh, fine, officer. I certainly was in luck. Mr. Taggert is from my town and he came along just as I got the flat."

She made it sound like she knew him. What a break! The policeman's expression changed. "You're lucky ma'am to be helped by a friend. It's not safe for women to be alone in disabled cars these days."

The cop got back in the patrol car but stayed there watching. "Will you fix the tire for me?" she asked. "I'm Nina Peterson. We live on Driftwood Lane."

"Sure. Be glad to." He got back in his car, very indifferent, very casual, like this was just another cheap repair job, never showing that he *had* to see her again. He could tell the way she looked at him that she was sorry the cop had come along too. But it was important to get away before the cop started thinking about Jean Carfolli and

Mrs. Weiss; before the cop asked, "You in the habit of stopping to help out ladies who are alone, mister?"

So he'd driven away and the next morning just when he was thinking about calling her, she called him. "My husband just gave me what-for about driving on the spare," she said, and her voice was very warm and intimate and amused like they had a private joke. "When can I pick up my tire?"

He thought fast. Driftwood Lane was in a quiet area; the houses weren't close together. If she came to his place, there'd be no way of getting friendly with her. That would be too dangerous.

"I have to go out on a job right now," he lied, "I'll bring it by late this afternoon, maybe about five." It got dark by five.

"Wonderful," she said, "just as long as the darn thing is back on the car before I go to pick up my husband at half-past six."

He was so excited that day that he could hardly think. He went out for a haircut and bought a new checkered sportshirt. When he got back he didn't bother at all with work. He just showered and dressed and while he waited he listened to some of his cassettes. Then he put a fresh new cassette in the recorder and labeled it "Nina." He made sure his camera was loaded and reflected on the pleasure of developing pictures, watching the images forming on the prints . . .

At ten after five he left for Driftwood Lane. He cruised around her street before deciding to park in the woods next to her house. Just in case . . .

He walked through the woods near the shore. He remembered how the water was lapping on the beach, a friendly sound that thrilled and warmed him even on the cold night.

Her car was in the driveway behind the house; her keys were in the ignition. He could see Nina through the kitchen window; moving around, unpacking groceries. The globe was off the fixture so the room was very bright. And she was so beautiful with that pale blue sweater over her slacks and that scarf knotted at her throat. He changed the tire very fast, keeping an eye out for any signs of other people in the house. He knew he'd make love to her and that secretly she wanted him to. Just the way she hinted that her husband had been angry at her showed she needed a sympathetic man. He turned on the recorder and began to whisper into it his plans for making Nina happy when he told her his feelings about her.

He went up to the kitchen door and knocked on it softly. She ran over, looked startled, but he held up her keys, smiling at her through the glass. Right away she began to smile and opened the door, all warm and friendly, her voice like arms around him, inviting him in, telling him how nice he was.

Then she asked him what she owed him. He reached his hand up, he had his gloves on, of course, and switched off the kitchen light. He put his hands on her face and kissed her. "Pay me like this," he whispered.

She slapped him, a stunning slap, impossibly hard from that small hand. "Get out of here," she said, spilling the words out like he was dirt, like he hadn't gotten all dressed up for her, like he hadn't done her a favor.

He went wild. Like the other times. Rejection did that to him. She should have known better than to lead him on like that. He stretched out his hands, wanting to hurt her, to squeeze that nastiness out of her. He reached for her scarf. But somehow she slipped away from him and ran into the living room. She never uttered a sound, never screamed for help. Afterward he understood why. She didn't want him to know the child was in the house. But she tried to pick up a poker from the fireplace.

He just laughed. He talked to her very low telling her what he would do. He held both her hands in one of his and put the poker back. Then he grabbed her scarf and twisted it around her neck, twisted while she gurgled and gagged, and her hands like a doll's hands waved and dropped and went limp, while her great brown eyes widened and glazed and accused, while her face turned blue.

The gurgling stopped. He was holding her with one hand, snapping the picture, wishing her eyes would close, when somewhere behind him the gurgling, choking sound began again.

He swung around. The boy was standing in the foyer, staring at him with huge brown eyes that burned through him. The boy was gasping just like she'd been gasping.

It was like he hadn't killed her at all; like she'd moved into the boy's body and was going to punish him, was taunting him, promising revenge.

He started across the room for the boy. He'd make him stop that noise, he'd close those eyes. He cupped his hands, bent over the boy . . .

The bell rang.

He had to run. He raced through the foyer into the kitchen, slipped out the back door while he heard the bell ring again. He was out through the woods, in his car, back in his shop in a few minutes. Calm. Be calm. He went to the Mill for a hamburger and beer, was there when the news of the murder on Driftwood Lane swept through the town.

But he was scared. Suppose that trooper recognized Nina's picture in the paper, said at headquarters, "Funny thing, last night I saw her on the road, some guy named Taggert was fixing her car . . ."

He decided to get out of town. But when he was packing he heard on the news that an eyewitness, a neighbor, had been knocked down by someone running out of the Peterson house, that she had positively identified him as Ronald Thompson, a local seventeen-year-old, and that Thompson had been seen talking to Mrs. Peterson a few hours before the crime.

Arty put his camera and recorder and prints and film and cassettes inside a metal box and buried it under a bush behind his shop. Something told him to wait.

Then Thompson was caught at that motel in Virginia, and the kid identified him, too.

The luck. The incredible luck. The living room had been dark. The boy might not have seen his face clearly and then Thompson had gone into the house.

But he'd started to go for the kid; he'd gotten close to him. Neil must have been in shock. But suppose he remembered some day.

The thought haunted Arty's dreams. The eyes followed him all through his restive nights. Sometimes he woke up in the middle of the night, sweating, trembling, thinking the eyes were looking in his bedroom window, or the wind would be making that same gurgling sound.

He never went looking for girls after that. Never. He just went to the Mill Tavern most nights and got friendly with the guys there and especially with Bill Lufts. Bill talked a lot about Neil.

Until last month; until he knew he had to dig out his cassettes from where he'd buried them and listen to them again.

That night on his C.B. he heard the Callahan girl saying

she had a blowout, and he went looking for her. Two weeks later he went out when Mrs. Ambrose got on the C.B. looking for directions, saying she was almost out of gas.

Now Fairfield County was in an uproar again, looking for a guy they called the C.B. killer. You didn't leave any trace, he told himself.

But after these last two, the dreams of Nina came every single night. Accusing. Then a couple of weeks ago, Bill Lufts drove up to his place with the boy Neil beside him in the wagon. Neil stared at Arty.

That was when he knew he had to kill Neil before he left Carley. And when Lufts bragged about the trust fund in Neil's name—his wife had seen the bank statement on Peterson's desk—he'd known how to get the money he needed.

Whenever he thought about Nina, he hated Steve Peterson more. Peterson had been able to touch her without getting slapped; Peterson was a big-shot editor; Peterson had people to wait on him; Peterson had a good-looking new girlfriend. He'd show him.

The room in Grand Central had always been there in his consciousness. A place to hide if ever he needed it, or a place to take a girl where no one would find her.

He used to think all the time about blowing up Grand Central Station when he was working in that room. He'd think about how scared and shocked the people would be when a bomb went off, when they felt the floor give way under them and the ceilings fall in; all those people who ignored him when he was trying to be friendly, who never smiled at him, who rushed past him, who looked through him, who ate off the dishes he had to wash and left them greasy with shells and salad dressing and smears of butter.

Then everything came together. The plan. The August *Rommel* Taggert plan. A fox's plan.

If only Sharon didn't have to die; if only she'd loved him. But in Arizona many girls would be friendly. He'd have so much money.

It was a good idea to have Sharon and Neil die just at the minute the Thompson kid was executed. Because he was executing them, too, and Thompson deserved to die for having interfered that night.

And all those people in Grand Central—tons of rubble falling on them! They'd know how it felt to be trapped.

And he'd be free.

Soon. Soon it would be over.

Arty narrowed his eyes realizing that much time had passed. It was always like that when he began to think of Nina. It was time to go.

He turned the ignition key in the Pontiac. At quarter of two he drove to the toll booth and handed over the ticket he'd taken at the automatic gate for his Volks. The collector looked sleepy. "Two hours and twenty-five minutes —that'll be two bucks, mister."

He drove out of the airport to a phone on Queens Boulevard. Promptly at two, he called the payphone outside Bloomingdale's. As soon as Peterson answered, he directed him to the public phone at Ninety-sixth Street.

He was getting hungry and he had fifteen minutes.

In an all-night diner, he gulped down coffee and some toast as he watched the clock.

At 2:15, he dialed the Ninety-sixth Street public phone and tersely directed Steve to the meeting place he'd selected.

Now for the really dangerous part.

At 2:25 he began driving toward Roosevelt Avenue. The

233

streets were nearly deserted. There was no sign of un-marked cop cars. He'd be able to pick them out; he was the master of cruising around on roads without looking sus-picious.

Last week he'd selected Roosevelt Avenue for the meet-ing place. He'd timed how long it would take to get back to LaGuardia Airport from there. Exactly six minutes. Just in case the cops came along with Peterson, he'd have a good chance of getting away from them.

Because of the elevated train, Roosevelt was filled with pillars that obstructed the view, that made it hard to see what was happening across the street or down the block. It was the best place to make contact.

At exactly 2:35 he parked on Roosevelt Avenue, facing the Brooklyn Queens Expressway, less than half a block to the access road.

At 2:36, he saw the lights of a car coming off the BQE from the opposite direction. Instantly he slipped the stock-ing mask over his face.

It was Peterson's Mercury. For a second he thought Peterson was going to pull up to him, the car swerved right at him. Or was he trying to take a picture of the Pontiac? A lot of good that would do.

Peterson's car stopped almost directly across the street. He swallowed nervously. But there were no other head-lights coming off the expressway. He had to move fast. He reached for the duffel bag. In his electronics magazine he'd read that in payments of ransom, suitcases were usually bugged. He wasn't taking any chances.

The feel of the duffel bag, light, empty, ready to be filled, was reassuring. He opened the car door and crossed the street noiselessly. He needed just sixty seconds and then he'd be safe. He tapped on the window of Peterson's car, motioned him to open it. As the window slid down he looked quickly into the car. Peterson was alone. He shoved in the duffel bag.

The dim street lights threw shadows of the pillars against the car. In the soft, whispery voice he'd practiced, he told Peterson not to look at him, to put the money in the duffel bag.

Peterson didn't argue. Behind the stocking mask, Foxy's eyes roamed the area. His ears strained. But there was no sound of anyone coming. The cops had to be tailing Peterson, but probably wanted to be sure he made contact.

He watched Peterson drop the last packet of bills in the duffel bag and told him to close it and hand it over. Greedily, he felt its weight. Remembering to speak very low, he warned Peterson to wait fifteen minutes and told him that Sharon and Neil could be picked up at 11:30.

"Did you have anything to do with my wife's death?"

The question startled Foxy. How much were they beginning to suspect? He had to get away. He was sweating now, heavy beads of perspiration that soaked his suit under the brown coat, that warmed the soles of his feet even while the sharp wind bit at his ankles.

He crossed the street, got back in the Pontiac. Would Peterson dare to follow him?

No. He was still parked in the dark, silent car.

Foxy floored the accelerator of the Pontiac, shot onto the access road to the Brooklyn Queens Expressway, drove on that two minutes to the Grand Central Parkway, slipped into the light eastbound traffic and three minutes later exited at LaGuardia Airport.

At 2:46 he was reaching for a parking ticket at the automatic entry to parking lot five.

Ninety seconds later, the Pontiac was parked exactly

where he'd found it, the only perceptible difference a fraction less gas and six more miles registered on the odometer.

He got out of the Pontiac, carefully locked it, and carried the duffel bag to the dark-green Beetle. His first easy breath came when he was inside the Volks and clawing at the cord of the duffel bag.

Finally he had it loose. He switched the beam of his flashlight inside the bag. A smile, humorless as a jack-o'-lantern's, played on his lips. He reached for the first packet of money and began to count.

It was all there. Eighty-two thousand dollars. He reached for the empty suitcase in the back seat and neatly began to pile the packets inside it. This bag he'd carry on the plane.

At 7:00 A.M. he pulled out of the parking lot, blended with the early morning commuter traffic into Manhattan, parked the car in the Biltmore garage, and hurried upstairs to his room for a shave and shower and room service.

36

By 4:00 A.M. IT WAS CLEAR that the one lead they had, the license number of the car the abductor had used, was going sour.

The first blow was to find that the car was registered to Henry A. White, a vice-president of the International Food Company of White Plains.

Agents rushed to White's home in Scarsdale and put it under surveillance. But the Pontiac was not in the garage and the house had a closed-up look. Not one window in the sprawling house was open even a fraction and the single light shining through the drawn drapes was probably on a timer.

The security guard at International Food was contacted. He called the head of the personnel department. In turn a product manager from White's department was reached.

In a sleepy voice, he told investigators that White had just returned from a three-week stay at their world headquarters in Switzerland; that he'd had dinner with two of his staff in Pastor's Restaurant in White Plains and was leaving directly from there to join his wife for a brief skiing vacation. She was staying either in Aspen or Sun Valley with friends.

At five o'clock, Hugh and Steve started for Carley. Hugh drove. Steve watched the road thread through Westchester, approach Connecticut. There were so few cars out. Most people were in bed, able to reach for their wives, able to make sure their children were covered, that open windows weren't too drafty. Were Neil and Sharon in a drafty, cold place now?

Why am I thinking that? he wondered. Vaguely he remembered reading that when people couldn't control overwhelming events, they became concerned about small problems. Were Sharon and Neil still alive? That's what he should be worrying about. Spare, oh Lord in mercy, spare them . . .

"What do you make of the Pontiac?" he asked Hugh.

"It'll probably turn out that White's car was stolen from wherever he left it," Hugh replied.

"What do we do next?"

"We wait."

"For what?"

"He may release them. He did promise. He has the money."

"He's covered his tracks so carefully. He's thought of everything. You don't really expect him to release two people who could identify him, do you?"

"No," Hugh admitted.

"Is there nothing else we can do?"

"If he doesn't keep his word and let them go, we have

238

to consider blowing this open, releasing it to the media. Maybe somebody saw or heard something."

"What about Ronald Thompson?"

"What about him?"

"Suppose he's been telling the truth. Suppose we find that out after eleven-thirty?"

"What is your point?"

"My point is, do we have the right not to admit that Neil and Sharon have been kidnapped?"

"I doubt that it would affect the Governor's decision about Thompson. There's absolutely no proof that this is a hostage situation but if she thinks it is, it might only make her anxious to get the execution over with. She already been criticized for granting Thompson two stays. Those kids in Georgia had the switch pulled on them right on the dot. And there still may be a simple explanation of how Foxy managed to get a tape or cassette with your wife's voice on it . . . an explanation that has nothing to do with her death."

Steve stared ahead. They were passing Greenwich. He and Sharon had been at a party in Brad Robertson's house in Greenwich during the holidays. Sharon wore a black velvet skirt, a brocaded jacket. She looked lovely. Brad said to him, "Steve, if you have any sense, you'll latch onto that girl.'

"Could publicity panic the kidnapper?" He knew the answer. Even so he had to ask.

"I would say so." Hugh's inflection was different, crisper. "What's on your mind, Mr. Peterson?"

The question. Flat. Direct. Steve felt his mouth go dry. It's only a hunch, he told himself. It's probably irrelevant. If I begin this, I can't stop it. It may cost Neil and Sharon their lives.

Bleakly, miserably, he waited, poised like a diver for a

leap that would throw him into an uncontrollable current. He thought of Ronald Thompson at the trial, the young face, scared but adamant. "I didn't do it. She was dead when I got there. Ask the kid. . . ."

"How would you feel if it were your only child? How would you feel . . ."

It is my only child, Mrs. Thompson, he thought.

He began to speak. "Hugh, do you remember what Bob Kerner said, that he thought the murders of those four women and Nina's murder were tied together?"

"I heard him and I told you what I think. He's grasping at straws."

"Suppose I told you that Kerner may be right, that there may be a link between Nina's death and the others."

"*What are you talking about?*"

"Remember Kerner said that the only thing he couldn't understand is that the others had car trouble and Nina didn't; that she'd been strangled at home, not somewhere on the road?"

"Go on."

"The night before she was murdered, Nina got a flat. I was at a late meeting in New York and didn't get home till well after midnight. She was asleep. But the next morning when she drove me to the train, I noticed the spare was on her car . . ."

"Go on."

"Remember that transcript Kerner left? The Thompson boy said something about joking with Nina about bad luck turning into good luck and she said something about the groceries all fitting in the trunk."

"What are you saying?"

"Her trunk was small. If she had extra room in it, it can only mean that the spare tire hadn't been put back. That was after four o'clock and she must have gone directly

240

home. Dora was at the house cleaning that day and she said Nina drove her home shortly before five."

"Then she and Neil went straight back to your house?"

"Yes, and he went up to play with his trains. Nina unloaded the car. Remember all those bundles were on the table? We know she died in the next few minutes. I looked at her car that night. The spare tire was in the trunk. The new radial was back on her front wheel."

"You're saying that someone brought the tire back, changed it, then killed her?"

"When else could the tire have been changed except right at that time? And if that happened, that Thompson boy may be innocent. He may even have frightened off the killer by ringing the bell. For God sake, find out if he remembers whether the spare was in the trunk when he loaded those groceries. I should have realized that tire might be important when I checked it that night. But I hated remembering that I'd blown up at Nina the very last minute I was with her."

Hugh pressed his foot on the accelerator. The speedometer climbed from sixty to seventy to eighty. The car screeched into the driveway as the first hint of dawn cut across the somber sky. Hugh rushed to the phone. Before he took off his coat, he dialed the prison at Somers and demanded to speak to the warden. ". . . no, I'll hold on." He turned to Steve. "The warden's been in his office all night, just in case the Governor decided to call. They're shaving the kid now."

"Good God."

"Even if he claims that the trunk was empty, it's not proof. Everything is still supposition. Somebody could have dropped off that tire, changed it for her, been gone. It still doesn't let Thompson off the hook."

"We both believe Thompson is innocent," Steve said.

241

Dully he thought, I have always believed it. Dear God, in my heart I have always believed it, and never faced it.

"Yes, I'm here . . ." Hugh listened. "Thank you very much." He slammed down the phone. "Thompson swears the spare was missing when he loaded the groceries."

"Call the Governor," Steve pleaded. "Tell her, beg her, to at least delay the execution. Put me on if it will help."

Hugh was dialing the State House. "It's not evidence," he said. "It's a string of coincidences. I doubt she'll postpone it on this. When she hears that Sharon and Neil are missing —and you have to tell her that now—she may be convinced this is some kind of last-ditch trick."

The Governor absolutely could not be reached. She had referred all requests for further postponements of the execution to the Attorney General to appraise. He would be in his office at eight o'clock. No, his private phone number would not be given out.

There was nothing to do except wait. Steve and Hugh sat silently in the den as faint, watery light began to filter through the window. Steven tried to pray, could only think Dear God, they are so young, all three so young, please . . .

At six o'clock Dora came down the stairs, her footsteps heavy and unsteady. Looking aged and infinitely weary, she silently began to make coffee.

At six-thirty Hugh spoke to FBI headquarters in New York. There were no new leads. Henry White had taken a 1:00 A.M. flight to Sun Valley. They'd been too late to catch him at the airport there. He'd been driven away in a private car. They were checking motel registrations and condominium rentals. The APB for the Pontiac hadn't produced any results. They were still checking the regulars from the Mill Tavern.

At seven-thirty-five Bob Kerner's car plummetted down

the road and pulled into the driveway. He rang the bell furiously. stalked past Dora and demanded to know why Ronald had been asked about the spare tire.

Hugh glanced at Steve. Steve nodded. Tersely Hugh explained.

Bob paled. "Do you mean to say that your son and Sharon Martin were kidnapped. Mr. Peterson, and you've been covering it up?" he demanded. "When the Governor knows this, she'll have to postpone the execution. She has no choice."

"Don't count on it," Hugh warned.

"Mr. Peterson. I'm sorry for you. but you had no right not to tell me about this last night," Bob said bitterly. "My God, can't we reach the Attorney General before eight?"

"That's only twenty minutes."

"Twenty minutes is a lot when you've got only three hours and fifty minutes left to live, Mr. Taylor."

At exactly eight o'clock Hugh reached the Attorney General. He spoke for thirty-five minutes, his voice forceful, arguing, pleading. "Yes sir, I realize the Governor has already granted two stays. . . . I understand that the Connecticut Supreme Court unanimously confirmed the verdict. . . . No sir, we don't have *proof*. . . . It's more than *speculation* though . . . the cassette. . . . Yes sir, I'd appreciate if you'll call the Governor. . . . May I put Mr. Peterson on . . . ? All right, I'll hold.

Hugh cupped his hand over the phone. "He's going to call her but let me tell you, he's not going to recommend a stay."

Three minutes passed slowly. Steve and Bob did not look at each other. Then Hugh said, "Yes, I'm here . . . but . . . "

He was still protesting when Steve heard the unmistakable sound of the dial tone. Hugh let the phone drop. "The execution's on," he told them flatly.

37

THE PAIN. It was so hard to think with the pain shooting up through her body. If she could only unzip her boot. Her ankle was a mass of burning concrete, swelling against the boot, against the biting twine.

She should have taken a chance and screamed when they were going through the terminal. Better to have risked it then. What time was it? Time didn't exist. Monday night. Tuesday. Was it still Tuesday? Was it Wednesday yet?

How could they get out of here?

Neil. She could hear the rasping breath close to hers. He was trying to breathe slowly, trying to obey her. Sharon heard the moans coming from her lips, tried to bite them back.

She felt Neil sliding closer to her, trying to comfort her.

Neil would be so like Steve when he grew up. *If* he grew up . . .

Steve. What would it be like to live with Steve, to make a life with him and Neil? Steve who had known so much pain.

Everything had always been so easy for her. Her father saying, 'Sharon was born in Rome, Pat in Egypt, Tina in Hong Kong." Her mother, "We have friends all over the world." Even when they found out that she was dead, they'd have each other. When Steve lost Neil, he'd have no one.

Steve asking, "How come you're still single?" Because she hadn't wanted the responsibility of loving someone else.

Neil. So afraid that the Lufts would take him with them. So afraid that she'd take Steve away from him.

She had to get him out of here.

Again she tried rubbing her wrists against the cinder-block wall. But the cords were too tight, biting into her wrists. She couldn't get them in contact with the wall.

She tried to think. Her only hope was to get Neil free, to get him out of this room. If he opened the door from the inside, would the bomb explode?

The knob in the bathroom. If Foxy came back, if he let her go into the bathroom again, maybe she could pull the knob, break it off.

What would he do with them when he got the money? She was drifting off. Time . . . how much time . . . time passing . . . was it day or night? . . . muted train sounds . . . come for us, Steve . . . I blame you, Miss Martin . . . it is the issue, Miss Martin . . . none so blind as those who will not see . . . I love you, Sharon, I've missed you terribly . . . big, gentle hands on her face . . .

Big gentle hands on her face. Sharon opened her eyes.

Foxy was bending over her. With horrible gentleness his hands were running over her face, her neck. He slipped the gag from her mouth and kissed her. His lips were poker-hot, his mouth mushy. She tried to turn her head. It was such an effort.

He whispered, "It's all finished, Sharon. I have the money. I have to go now."

She tried to focus her eyes. His features emerged from the blur, glittering eyes and a throbbing pulse and narrow lips.

"What are you going to do to us?" It was so hard to talk.

"I'm going to leave you right here. I'll tell Peterson where to pick you up."

He was lying. It was like before, when he'd been leading her on, toying with her. No, she'd tried to trick him and then he'd pushed her down.

"You're going to kill us."

"That's right, Sharon."

"You killed Neil's mother."

"That's right, Sharon. Oh, I almost forgot." He was moving away from her, reaching down, unfolding something. "I'll put this picture up with the others." Something was floating over her head. Neil's eyes were staring down at her, eyes that were part of a sprawled body, a body with a scarf around its neck. A shriek tore her throat, pushing back pain and dizziness. Suddenly she was completely rational, focusing, looking at the picture, at the glittering, mad eyes of the man holding it.

He was hanging it next to the others on the wall over the cot, hanging it carefully, ritualistic in his exactness.

Fearfully, she watched him. Would he kill them now, strangle them as he'd strangled those women?

"I'm going to set the clock for you now," he told her.

"The clock?"

"Yes. It will make the bomb go off at eleven-thirty. You won't feel anything, Sharon. You'll just be gone, and Neil will be gone, and Ronald Thompson will be gone."

Carefully, delicately, he was opening the suitcase. She watched as he took a clock out, as he consulted his wristwatch and set the clock to 9:30. It was 9:30 Wednesday morning. The alarm—he was setting the alarm to 11:30. Now he was attaching wires to the clock.

Two hours.

Carefully, he lifted the suitcase, put it on top of the deep sinks near the door. The face of the clock was directly opposite her across the room. The hands and numerals glowed.

"Do you want to have anything before I go, Sharon, a glass of water? Would you like me to kiss you goodbye?"

"Could I . . . would you let me go into the bathroom?"

"Sure, Sharon." He came over, untied her hands, picked her up. Her legs crumbled under her. Pain made her shiver. Black curtains closed over her eyes. No . . . no . . . no . . . she could not faint.

He left her inside the dark cubbyhole, holding onto the doorknob. She twisted it around, around, around, praying the sound wasn't carrying. A faint cracking sound. The handle broke off.

Sharon ran her fingers over the separated end, felt the jagged edge of the broken metal. She slipped the handle in the deep pocket of her skirt. When she opened the door she had one hand in her pocket. If he felt anything when he carried her back to the cot, he'd think it was her fist.

It worked. He was hurrying now, anxious to be out of there. He tossed her back down; retied her hands quickly. She was able to keep them a little separated, those cords were not as tight as the others. The gag was yanked over her mouth.

He was bending over her. "I could have loved you very much, Sharon, as I think you could have loved me."

With a quick movement he pulled off Neil's blindfold. Neil blinked, his eyes swollen, his pupils enormous.

The man looked directly into the eyes; his gaze slid to the picture on the wall then back to Neil's face.

Abruptly he dropped the child's head, turned and clicked off the lights as for the last time he slipped out of the room.

Sharon stared at the glowing face of the clock. It was 8:36.

38

GLENDA'S BED WAS STREWN WITH PAGES, pages crumbled, begun again. "No . . . on the fourteenth I didn't go straight to the doctor. I stopped at the library . . . put that in, Roger, I spoke to a couple of people there. . . ."

"I'll start a new sheet. This one's too cluttered. Who did you talk to in the waiting room at the doctor's?"

Minutely they reviewed every detail of the past month. Nothing triggered awareness in Glenda of the man who called himself Foxy. At 4:00 A.M. at her persuasion, Roger called FBI headquarters and asked to speak to Hugh. Hugh told him about the contact.

"He says that the kidnapper has promised that Sharon and Neil can be picked up at eleven-thirty," Roger told her.

"They don't trust him, do they?"

"No, I don't think they do."

"If it is someone familiar to me, it might be someone Neil knows from this area. He couldn't let Neil go."

"Glenda, we're both so tired we're incapable of thinking. Let's try to sleep for a few hours. Then maybe something will come to you. Your subconscious works when you're sleeping. You know that."

"All right." Wearily, she started to stack the sheets of paper in chronological order.

He set the alarm for seven. For three hours they slept—exhausted, troubled sleep.

At seven Roger went down to make tea. Glenda slipped a nitroglycerin tablet under her tongue, went into the bathroom, washed her face, got back into bed and picked up her pad.

At nine Marian arrived. At 9:15 she came up to see Glenda. "I'm sorry you're not feeling well, Mrs. Perry."

"Thank you."

"I'll stay out of your way. If it's all right, I'll concentrate on one room at a time downstairs."

"That would be fine."

"That way by the end of the week, downstairs will be shipshape. I can tell you like a house kept nice."

"Yes, I do. Thank you."

"I'm just glad to be here, that I didn't have to disappoint you with the trouble we had over our car . . ."

"My husband mentioned something." Deliberately, Glenda raised her pen, held it poised.

"Really awful. After just spending four hundred dollars to get it fixed. Normally we wouldn't spend that much on an old car, but Arty's such a good mechanic that my husband said it was worth it. Well, I see you're busy. I shouldn't be gabbing. Would you like a little breakfast?"

"No thank you, Mrs. Vogler."

The door closed behind her. A few minutes later Roger came back in. "I spoke to a couple of people at the office. Said I had a touch of flu."

"Roger . . . wait a minute." Glenda depressed the button on the recorder. The now familiar sentence filled their ears: *Be at the Exxon service station. . . .* Glenda snapped the machine off. "Roger, when did we get my car serviced?"

"A little over a month ago, I think. Bill Lufts took it over to that place he recommended."

"Yes, and you dropped me off on your way to work when it was ready. *Arty*, that was the name wasn't it?"

"I believe so. Why?"

"Because the car was ready but he was just about to fill it with gas. I was talking to him, standing next to it. I noticed his sign said 'A. R. Taggert' and asked if the 'A' stood for Arthur, because I'd heard Bill call him Arty.

"Roger," Glenda's voice became high-pitched. She sat up and grabbed his hand, "Roger, he told me that people around here started to call him Arty because of the sign 'A. R. Taggert,' but that his name really was August Rommel Taggert.

"And I said, 'Rommel—wasn't he the famous German General?'

"And he said, 'Yes, Rommel was the Desert *Fox*.' The way he said *fox* . . . and the way he said *foxy* on the phone the other night. Roger. I swear to you, that mechanic is Foxy and he's the one who kidnapped Neil and Sharon!"

It was 9:31 A.M.

39

SHE WAS GOING TO HER ROOM. Olendorf was off today and the other guard would never bother her. Lally hadn't slept all night. She was getting sick. The arthritis was murder, but it was more than that. There was something inside her winding down. She could feel it. She just wanted to get into her room and lie down on the cot and close her eyes.

She *had to.*

She drifted down with the 8:40 Mount Vernon passengers and slipped around to the ramp. She had extra newspapers in her shopping bag to cover herself, but she didn't stop for coffee. She wasn't hungry for anything, just her room.

It didn't even matter if the man was there. She'd take her chances. The comforting noise of the generators and vents greeted her. It was gloomy here like always, and that was good with her. Her heavy sneakers were silent as she padded across to the staircase.

And then she heard it.

The muffled sound of a door opening slowly. Her door. Lally shrank behind the generator into the shadows.

Soft, low footsteps. He was coming down the metal steps, the same man. She melted back, pressed her bulk against the wall. Should she confront him? No . . . no. Every instinct warned her to hide. She watched him stand, listen intently, then move swiftly toward the ramp. In a minute he'd be gone and she'd be in her room. If the girl was still there, she'd scare her off.

Her arthritic fingers started to pull the key from her pocket, fumbled. It fell with a ping at her feet.

She held her breath. Had he heard? She didn't dare to look out. But the footsteps were completely gone. There was no sound of anyone coming back. She waited ten minutes, ten long minutes, trying to calm the pounding of her heart. Then slowly, painfully, she bent down, felt on the ground for her key. It was so dark here; her eyes were so bad now. She felt the outline of the key and sighed with relief.

Lally was just beginning to straighten up when something grazed against her back, something shivery cold. She gasped as it touched her skin, touched and slipped in, so sharp, so quickly that she barely felt the blinding pain, the warm gushing of her blood as she clumsily sank to her knees and slumped forward. Her forehead took the impact of the fall; her left arm arced out. As she slipped into unconsciousness, her right fist closed around the key to her room.

40

At 9:30 an agent from FBI headquarters phoned Hugh Taylor at Steve's home. "We think we have something, Hughie."

"What is it?"

"That Arty—the mechanic, Arty Taggert."

"Yeah."

"There used to be a guy known as Gus Taggert who got picked up for hanging around the Port Authority about twelve years ago. Suspect in disappearance of some sixteen-year-old runaway. We couldn't pin anything on him, but a lot of guys thought he did something to her. He was questioned about disappearances of other young girls, too. His description matches the one you gave us."

"Good work. What else have you got on him?"

"We're trying to check out where he used to live. He

had a bunch of jobs in New York, pumping gas on the west side, busboy in an Eighth Avenue joint, dishwasher in the Oyster Bar . . ."

"Concentrate on where he lived; find out if he has any family."

Hugh hung up the phone. "Mr. Peterson," he said carefully, "there's a chance we have a new lead. A mechanic who hangs around Mill Tavern seems to have been a suspect in several cases of young girls disappearing about twelve years ago. Name of Arty Taggert."

"A mechanic." Steve's voice rose. "*A mechanic.*"

"Exactly. I know what you're thinking. It's a slim chance, but if someone fixed your wife's tire that day, is it possible she'd have written a check in payment? Do you have your canceled checks or stubs from January two years ago?"

"Yes, I'll look."

"Remember, we're only examining any lead we can. We have no proof at all of anything about this Arty except that he was questioned once years ago."

"I see." Steve walked over to his desk.

The phone rang. It was Roger Perry shouting the news that Glenda was positive a mechanic called A. R. Taggert was Foxy.

Hugh slammed the phone down, was about to pick it up to dial New York when it rang again. Impatiently he barked "Yes." His expression changed, became inscrutable. "What? Hold it, start again."

Steve watched as Hugh's eyes hardened into slits of concentration. When Hugh whipped out a pen, he held the memo pad for him. Ignoring the other man's attempt to screen what he was writing, Steve stared at the pad, digesting the words as they went down.

Thank you for the money. It is all there. You have kept your promise. Now I will keep mine. Neil and Sharon are alive. At 11:30 they will be executed during an explosion in New York State. In the rubble from that explosion you can dig for their bodies.

FOXY

Hugh said, "Repeat that again so I'm sure I have it straight." A moment later he said, "Thank you. We'll be in touch with you shortly." He hung up the phone.

"Who took the call?" Steve asked. Merciful numbness was paralyzing his capacity to think, to fear.

Hugh waited a long minute before answering. When he did his voice was infinitely weary. "The mortician in Carley who handled your wife's funeral arrangements," he said.

It was 9:35 A.M.

41

If that old hag hadn't made that noise! Arty was drenched in perspiration. His new green suit smelled really bad now, just the way it always did after . . .

Suppose he hadn't heard her? She must be the one who'd been staying in the room, who dragged that cot in. That meant she must have a key. If he hadn't heard her, she'd have gone in, found them. They'd have time to get experts to deactivate the bomb.

He walked rapidly through the terminal to the arcade that led to the Biltmore and picked up the car from the Biltmore garage. The suitcase and radio were already packed in it. He drove swiftly up the East Side Drive to the Triborough Bridge. It was the quickest way to La-Guardia. He was frantic now to get out of New York. The plane to Phoenix left at 10:30.

He returned to the parking lot he'd left only hours before. The thought of how successful his plan had been to pick up the ransom soothed him. This time he parked the Volks far away from the tollgate in the area where people parked for the Eastern Shuttle. That section was always crowded. He'd filed the engine number off the Volks and the license plate could never be traced to him. He'd taken it off a junked car five years ago. Anyhow, it might be a month before someone noticed that the Volks had been here a long time.

He pulled his two suitcases, the light one with the clothes and cassettes and the heavy one with his money, and the crated C.B. radio out of the trunk. Now there was absolutely nothing to link him with the car.

He walked swiftly over to the bus stop. The courtesy airport bus came along and he got on it. The other passengers glanced at him indifferently. He could feel their dismissal. Just because he wasn't all dressed up. He sat next to a girl about nineteen years old, a very attractive girl. He didn't miss the wrinkle of distaste, the way the girl turned away from him. Bitch. Little did she know that he was a clever, wealthy man.

The bus stopped at the domestic terminal. He walked two hundred feet to the American Airlines special entrance. An attendant was checking in luggage. He wouldn't have to drag all this stuff around. He yanked out his ticket. The name on the ticket was Renard. That meant fox in French. It was the name he planned to use in Arizona.

"Check all three pieces, sir?"

"No! Not that one." He yanked the suitcase with the money out of the reach of the attendant.

"Sorry, sir. I'm not sure you can carry one that big on board."

"I must!" Deliberately, he tried to curb the intensity in his voice. "I have papers I have to work on."

The attendant shrugged. "All right, sir. I guess the stewardess can always put it in the cabin closet if necessary."

It was 9:28 and he was hungry again. But first he had the call to make. He selected a phone booth in a far corner of the terminal and wrote down what he wanted to say so there'd be no mistake. He pictured what Steve Peterson would think when he got the message.

The funeral home phone was picked up promptly. His voice low, Foxy said, "You will be needed to pick up remains."

"Of course, sir. Who is calling?" The other voice was subdued.

"Are you ready to write this down?"

"Certainly."

Foxy's voice changed, became harsh. "Write it down, then read it right back to me and make sure you have it straight." He began to dictate, enjoying the shocked gasp he heard on the other end of the phone. "Now read it back," he demanded. A trembling voice obeyed then said, "My God, please . . ."

Smiling Foxy hung up.

He went into a cafeteria in the terminal and selected bacon, rolls, orange juice and coffee. He ate slowly, watching the people hurrying fast.

Now he was beginning to relax. The thought of the phone call to the funeral home made him chuckle deep in the pit of his stomach. At first he was going to warn them of an explosion in New York *City*. At the very last minute he'd changed it to New York *State*. He could just imagine the cops going nuts now. A lot of good it would do them.

263

Arizona, land of the painted desert.

Looking into the boy's eyes had been necessary. He wouldn't have to run away from them ever again. He imagined what it would be like at 11:30 in Grand Central. The explosion would go upward. The whole ceiling would come crashing down on Neil and Sharon, tons and tons and tons of cement.

It was easy to make a bomb just like it was easy to fix an engine. All you did was read everything about it. Now the whole world would want to know who Foxy was. They'd probably write about him the way they did about Rommel.

He finished his coffee, wiped the back of his hand over his mouth. From the window he watched as people carrying bags hurried across the terminal to departure gates. He remembered the bombing of LaGuardia at Christmastime a couple of years before. That had caused panic, closed the airport. He's seen it on television.

He was already looking forward to being in a bar tonight in Phoenix watching the news reports of the explosion in Grand Central. It would be on television all over the world. But it would be even better if the cops had some place to start looking. The people who put those bombs in the office buildings did it that way. They called up and gave a big list of where they'd put bombs and the cops didn't know where to go first. They'd had to make people leave every building they talked about.

He could still do something like that. What should he tell them? He stared out. This was a busy airport. People running back and forth all over the place and it wasn't even as big as Kennedy.

Just like Grand Central. Or the bus terminal. Everybody rushing. Paying no attention to anybody. Just wanted to get where they were going. Didn't notice anybody. Didn't smile back.

An idea slowly took shape. Suppose he warned the cops. Suppose he told them that Sharon and Neil and the bomb were in a transportation center in New York City. That would mean they'd have to clear out both airports and the two bus terminals and Penn Station as well as Grand Central. They'd start searching under seats in the waiting rooms and opening lockers. They wouldn't know where to start. And all these people, these lousy people would be made to get out of all those places, to miss their trains and planes and buses.

They'd never find Sharon and Neil. Never. The only one who knew about that room was the old hag and he'd taken care of her. All by himself he could keep people in or out of the biggest city in the world with one more phone call. Peterson thought he was a big shot with his magazine and his trust fund and his girlfriend. Foxy laughed aloud. The couple sitting at the next table looked at him curiously.

He *would* call, just before he got on the plane. Who would he call?

The funeral home again? No.

Who else would be sure the call wasn't a fake?

He knew. Smiling, anticipating the reaction he'd get, he went for another coffee. At twelve minutes past ten he left the cafeteria, the suitcase gripped in his hand. He deliberately waited that long so that when they were x-raying the carry-on luggage they'd be hurrying. No one would be curious about his suitcase. Airlines loved to keep to their schedules.

At 10:15 he slipped into a phone booth near departure gate 9, pulled out quarters and dimes and dialed a number. When the receiver at the other end was picked up, he whispered a message. He replaced the receiver gently, walked to the check-in desk and went through the inspection without a hitch.

The "boarding" sign was flashing as he walked across the waiting area to the covered ramp leading to the plane.

It was 10:16 A.M.

42

HER CLOTHES FELT WET AND WARM AND STICKY. Blood. She was bleeding to death.

Death. She was going to die. Lally knew it. Through the dim fading light in her mind, she sensed it. Someone had killed her . . the man who had taken her room had taken her life.

The room. Her room. She wanted to die in it. She wanted to be there. He'd never come back. He'd be afraid. Maybe no one would find her. Entombed. She'd be entombed in the only home she'd ever had. She'd be here sleeping forever with the comforting roar of her trains. Her mind was clearing . . . but she didn't have long. She knew it. She had to get to her room.

Aware of the key in her right fist, Lally tried to drag herself up. Something was pulling . . . the knife . . . the knife was still plunged into her. She couldn't reach it. She began to crawl . . .

She had to arc around. She'd been laying facing away from where the room was. The effort of turning her body . . . too much, too much. Slowly, inch by inch, she crawled until she was in the direction of her room. Twenty feet at least to the staircase. And then the stairs. Could she? Lally shook her head trying to clear away the darkness. She could feel blood running from her mouth. She tried to clear it from her throat.

Right hand . . . keep gripping the key . . . left hand forward . . . right knee, drag it forward . . . left knee . . . right hand . . . She would do it. Somehow she would manage to get up those stairs.

She kept in her mind the vision of opening the door, closing it . . . crawling inside . . . pulling herself up on the cot . . . lying there . . . closing her eyes . . . waiting.

In her room death would come as a friend, a friend with cool and gentle hands . . .

43

THEY ARE DEAD, Steve thought. When you are condemned you are already dead. This afternoon Ronald Thompson's mother would claim her son's body. This afternoon the Sheridan Funeral Home would go to the site of an explosion and wait for Sharon's and Neil's bodies.

Somewhere in New York State, digging in the rubble . . . He was standing by the window. A knot of reporters and television cameras was grouped outside. "The word goes fast," he said. "We vultures of the media love a good story."

Bradley had just phoned. "Steve, what can I do?"

"Nothing. Nothing. Just let me know if you happen to see a Volks beetle, dark green, with a guy about thirty-eight years old in it. He probably has the license plates changed

269

so that won't help. We have an hour and twenty minutes—an hour and twenty minutes."

"What have you done about the bomb threat?" he had asked Hugh.

"Alerted every major city in the state to stand by for an emergency. There's nothing more we can do. An explosion in New York State. *New York State.* Do you know how many thousands of square miles that covers? Mr. Peterson, there's still a chance this is a hoax. I mean, the threat of the explosion, the call to the funeral parlor."

"No, no, it's too late for them, too late." Steve thought, Bill and Dora Lufts moved in because of Nina's death. They were staying here to do him a favor, to take care of Neil for him. But Bill Lufts discussing his affairs may have caused Neil and Sharon's kidnapping—their death. Circle of death. No, please let them live, help us to find them . . .

Restlessly, he turned from the window. Hank Lamont had just come in with Bill. They were going over his story again. Steve knew it by heart.

"Mr. Lufts, you've talked to this Arty a lot. Please try to remember. Has he ever mentioned wanting to go to some particular place? Has he ever talked about some place a lot, like Mexico . . . or Alaska?"

Bill shook his head. All this was too much for him. He knew that they thought Arty had kidnapped Neil and Sharon. Arty, a quiet fellow, a good mechanic. Just a couple of weeks ago he'd driven over to his place. Neil rode with him. He could remember the day exactly because Neil had a bad asthma attack that night. Desperately, he tried to remember what Arty talked about, but it seemed as though he never said much, just seemed real interested in Bill's stories.

Hank was furious at himself. He'd been sitting in the

Mill Tavern buying that guy beers. He'd even told the office not to bother much about checking him. Lufts *had* to remember something. Like Hughie said, everything a man does leaves traces. He could see that guy walking out of the Mill—and he, Hank, not suspecting. Hank frowned. There had been some kind of crack Arty made when he said goodbye. What was it?

Bill was saying, ". . . and a nice quiet fellow, like I tell you. Minds his business. Maybe he did ask questions, just seemed friendly and interested like . . ."

"Hold on." Hank interrupted.

"What is it?" Hugh turned quietly to the younger agent. "You've got something?"

"Maybe. When Arty left with the others . . . and they said something about not having the chance to see Bill before he left for Rhode Island . . ."

"Yeah. And in a pig's eye Arty's heading for Rhode Island."

"That's what I mean. He said something else . . . and that advertising guy Allan Kroeger made a crack on top of it. A crack about . . . about the painted desert. That's it!"

"What?" Hugh demanded.

"When they said, 'too bad Bill Lufts isn't around to say goodbye,' Arty said, 'Rhode Island's not Arizona.' Could that have been a slip?"

"We'll find out soon." Hugh ran for the phone.

Roger came in, put his hand on Steve's shoulder and listened with him as Hugh barked orders into the phone, putting the awesome power of the Federal Bureau of Investigation into tracking down the new lead.

Finally Hugh put the phone down. "If he's heading for Arizona, we'll get him, Mr. Peterson. I can promise you that."

"When?"

Roger's face was the color of the bleak morning. "Steve, get out of here," he said. "Glenda wants you to come over. Please."

Steve shook his head.

"We'll both go," Hugh said briskly. "Hank, take over here."

Steve considered. "All right." He started toward the front door.

"No, let's go out the back way and through the woods. You'll be able to avoid the reporters."

A ghost of a smile touched Steve's lips. "But that's just it. I don't intend to avoid them."

He opened the door. The cluster of reporters broke past the agents stationed on the walk and raced to him. Microphones were shoved in front of his face. Television cameras angled to catch his drawn, tired face.

"Mr. Peterson, has there been any further word?"

"No."

"Do you think the kidnapper will carry out his threat to execute your son and Sharon Martin?"

"We have every reason to believe he's capable of this kind of violence."

"Do you think it's more than coincidence that the threatened explosion will occur at the exact minute Ronald Thompson is executed?"

"I do not think it is coincidence. I think the kidnapper Foxy may very well have been involved in my wife's death. I have tried to get that word to the Governor, who refuses to speak with me. I now publicly implore her to delay the Thompson execution. That boy may very well be innocent—I think he is."

"Mr. Peterson, has your position on capital punishment changed in view of your terrible worry over your son and

Miss Martin? When this kidnapper is apprehended would you want to see him executed?"

Steve reached down and pushed the microphones back from his face. "I want to answer your questions. Please give me the opportunity." The reporters became quiet. Steve looked directly into the camera. "Yes. I have changed my mind. I say this knowing that it is very unlikely that my son and Sharon will be found alive. But even if their kidnapper is apprehended too late to save them, I have learned something in these past two days. I have learned that no man has the right to determine the time of death of one of his fellow human beings. I believe that power rests only with Almighty God and . . ." his voice broke, "I only ask you to pray to God that Neil and Sharon and Ronald will be spared this morning."

Tears streamed down his cheeks. "Let me pass."

Quietly the reporters separated. Roger and Hugh ran behind him as he darted across the street.

Glenda was watching at the door. She opened it for them, put her arms around Steve. "Let it out, dear," she said quietly. "Go ahead."

"I can't let them go," he cried brokenly. "I can't lose them . . ."

She let him cry, hugging him as the broad shoulders heaved. If I had only remembered sooner, she agonized. Oh God, I've been too late to help him. She felt the shuddering of his body as he tried to stifle his sobs.

"Sorry, Glenda, you've had enough . . . you're not well."

"I'm all right," she said, "Steve, like it or not, you're going to have a cup of tea and some toast. You haven't eaten or slept in two days."

Somberly, they went into the dining room.

"Mr. Peterson," Hugh said carefully, "remember that pictures of Sharon and Neil are coming out on special editions of morning newspapers; they're being shown on every television station. Someone may have seen them, seen something."

"Do you think whoever has them paraded them in public?" Steve asked bitterly.

"Someone may have seen unusual activity; someone may have heard one of those phonecalls being made; may have heard people talking in a bar . . ."

Marian poured water from the kettle into the teapot. The door between the kitchen and dining room was open and she could overhear the conversation. That poor, poor, Mr. Peterson. No wonder he'd seemed so rude when she spoke to him. He'd been all choked up about the little boy being kidnapped and she'd only upset him by talking about Neil. Shows you should never judge people. You don't know what kind of grief they're carrying around inside them.

Maybe if he'd just have some tea.

She brought in the teapot. Steve's face was buried in his hands.

"Mr. Peterson," she said gently, "let me fix you a nice hot cup of tea."

She picked up his cup. With the other hand she began to pour.

Slowly Steve lowered his hands from his face. The next instant the teapot was flying across the table; spilling down into the sugar bowl, running across the flowered placemats, a bubbling, tawny stream.

Glenda, Roger and Hugh jumped up. Shocked, they stared at Steve, who was gripping a terrified Marian's arms. "Where did you get that ring?" he shouted. "Where did you get that ring?"

44

AT SOMERS STATE PRISON, Kate Thompson kissed her son
goodbye. She stared unseeingly at the shaven spot like a
monk's tonsure on his head, the slits in the side of his
trousers.

She was dry-eyed as she felt his strong young arms
around her. She pulled his face down. "Be brave, dear."

"I will. Bob said he'd look out for you, Mama."

She left him. Bob was going to stay until the end. She
knew it was easier if she went now . . . easier for him.

She walked out of the prison, along the cold, windswept
road to town. A police car came by. "Let me drop you,
ma'am."

"Thank you." With dignity, she got in the car.

"You're staying at the motel, Mrs. Thompson?"

"No. Take me to St. Bernard's, please."

The morning masses were over; the church was empty. She knelt at the statue of the Virgin. "Be with him at the end. Take the bitterness from my heart. You who gave up your innocent Son, help me if I must give up mine. . . ."

45

A TREMBLING MARIAN TRIED TO SPEAK. But she couldn't talk over the dryness in her mouth, the knot in her throat. Her tongue was so heavy. The tea had burned her hand. Her finger hurt where Mr. Peterson had wrenched the ring from it.

They were all looking at her as though they hated her. Mr. Peterson's grip on her wrist tightened. "Where did you get that ring?" he shouted again.

"I . . . I . . . I found it." Her voice quivered, broke.

"You *found* it!" Hugh shoved Steve away from Marian. His voice dripped with scorn. "You *found* it."

"Yes."

"Where?"

"In my car."

Hugh snorted and looked directly at Steve. "Are you positive this is the ring you gave Sharon Martin?"

"Absolutely. I bought it in a village in Mexico. It's one of a kind. Look!" He tossed it at Hugh. "Feel for a ridge on the left side of the band."

Hugh ran his finger over the ring. His expression hardened. "Where's your coat, Mrs. Vogler? You're coming in for questioning." Rapidly he spat out the Miranda warning. "You are not obliged to answer questions. Anything you say may be used against you. You have the right to call a lawyer. Let's go."

Steve shouted, "Damn you! Don't tell her she doesn't have to answer questions! Are you crazy? She's *got* to answer questions!"

Glenda's face was stony. She stared at Marian with angry disgust. "You talked about Arty this morning," she accused. "You talked about him fixing your car. How *could* you? How could you, a woman with children of her own, be part of this?"

Hugh spun around. "She talked about Arty?"

"Yes."

"Where is he?" Steve demanded. "Where has he got them? My God, the first minute I met you, you talked about Neil."

"Steve, Steve, calm down." Roger gripped his arm.

Marian knew she was going to faint. She had kept the ring and it wasn't hers. Now they thought she had something to do with the kidnapping. How could she make them believe her? Waves of dizziness made her vision cloudy. She'd make them call Jim. They had to call Jim. He'd help her. He'd come here and tell them about the car being stolen and that she'd found the ring in it. He'd *make* them believe her. The room started spinning. She clutched at the table.

Steve jumped forward to catch her before she fell. Through blurring eyes, she looked into his eyes, saw the

278

agony in them. Pity for him calmed her. She grabbed him for support, forced herself to push back the dizziness. "Mr. Peterson." She could speak now. She had to speak. "I couldn't harm anybody. I want to help you. I *did* find the ring. In our car. Our car was stolen Monday night. Arty had just fixed it for us."

Steve looked down into the frightened, earnest face, the truthfilled eyes. Then the impact of what he had just heard sank into him. "Stolen! Your car was stolen Monday night?" Oh God, he thought, is there still a chance to find them?

Hugh snapped. "Let me handle this, Mr. Peterson." He pulled over a chair, helped Marian into it. "Mrs. Vogler, if you are telling the truth, you must help us. How well do you know Arty?"

"Not well. He's a good mechanic. I picked the car up from him on Sunday. Then on Monday I went to the four o'clock movie at the Carley Square. I parked it in the movie lot. It was gone when I got out just before seven-thirty."

"So he knew the condition of the car," Hugh said. "Did he know you'd be going to the movie?"

"He might have." Marian frowned. "Yes, we were talking about it at his place. And then he filled up the car with gas. He said it was a bonus because it was such an expensive job."

Glenda murmured, "Remember I said that it was a dark car, a wide one."

"Mrs. Vogler," Hugh said, "this is very important. Where was your car recovered?"

"In New York City. The police towed it. It was illegally parked."

"*Where?* By any chance do you know where they found it?"

Marian tried to think. "By a hotel, by some hotel."

279

"Mrs. Vogler, try to remember. Which hotel? You can save us so much time."

Marian shook her head. "I can't."

"Would your husband remember?"

"Yes, but he's on an outside job today. You'll have to phone the plant and see if they can reach him."

"What is the license number of your car, Mrs. Vogler?"

Quickly Marian gave it to him. What hotel? Jim had said something about the street it was on? Why? It would take them so long to reach Jim . . . to check the towing records. . . . She had to remember. It was something about an old car on easy street. That's what Jim said. No, he said the *block* was named after a family that's always been on easy street. "Vanderbilt Avenue," she cried, "that's it. My husband told me the car was parked on Vanderbilt Avenue in front of some hotel . . . the . . . the *Biltmore* Hotel."

Hugh grabbed the phone and dialed FBI headquarters in New York. He issued rapidfire orders. "Get back to me fast." He hung up the phone.

"An agent is rushing over to the Biltmore with an old mug shot we have of Taggert," he said. "Let's hope it still looks like him and let's hope they can tell us something."

Tensely they waited.

"Please," Steve prayed. "Dear God, please!" The phone rang.

Hugh yanked the receiver off the hook. "What have you got?" He listened, then yelled, "Sweet Jesus. I'll take the copter down." He dropped the phone. looked at Steve. "The room clerk positively identified the picture as an A. R. Renard who checked in on Sunday night. He had a dark green Beetle in the Biltmore garage. He checked out this morning."

"*Renard*. That's French for fox!" Glenda cried.

"Exactly," Hugh said.

"Was he?" Steve gripped the table.

"He was alone. But the clerk remembers that he's been going in and out of the hotel at odd hours. Sometimes he's only been gone a short time, which could mean that he's been keeping Neil and Sharon somewhere in midtown. Remember that John Owens picked up a lot of train noises in the background of the cassette.

"We've got no time, no time." Steve's voice was bitter. "What good will knowing this do?"

"I'm taking the copter down to the Pan Am building. They'll clear us for an emergency landing there. If we can get Taggert in time, we'll make him talk. If we don't our best bet is still to concentrate our search in the area of the Biltmore. Do you want to come?"

Steve didn't bother to answer. He ran to the front door.

Glenda looked at the clock. "It is half past ten," she said tonelessly.

46

FATHER KENNEDY SAT AT HIS DESK in St. Monica's rectory listening to the news bulletins. He shook his head thinking of the agonized face of Steven Peterson when he picked up the package at the rectory last night. No wonder he'd been so upset.

Could they possibly find that child and young woman in time? Where would that explosion occur? How many others would be killed?

The phone rang. Wearily, he picked it up. "Father Kennedy."

"Thanks for delivering the package I left on your altar last night, Father. This is Foxy."

The priest felt his throat constrict. The press has been told only that the cassette was found in the church. "What . . ."

"Never mind any questions. You just call Steve Peterson for me and give him another hint. Tell him I said the bomb will go off at a major transportation center in New York City. He can do his digging there."

The phone went dead.

47

Foxy moved slowly across the waiting area of gate 9 toward the enclosed ramp that led to the plane. A presentiment of danger as definite as a tripped alarm was jangling nerves through his entire system. His eyes moved restlessly around the area. His fellow passengers were ignoring him, intent on juggling on-board luggage with pocketbooks or attaché cases while preparing to present boarding passes.

He glanced down at his own boarding pass neatly protruding from the ticket envelope he'd presented at the desk. In his other hand he was firmly gripping the old black suitcase.

Sound! That was it. The sound of running feet. Police! He dropped the ticket, vaulted the low divider between the boarding area and corridor. Two men were running swiftly down the corridor toward him. Desperately, he glanced around and noticed an emergency exit door some fifty feet away. It had to lead to the field.

The suitcase. He couldn't run with the suitcase. With only the briefest hesitation, he threw it backward. It thumped against the stone floor, slid a few inches and burst open. Money scattered over the corridor.

"Stop or we'll shoot!" a commanding voice shouted.

Foxy threw open the emergency door, setting off a loud pealing sound. He yanked it closed behind him and wove across the field. The Phoenix-bound plane was in his path. He ran around it. A small service van, its engine running, was near the left wing of the plane. The driver was just getting back in. Foxy grabbed him from behind, punched him viciously in the neck. The man grunted and collapsed. Foxy shoved him aside and jumped into the van. Pressing his foot down on the accelerator, he zigzagged around the plane. They wouldn't dare shoot with that plane in the way.

The cops would be following him in a car any second. Or they'd send cars from other areas to head him off. It was risky to get out of this car, more risky to stay in it. The runways were fenced off or ended at the Sound. If he drove down one of them, he'd be trapped.

They were looking for a man driving a service van on the field. They'd never look for him in the terminal. He spotted an identical van parked near a hangar, swung next to it and stopped. On the seat beside him a looseleaf book was open. He glanced at it swiftly. Something about requisitions, supplies. He grabbed it and got out of the van. A door marked "authorized personnel only" was opening. Bending his head over the book, he reached for it, prevented it from closing. A brisk-looking young woman in an airline uniform came out, glanced at the book in his hand, and sped past him.

Now his walk became authoritative, swift. He strode through the small corridor with the individual offices and an instant later was in the departure area. Airport police were running past him toward the field. Ignoring them, he walked through the terminal, out to the curb and hailed a cab.

"Where to?" the driver asked.

"Grand Central Station." He pulled out a twenty-dollar bill, the last of his money. "How fast can you get there? My plane's been canceled and I gotta make a train before eleven-thirty."

The driver was a kid, not more than twenty-two. "Mister, that's calling it a little close, but I'll do it. The roads are pretty good now and the traffic is real light." He pressed his foot on the gas pedal. "Hang on."

Foxy leaned back. Icy perspiration chilled his body. They knew who he was now. Suppose they'd looked up his old record. Suppose someone said, "He used to work in the Oyster Bar. He was a dishwasher." Suppose they thought about the room and went to look in it.

The bomb was attached to the clock now. That meant that if anyone went into the room, they'd have time to get Sharon and Neil out; maybe time to deactivate the bomb. No, it would probably go off if anyone touched it; it was that sensitive. But what good if Sharon and Neil got out?

He shouldn't have made that last phonecall. It was Sharon's fault. He should have strangled her yesterday. He remembered the feeling of his hands squeezing her neck, reaching for the soft pulse in her throat. He hadn't touched any of the others with his hands; he'd just knotted and twisted their scarves or belts. But her! His hands burned with the need to surround that throat. She had ruined it for him. She had tricked him, pretending to be in love with him. The way she'd looked at him, even from the television, acting like she wanted him, wanted him to take her away. Then yesterday she'd put her arms around him and tried to get his gun. She was no good. She was the worst of all of them, all the women in the foster homes, the matrons in the detention homes, all of them, pushing him away when he tried to kiss them. "Stop that! Don't do that!"

He shouldn't have taken Sharon to the room. If he'd just taken the boy, this wouldn't have happened. She'd made him take her, and now the money was gone and they knew who he was and he'd have to hide somewhere.

But he'd kill her first. By now they were probably just starting to evacuate the terminals and airports. They probably wouldn't think of the room this fast. The bomb was too good for her. She had to look up and see him and feel his hands on her throat. He had to look down at her and see her die. He had to talk to her and tell her what he was going to do and listen to her beg him not to, and then he'd squeeze.

He closed his eyes and swallowed over the dryness in his mouth, the shiver of ecstasy that made the perspiration tingle.

He only needed four or five minutes inside the terminal. If he got into the room by 11:27, he'd have enough time. He'd get away through the Park Avenue tunnel.

And even though he didn't have his recorder, he'd remember how Sharon sounded. He wanted to remember. He'd fall asleep remembering how she sounded when she died.

The boy. He'd just leave him there. Let the bomb take care of him, him and all the stinking cops and all the people

288

who wouldn't get out in time. Didn't even know what was going to happen to them.

They were entering the midtown tunnel. This kid was a good driver. It was only ten minutes of eleven. Another ten or fifteen minutes and he'd be on Forty-second Street. He'd have plenty of time. Plenty of time for Sharon.

The cab came to an abrupt halt halfway through the tunnel. Foxy looked up from his meditation. "What's the matter?"

The cabby shrugged. "Sorry, mister. There's a disabled truck up there. Looks like he lost some of his cargo too. Both lanes are blocked. But it shouldn't take long. Don't worry I'll get you there for your train."

Frantic with impatience to get to Sharon, Foxy waited. His hands were burning so much now, like they were on fire. He thought about getting out and walking the rest of the way but rejected the idea. The cops would stop him sure.

It was seventeen minutes past eleven when they inched out of the tunnel and turned north. The traffic began to back up at Fortieth Street. The driver whistled. "This is some mess. I'll try cutting west here."

At Third Avenue they came to a complete stop. Motionless cars blocked the intersections. Horns tooted angrily. Tense-looking pedestrians, scurrying east, tried to make their way around the cars. "Mister, there must be something wrong. Looks like some streets are closed off up there. Wait. I'll turn on the radio. Maybe it's another bomb threat."

They were probably clearing out the terminal. Foxy tossed the twenty-dollar bill at the driver, opened the door and slid out into the traffic.

At Forty-second Street he saw them. Cops. Cops all over

289

the place. Forty-second Street closed off. He pushed and shoved his way through. Bomb. Bomb. He stopped. People were talking about a bomb in the station. Had they found Sharon and the boy? The thought sent black fury gushing through him. He shouldered people aside, forced his way through the crowd.

"Stand back, buddy. You can't go any further." A burly, young policeman tapped his shoulder as he tried to cross Third Avenue.

"What's the matter?" He had to know.

"Nothing, we hope, sir. But there's been a bomb threat phoned in. We have to take precautions."

Phoned in. His phonecall to that priest. *Threat!* That meant they hadn't found the bomb. It was all right. Exultation leaped through him. His fingers and palms tingled the way they always did when he started to go to a girl and knew nothing could stop him. His voice was smooth, his expression concerned when he spoke to the cop. "I'm a surgeon. I'm joining the emergency medical squad in case it's needed."

"Oh, sorry, Doctor. Go right through."

Foxy ran up Forty-second Street, taking care to keep close to the buildings. The next cop who stopped him might be smart enough to ask for identification. People were streaming out of office buildings and shops, prodded by the urgency of the bullhorns the police were using. "Move quickly but do not panic. Walk to Third or Fifth Avenue. Your cooperation may save your life."

It was exactly 11:26 when Foxy, pushing his way through the confused and frightened crowds, reached the main entrance to the terminal. The doors had been wedged open to speed the exodus. A veteran policeman was standing guard at the far left door. Foxy tried to duck past him. His arm was grabbed. "Hey, you can't go in there!"

290

"Terminal engineer," Foxy said crisply. "I've been sent for."

"You're too late. The searchers will be clearing out in a minute."

"I've been sent for," Foxy repeated.

"Suit yourself." The cop dropped his arm.

The deserted newsstand beyond the doors was piled with morning papers. Foxy saw the huge black headline. *Kidnap.* It was about him, what he'd done—the fox.

He ran past the stand and looked down into the main terminal. Grim-faced policemen with construction hats were searching behind counters and booths. There were probably dozens more all over the station. But he'd outsmarted them! All of them!

A small group of people was clustered near the information desk. The taller one, a broad-shouldered, sandy-haired man, hands shoved in his pockets, was shaking his head. Steve Peterson! It was Steve Peterson! Sucking in his breath, Foxy raced down to the main floor and dashed for the staircase to the lower level.

Now he only needed two more minutes. His fingers throbbed and burned. He curled and uncurled them as he rushed down the stairs. Only his thumbs were rigid as he ran, unchallenged, across the lower terminal and disappeared down the steps leading to the Mount Vernon platform and the room beyond it.

48

THE NEWS OF FOXY'S PHONECALL reached Hugh and Steve as the helicopter passed over the Triborough Bridge.

"*Major transportation center, New York City,*" Hugh snapped into the phone. "Christ, that includes both airports, both bus terminals, Penn Station, and Grand Central. Have you started evacuating them?"

Steve listened, his shoulders slumped forward, his hands restlessly clasping and unclasping. Kennedy Airport! La-Guardia Airport! The Port Authority bus terminal took up a square block; the one at the bridge was probably bigger. Sharon . . . Neil . . . oh God, it was hopeless . . . may the fox build his nest on your hearthstone. . . .

Hugh hung up the phone. "Can't you push this thing any faster?" he urged the pilot.

"That wind is getting awful strong," the pilot replied, "I'll try going lower."

"Wind velocity, just what we need if there's a fire when that thing goes off," Hugh muttered. He looked over at Steve. "There's no use kidding. It's bad. We have to assume he's carried out his threat to set that bomb."

"With Sharon and Neil somewhere near it?" Steve's voice was ragged. "Where do you start looking?"

"We're gambling," Hugh said tersely. "The main search will be in Grand Central. Remember, he parked the car on Vanderbilt and stayed at the Biltmore. He knows the terminal like a book. And John Owens says the train sounds he heard on the cassette are more consistent with commuter trains than subways."

"What about the Thompson boy?"

"If we don't catch Foxy and get a confession out of him, he's finished."

At 11:05 the helicopter landed on the Pan Am building. Hugh threw open the door. A thin-faced agent ran over to them as they jumped to the ground. White with anger, lips tightly compressed, he briefed them on Foxy's escape.

"What do you mean, *escaped?*" Hugh exploded. "How the hell did that happen? How sure are you that it was Foxy?"

"Absolutely sure. He dropped the ransom. They're searching the field and terminal for him now. But the whole airport is being evacuated so it's a mess out there."

"The ransom doesn't tell us where he set that bomb and it can't help the Thompson kid," Hugh snapped. "*We've got to find Foxy and make him talk.*"

Foxy escaped. With numb disbelief, Steve absorbed the words. Sharon. Neil. "Steve, I was wrong, forgive me." "Mommy wouldn't want me to be here." Was that bizarre cassette to be his last contact with them?

The cassette. Nina's voice . . .

He grabbed Hugh's arm. "That cassette he sent. He must have dubbed Nina's voice on it. You said he'd cleared everything out of the garage. Did he have any luggage? He may have been carrying a suitcase, something with him. Maybe he still has the other cassette with Nina's voice, maybe he has something that would show where Sharon and Neil are."

Hugh spun around to the other agent. "What about any luggage?"

"There are two stubs clipped onto the ticket he dropped. But the plane took off about twenty-seven minutes ago. No one thought to stop it. We'll get those bags in Phoenix."

"That's not good enough," Hugh shouted. "Sweet Christ, that's not good enough. Get that goddamn plane back. Have every baggage handler in LaGuardia ready to unload it. Tell the control tower to clear a runway. Don't let any dumb ass stand in your way. Where's a phone?"

"Inside."

Hugh pulled out his notebook as he ran. Rapidly he dialed Somers prison and got the Warden's office. "We're still trying to locate evidence to prove Thompson's innocence. Have a phone manned to the last split second."

He called the Governor's office, got through to her private secretary. "Make damn sure the Governor's available and that you have a phone open to our guys in La-Guardia and another to the prison. Or else, the Nutmeg State may go down in history for frying an innocent kid." He dropped the phone. "Let's go," he told Steve.

Nineteen minutes, Steve thought as they plummeted down in the elevator. Nineteen minutes.

The lobby of the Pan American building was jammed with people streaming from the terminal. Bomb threat . . . bomb threat . . . The words were on everyone's lips.

Steve and Hugh shoved their way through the surging bodies. How can anyone know where to search? Steve agonized. He'd been here only yesterday. Sitting in the Oyster Bar, waiting for his train. Had Sharon and Neil been here all along, helpless? Over the loudspeaker an urgent voice kept repeating, "Leave the buildings immediately. Walk to the nearest exit. Do not panic. Do not congregate at exits. Leave the area . . . leave the area. . . ."

The Information Booth on the upper level of the terminal, its red emergency lights flashing ominously, was the command desk for the investigators. Engineers were poring over charts and diagrams, issuing rapid-fire orders to searching parties.

"We're concentrating on the area between the floor of this level and the ceiling of the lower level now," a supervisor told Hugh. "It's accessible from all the platforms and a good hiding place. We've done a fast check on the platforms and we're hitting all the lockers. We figure that even if we find the bomb, it's probably too risky to try to dismantle it. The bomb squad brought over all the bomb blankets they could lay their hands on. They're distributed among the searching parties. We can count on one of them being ninety percent effective in containing an explosion."

Steve's eyes swept the terminal. The loudspeaker was off now and the vast area was becoming quiet, a hushed, mocking silence. The clock. His eyes searched out the clock over the information desk. Relentlessly the hands kept moving: 11:12 . . . 11:17 . . . 11:24 . . . He wanted to hold those hands back. He wanted to run into every platform, every waiting room, every cubicle. He wanted to shout their names, Sharon! Neil!

Frantically, he turned his head. He had to *do* something, search for them himself. His gaze fell on a tall, bony man who rushed in from the Forty-second Street entrance, ran down the stairs and disappeared down the second staircase that led to the lower level. There was something vaguely familiar about him—one of the agents maybe? What good could he do now?

The loudspeaker went on. "It is eleven-twenty-seven. All searchers immediately proceed to the nearest exit. Leave the terminal immediately. Repeat. Leave the terminal immediately."

"No!" Steve clutched Hugh's shoulders, spun him around. "No!"

"Mr. Peterson, make sense. If that bomb goes off, we may all be killed. Even if Sharon and Neil are here, we can't help them that way."

"I'm not leaving." Steve said.

Hugh grabbed his arm. Another agent took the other one. "Mr. Peterson, be reasonable. It may only be a precaution."

Steve wrenched himself free. "Let go of me, damn you," he shouted. "Let go of me."

49

IT WAS NO USE, NO USE, NO USE. Her eyes magnetized to the clock, Sharon frantically tried to jab the broken edge of the handle into the cords on her wrists. It was so hard to hold the handle in one fist. to try to push at the cords of the other.

More times than not, she missed the cords completely, and the metal cut into her hand. She could feel the warm, soft, sticky blood, running, crusting. She was beyond pain. But what if she jabbed an artery and passed out?

The blood was making the cord softer, more resilient. The metal jabbed at it, not in it. She'd been trying for over an hour now . . . it was twenty-five of eleven.

Twenty of eleven.

Ten of . . . five of . . . five after . . .

She worked on, her face clammy with perspiration, her

hands sticky with blood, not feeling pain anymore. She felt Neil's eyes watching her. Pray, Neil.

At ten after eleven, she felt the cord weakening, giving. Summing up a last reserve of energy, Sharon pulled her hands apart. They were free; the cords were dangling from them.

She held them up, shook them, tried to get feeling back into them. Fifteen minutes.

Leaning on her left elbow, Sharon dragged herself up. She swung just enough to support her back against the wall and managed to squirm to a sitting position. Her legs fell over the side of the cot. Raw pain screeched through her ankle.

Fourteen minutes.

Her fingers trembled with weakness as she tugged at the gag. The gauze was so tightly knotted. She couldn't get it loose. Tugging frantically, she managed to pull the gag down. Great gulping breaths of air helped to clear her head.

Thirteen minutes.

She couldn't walk. Even if she could drag herself over to the bomb she might jar it, trying to pull up on the sink, to reach it. Or she might set it off just by touching it. She remembered the infinite care Foxy had shown when he touched the wires.

There was no hope for her. She had to try to free Neil. If she could get him loose, he could get out, could warn people. She yanked his gag off.

"Sharon . . ."

"I know. I'm going to try to untie you. I can't help it if I hurt you."

"All right, Sharon."

And then she heard it. The sound. Something thudding against the door. Was he coming back? Had he changed his mind? Clutching Neil to her, Sharon stared at the door. It was opening. The light switch clicked.

In the dusty light, she saw what seemed to be an apparition stumbling toward her, a woman, an old woman with a trickle of blood coming from her mouth with deep sunken eyes that were out of focus.

Neil shrank back against her as the woman came toward them, stared in horror as the woman began to fall forward, to slump downward like an unsupported laundry bag.

The woman fell on her side, tried to speak, "Knife . . . still in my back . . . help . . . please . . . take it out . . . hurts . . . want to die here . . ."

The woman's head was against her foot. Her body angled grotesquely out. Sharon saw the handle of the knife between her shoulderblades.

She could free Neil with the knife. Shuddering, Sharon put both hands around the handle, pulled.

The knife held, then suddenly came free. She was holding it, the blade wickedly sharp, matted with blood.

The woman whimpered.

In an instant Sharon had cut Neil's bindings. "Neil . . . run . . . get out of here . . . yell to people that there's going to be an explosion . . . hurry . . . down those stairs . . . and there's a big ramp . . . run toward it . . . at the train platform, go up the stairs . . . you'll see people there . . . Daddy will come for you . . . hurry . . . get out of this building . . . get people out of it . . ."

"Sharon," Neil's voice was pleading. "What about you?"

"Neil . . . just go. Go!"

Neil slid off the cot. He tried to walk, stumbled, righted himself. "My legs . . ."

"Neil, hurry. Run! Run!"

With a last beseeching glance at her, Neil obeyed. He

ran out of the room, onto the landing. Down the stairs. Sharon had said to go down the stairs. It was so quiet here, so spooky. He was so afraid. The bomb. Maybe if he could find someone, they'd help Sharon. He had to make someone help Sharon.

He was at the foot of the stairs. Which way should he go? There were so many pipes around here. A ramp. Sharon said a ramp. That must be it. Like the ramp they had in school between the classrooms and the auditorium.

He raced along it. He wanted to shout for help. But he had to hurry. He had to find someone. He was at the end of the ramp. He was in a station, a train station. The tracks were right there. Sharon said to go upstairs. He ran around the platform where the tracks ended.

A voice started to talk. It sounded like when the principal talked on the loudspeaker at school. It was telling everyone to get out. Where was the man who was talking?

He could hear footsteps coming down a staircase. Someone was coming, someone who would help Sharon. He was so relieved he tried to yell and couldn't. He had no breath from running. His legs hurt so much it was hard to run. He stumbled toward the stairs and began to climb. He had to tell whoever was coming about Sharon.

Neil looked up and saw the face that had stalked his dreams rushing down at him.

Foxy saw Neil. His eyes narrowed. His mouth twisted. He stretched out his hands . . .

Neil jumped to one side, stuck out his foot. The man's flailing leg jammed against his sneaker. The man sprawled down the last three steps. Eluding the arms that swung out at him, Neil ran up the steps. He was in a big, empty place. There was no one here. Another staircase. Over there. Maybe there were people upstairs. The bad man was going to Sharon.

Sobbing, Neil ran up the stairs. Daddy, he tried to yell, Daddy. Daddy. He was on the last step. There were policemen all over here. They were all running away from him. Some of them were pushing another man.

They were pushing Daddy.

"Daddy," Neil shouted. "Daddy!"

With a last, final burst of energy. he stumbled across the terminal. Steve heard him, turned, ran to him, grabbed him.

"Daddy," Neil sobbed. "that man is going to kill Sharon now . . . just like he killed Mommy."

50

A DETERMINED ROSIE was fighting the efforts to put her out. Lally was down in Sing Sing. She knew it. Cops were all over the place. There was a bunch of them right at the Information Desk. Rosie spotted Hugh Taylor. He was the nice FBI guy who always talked to her when he was around the station. She ran to him, tugged his arm. "Mr. Taylor, Lally . . ."

He glanced down at her, pulled his arm free. "Get the hell out of here, Rosie," he ordered.

A loudspeaker came on, ordering everyone out. "No!" Rosie sobbed.

The tall man near Hugh Taylor grabbed him, turned him around. She watched as Hugh and another cop wrestled with him.

"Daddy! Daddy!"

Was she hearing things? Rosie spun around. A little boy was weaving across the terminal. Then the big guy who was shouting at Mr. Taylor ran past her to the child. She heard the boy say something about a bad man and rushed over. Maybe he'd seen the guy she and Lally were watching.

The boy was crying. "Daddy, help Sharon. She's hurt. She's all tied up and there's a sick old lady . . .

"Where, Neil, where?" Steve begged.

"A sick old lady," Rosie shrieked. "That's Lally. She's in her room. You know it, Mr. Taylor, in Sing Sing—the old dishwasher room."

"Come on," Hugh shouted.

Steve thrust Neil at a policeman. "Get my son out of here," he ordered. He ran behind Hugh. Two men struggling with a heavy metal sheet followed them.

"Christ, let's get out of here!" Someone thrust an arm around Rosie's waist and dragged her toward an exit. "That bomb will go off any minute!"

51

SHARON HEARD THE PADDING OF NEIL'S SNEAKERS as he ran down the steps. Please God, let him be safe. Let him get away.

The old woman's moans stopped, resumed, stopped for a longer instant. When the sound began again, it was lower, softer; it had a fading quality.

With detached clarity, Sharon remembered what this woman said about wanting to die here. Leaning down, she felt the matted hair, patted it gently. Her fingertips smoothed the wrinkled forehead. The skin felt damp and cold. Lally shuddered violently. The moaning stopped.

Sharon knew the woman was dead. And now she was going to die. "I love you, Steve," she said aloud. "I love you, Steve." His face filled her mind. Her need for him was physical pain; primal, acute, transcending the throbbing agony of her leg and ankle.

She closed her eyes. "Forgive us our trespasses as we forgive those who trespass against us . . . Into Your Hands, I commend my spirit."

A sound.

Her eyes flew open. Foxy was framed into the doorway. An ear to ear smile slashed his face. His fingers curved, his thumbs rigid, he started toward her.

52

Hugh led the way down to the Mount Vernon platform, around the tracks, down the ramp into the lowest depths of the terminal. Steve raced beside him. The men carrying the bomb blanket struggled to keep up with them.

They were on the ramp when they heard the screaming.

"No . . . no . . . no . . . Steve . . . help me . . . Steve . . ."

Steve's track team days were twenty years in the past. But once again he felt that tremendous surge of power, that terrible burst of energy he had always summoned in a race. Crazed with the need to reach Sharon in time, he flew past the others.

"Steeeeeevvvvveeee . . ." The scream choked off.

Stairs. He was at the foot of a staircase. He lunged up it, burst through an open door.

His brain absorbed the nightmarish quality of the scene,

the body on the floor, Sharon half-lying, half-sitting, her legs tied, her hair dangling behind her, trying to pull away from the figure bent over her, the figure with the thick fingers that were squeezing her throat.

Steve threw himself on the man, butted his head into the arched back. Foxy sprawled forward. They both fell on Sharon. Under their weight, the sagging cot broke and they rolled together on the floor. The hands were still on Sharon's throat but broke loose under the impact of the fall. Foxy stumbled to his feet, crouched. Steve tried to leap up, tripped on Lally's body. Sharon's breathing was a tortured, choking grasp.

Hugh raced into the room.

Cornered, Foxy backed away. His hand found the door to the toilet cubicle. He jumped past it, slammed it shut. They heard the bolt slide into place.

"Get out of there, you crazy fool," Hugh shouted.

The agents carrying the bomb blanket were in the room. With infinite care, they draped the black suitcase with the heavy metal sheet.

Steve reached for Sharon Her eyes were closed. Her head flopped backwards as he picked her up. Ugly welts were rising on her throat. But she was alive; she was alive. Holding her to him, he turned to the door. His eyes fell on the posters, on Nina's picture. He hugged Sharon tightly.

Hugh bent over Lally. "This one's gone."

The large hand of the clock was moving to six.

"Get out of here!" Hugh shouted.

They tumbled down the stairs.

"The tunnel. Head for the tunnel!"

They raced past the generator, past the vents, onto the tracks, through the darkness . . .

Foxy heard the retreating steps. They were gone. They were gone. He slid the bolt and opened the door. Seeing the metal blanket over the suitcase, he began to laugh, a deep, rumbling, staccato sound.

It was too late for him. But it was too late for them too. In the end the Fox always won.

He reached his hand to the metal blanket, tried to tug it off the suitcase.

A blinding flash, a roar that shattered his eardrums hurtled him into eternity.

11:42 A.M.

Bob Kerner burst into St. Bernard's Church, raced up the aisle and threw his arms around the kneeling figure.

"Is it over?" Her eyes were tearless.

"*Is it over!* Mamma, come on and take your kid home. They've got absolute proof that another guy committed the murder; they've got a tape of him doing it. The Governor said to get Ron out of that prison *now*."

Kate Thompson, mother of Ronald Thompson, staunch believer in the goodness and mercy of her God, fainted.

Roger Perry hung up the phone, turned to Glenda. "They were on time," he said.

"Sharon, Neil, both safe?" Glenda whispered.

"Yes, and the Thompson boy is going home."

Glenda raised her hand to her throat. "Thank God." She saw his expression. "Roger, I'm fine. Put away those damn pills and make me a good stiff old-fashioned!"

Hugh had his arm around a softly weeping Rosie. "Lally saved her station," he said. "And we're going to start a petition to put up a plaque for her. I'll bet Governor Carey himself will unveil it. He's a nice guy."

"A plaque for Lally," Rosie whispered. "Oh, she'd love that!"

A face was floating somewhere above her. She was going to die and never see Steve again. "No . . . no . . ."

"It's all right, darling, It's all right."

Steve's voice. It was Steve's face she was seeing.

"It's all over. We're on the way to the hospital. They'll fix up that leg."

"Neil . . ."

"I'm here, Sharon." A hand butterfly soft in hers.

Steve's lips on her cheeks, her forehead, her lips.

Neil's voice in her ear. "Sharon, just like you told me, I kept thinking the whole time about the present you promised me. Sharon, exactly how many Lionel trains have you got for me?"